D0475480

RECON TEAM ANGEL

The Assault

Task Force

Ice War

ALSO BY BRIAN FALKNER

The Tomorrow Code

Brain Jack

The Project

ICE WAR

RECON TEAM ANGEL 3

BRIAN FALKNER

Random House 🏠 New York

Text copyright © 2014 by Brian Falkner
Jacket art copyright © 2014 by Alan Brooks

All rights reserved. Published in the United States by Random House Children's Books, a division of Random House LLC, a Penguin Random House Company, New York.

Random House and the colophon are registered trademarks of Random House LLC.

Symbol art by snoopydoo

Visit us on the Web! randomhouseteens.com

Educators and librarians, for a variety of teaching tools, visit us at
RHTeachersLibrarians.com

Library of Congress Cataloging-in-Publication Data
Falkner, Brian.
Ice war / Brian Falkner.—First edition.
pages cm.—(Recon Team Angel ; 3)
Summary: "Recon Team Angel must stop the alien invasion across the frozen Bering Strait into the Americas—the last free human territory remaining—or all will be lost."—Provided by publisher.
ISBN 978-0-449-81303-4 (trade) — ISBN 978-0-449-81305-8 (ebook)
[1. Extraterrestrial beings—Fiction. 2. War—Fiction. 3. Undercover operations—Fiction.
4. Adventure and adventurers—Fiction. 5. Alaska—Fiction. 6. Science fiction.] I. Title.
PZ7.F1947Ic 2014 [Fic]—dc23 2013027907

Printed in the United States of America
10 9 8 7 6 5 4 3 2 1
First Edition

For Ray Richards, ONZM, DSC
1921–2013
An Officer and a Gentleman

▪ CONTENTS ▪

Prologue   1

BOOK 1—THE BERING STRAIT

1. Seal Team Two   5
2. Above the Ice   16
3. Heat   38
4. Tank   43
5. Arctic Tears   61
6. Nokz'z   75
7. Silent Angels   83
8. Ivrulik   89
9. Brogan   90
10. Fezerker   98

BOOK 2—DIOMEDE

11. The Briefcase   104
12. Nukilik   106
13. Monster Calls   112
14. Tanks   120
15. Lessons for the Dead   126
16. The Bunker   141
17. Melting the Ice   149

18. Ambush   166

19. Decoy   174

20. Snow Angels   185

21. Proof   208

22. Elders   213

23. Credentials   223

24. War Planning   230

BOOK 3—ICE WAR

25. Aftermath   240

26. Wilton   242

27. The Hunt   249

28. Spitfire   254

29. Angels   258

30. Attack Run   262

31. The Run   273

32. Sacrifice   278

33. The End   289

34. Greater Love   292

35. Russell   295

36. Chisnall   299

Glossary   301

Congratulations   305

PROLOGUE

THIS IS NOT A HISTORY BOOK.

The achievements of 4th Reconnaissance Team (designation: Angel) of the Allied Combined Operations Group, 1st Reconnaissance Battalion, from November 2030 through July 2035, during the Great Bzadian War, are well documented by scholars and historians. Less well known are the people behind the myth: the brave young men and women who earned the reputation and the citations for which Recon Team Angel became famous.

These are their stories, pieced together from Post-Action Reports and interviews with the surviving members of the team. The stories of the heroes whose skill, daring, and determination changed the course of history.

Where necessary to gain a full understanding of the situations these soldiers faced, accounts have been included from the forces they opposed: from interviews with prisoners and Bzadian reports of the battles.

The members of Recon Team Angel changed over time, due to injury and death, as happens in a combat arena. By the end of the war, over seventy young people had served in the unit. They were aged fourteen to eighteen—small enough to pass themselves off as alien soldiers but old enough to undertake high-risk covert operations behind enemy lines.

At its peak, this remarkable group boasted a core of twenty-five specialist operatives. But only six "Angels" were sent on a high-risk midwinter mission into the icy wilderness of the Bering Strait:

```
Angel One: Lieutenant Trianne (Phantom) Price—
    New Zealand
Angel Two: Sergeant Janos (Monster) Panyoczki—
    Hungary
Angel Three: Specialist Retha Barnard—Germany
Angel Four: Specialist Dimitri (the Tsar)
    Nikolaev—Russia
Angel Five: Specialist Hayden Wall—America
Angel Six: Private First Class Emile Attaya—
    Lebanon
```

May we always remember the names of those who fell in the pursuit of liberty for Earth.

BOOK I—THE BERING STRAIT

*Fighting an ice war is like
turning the military clock back 300 years.
In the frozen wastelands of the Bering Strait,
high-tech equipment fails, high-tensile steel
shatters like glass, communications are
intermittent or nonexistent.
This is war at its most primitive.
It is war at its most brutal.*
—*General Harry Whitehead*

1. SEAL TEAM TWO

[TRANSCRIPT OF RADIO COMMUNICATION BETWEEN US NAVY SEAL TEAM TWO (CODE NAME ICEFIRE) AND MISSION CONTROLLERS AT ACOG HEADQUARTERS, FEBRUARY 15, 2033. SCHEDULED RADIO CONTACT AT 0700 HOURS LOCAL TIME.]

ICEFIRE ONE: Icefire Actual, this is Icefire One. How copy?

ICEFIRE ACTUAL: Solid copy, Icefire One. What is your grid point reference? Over.

ICEFIRE ONE: Icefire Actual, we are in position at designated OP. Grid reference, Charlie November, four, three, five, niner, two, one.

ICEFIRE ACTUAL: Clear copy, Icefire One. Do you have eyes on the island? Over.

ICEFIRE ONE: That's an affirmative, Icefire Actual. Over.

ICEFIRE ACTUAL: Icefire One. Is there any sign of activity? Over.

ICEFIRE ONE: That's also affirmative, Icefire Actual. Lights are on and there is movement inside.

ICEFIRE ACTUAL: Can you confirm identity of the occupants? Over.

ICEFIRE ONE: Negative. It might be Goldilocks, or it might be the Big Bad Wolf. Over.

ICEFIRE ACTUAL: What about enemy activity around the island? Over.

ICEFIRE ONE: Ah, that's also a negative, Icefire Actual. We got nothing on the scopes and nothing eyes on. Looks all clear, but conditions are challenging. Over.

ICEFIRE ACTUAL: What is your visibility rating? Over.

ICEFIRE ONE: Visibility estimated at tango three. Lots of interference on the scopes. We got a lot of bad TV here. Over.

ICEFIRE ACTUAL: Solid copy, Icefire One. You are cleared to move to grid reference Charlie November, four, three, five, niner, three, two.

ICEFIRE ONE: Roger that, Icefire Actual. We are Oscar Mike to grid reference Charlie November, four, three, five, niner, three, two.

ICEFIRE ACTUAL: Icefire One, hold position. I say again, hold your position. We have a transmission coming in from Overlord. They have had a break in the cloud cover and say they are picking up some kind of activity to your west. Over.

ICEFIRE ONE: What kind of activity, Icefire Actual? Scopes are still clear down here.

ICEFIRE ACTUAL: Querying that now, Icefire One.

[TRANSMISSION BREAK: 23 SECONDS]

ICEFIRE ACTUAL: Icefire One, this is Icefire Actual. How copy?

ICEFIRE ONE: Clear copy, Icefire Actual. What have you got for us?

ICEFIRE ACTUAL: No further information, Icefire One. Activity has ceased. They could not get a visual on it and could not identify a heat signature. There is no indication of enemy activity. I repeat, no enemy activity. It could have been wildlife. Over. You are recleared to grid reference Charlie November, four, three, five, niner, three, two.

ICEFIRE ONE: [Garbled transmission, indeterminate noise]

ICEFIRE ACTUAL: Icefire One, zero copy on your last. You are coming in weak and unreadable. Please repeat your transmission. Over.

[TRANSMISSION BREAK: 16 SECONDS]

ICEFIRE ACTUAL: Icefire One, this is Icefire Actual. How copy?

ICEFIRE ONE: [Garbled transmission, indeterminate noise, possible screaming]

ICEFIRE ACTUAL: Icefire One, this is Icefire Actual. How copy?

[TRANSMISSION BREAK: 20 SECONDS]

ICEFIRE ACTUAL: Icefire One, this is Icefire Actual. How copy?

[TRANSMISSION BREAK: 20 SECONDS]

ICEFIRE ACTUAL: Icefire One, this is Icefire Actual. We are not receiving your transmissions. Please relocate to higher ground and resume radio traffic.

[TRANSMISSION ENDS AT 0707 HOURS]

The recording finished and the silence in the room was absolute.

General Whitehead pushed the transcript away from him as if he was somehow offended by it.

General Jake Russell, ACOG, Bering Strait Defense Force, picked up his copy and folded it in half so he could no longer see the words.

They were paper copies, an anachronism in an electronic age, but at the end of the meeting they would be collected and incinerated, with no risk of an electronic copy finding its way out into cyberspace.

The room was oval, as was the table in its center. There were no windows. Here, deep in the heart of the Pentagon, security was far too tight for that. Nor were there air-conditioning ducts through which microphones could be inserted. The room was swept every day for bugs.

The bombproof walls were plain and white, no photos, nor artwork. The table resembled wood, although it was made of a bulletproof composite fiber. Even the chairs, high-backed, comfortable, and leather, had built-in airbags to deal with a sudden traumatic incident, like a missile attack.

The workstations around the outside walls, where subordinates sat in a variety of uniforms, had no such luxuries. Their desks were plain and their seating simple low-backed swivel chairs.

Seated around the center table were ten people, a mixture of men and women. General Harry Whitehead, as commander of ACOG, occupied pride of place at the head of the table.

General Russell, second-in-command, was opposite him at the far end.

"They were the second Navy Seal team we sent in," Russell said. "Seal Team Two, specialists in arctic warfare. Frostiest sons of bitches I ever met in my life. These guys have ice cubes for testicles. Kick 'em in the nuts and you break your toe. They don't just survive—they thrive in the coldest, bleakest places on Earth."

"So where are they?" Whitehead asked.

"It's a dangerous place this time of year," Russell said. "And in the middle of a blizzard . . ."

Whitehead shook his head. "One team disappears, that could be a hole in the ice. Point man drags the rest of them in, bodies are never found. But two teams in a row . . ."

"What were they doing there in the first place?"

The speaker was Emily Gonzales, the new liaison officer from the ACOG Oversight Committee. Gonzales was a compact woman with bright blue eyes that shone with a glint of steel. The same steel was in her voice. "Why send in a Seal team—I'm sorry, two Seal teams—when you are still in contact with the station?"

"Your predecessor was fully up to date with all these details," Russell said. "Do we really have to go over this again?"

Gonzales turned her head slowly and impaled him with those eyes. "If you want the approval of the oversight committee, you do," she said.

General Whitehead looked as though he was about to say something to that, but thought better of it.

"I'll answer the question," Daniel Bilal said. A small, tidy man with a pencil-thin mustache, he had an air of calm, as though he were somehow removed from the tension in the room.

Gonzales raised an eyebrow.

"Daniel Bilal, military intelligence," Bilal said.

Gonzales made a note on her smartpad.

"It's a sensitive region," Bilal said. "When the Pukes come, they're going to come through the Bering Strait. And they're going to come now, in midwinter, while the strait is frozen over. So if a butterfly farts in the strait at this time of year, we want to know what it had for lunch."

"Thank you for that lesson in basic geography and biology," Gonzales said. "But that still doesn't explain the need for the Seal teams."

Bilal was unfazed. "The commander of the station on Little Diomede was Jared Legrand," he said. "A good man. Two days ago he fell into a crevasse. His body has not yet been recovered."

"How did it happen?" Gonzales asked.

"He was checking sensors with one of the other crew," Russell said. "It was an accident."

"The other crewmember, Nikolas Able, made it back alive," Bilal said. "Legrand did not."

"Even so, there was no reason to suspect foul play," Russell said.

"Perhaps," Bilal said.

The others at the table all turned to look at him.

"What haven't you told us?" Russell asked.

"Legrand was not a regular soldier," Bilal said.

"What kind of 'not regular'?" Gonzales asked.

"He was one of ours," Bilal said.

"Military intelligence." Russell said it like it was some kind of a disease.

"He was undercover," Bilal said. "Making sure that nothing at that station could possibly go wrong."

"So he was a spy," Russell said. "His death might still have been an accident."

"And it might not," Bilal said. "Can we afford that risk?"

"Any sign that the station has been infiltrated by the Bzadians?" Gonzales asked.

"All code signs were confirmed. No distress signals have been given," Russell said. "Comprehensive background checks were done on the crew. They all came up clean. The remaining crew on Little Diomede are solid."

"Could they be under duress?" Gonzales asked. "Are there Bzadians hiding in the shadows with guns in our guys' backs?"

"There are duress codes," Russell said. "None have been given. I repeat: there is no reason to think that anything is wrong out there."

"If it wasn't in the Bering Strait, then I might agree with you and we might just wait for the storm to pass," Bilal said. "But we don't have that luxury. If we don't stop the Bzadians on the ice, we sure as hell won't be able to stop them when they hit dry land. We've spent the last year building up our arctic warfare capabilities for exactly that reason."

"How sure are you that they will attack?" Gonzales asked. "We beat them back once, and they haven't tried again since."

"They weren't ready," Bilal said. "They learned their lesson in 2028. They would have attacked last year, but they didn't have the fuel, thanks to Operation Magnum."

He stood and moved to the map. "To the west, Big Diomede Island. To the east, Little Diomede. Right bang in the middle of the strait. A couple of kilometers apart. Little Dio is bristling with every kind of detector you could imagine and controls a string of sensor buoys that extend for kilometers in each direction. It's also home to our control and maintenance center here on the southwestern tip. This gives the Pukes a big problem. If they try to sneak across the strait, we'll know they're coming. If they take out Little Dio, we'll still know they're coming. But if they compromised our sensors in some way and slipped across under the cover of an ice storm, we wouldn't know about it until their battle tanks were spinning into Anchorage."

"Compromise our sensors?" Gonzales asked. "How?"

"On Operation Magnum, we replaced a couple of circuit boards in their SONRAD station and made our invasion fleet invisible to their scopes," Bilal said. "Who's to say they can't do the same to us?"

"What about Big Diomede?" Gonzales asked.

Russell shook his head. "Deserted. It used to be a Russian outpost, but the Bzadians have never had a use for it. The only people who set foot on that rock are the local native Inupiat people."

"You're sure they're Inupiat and not Bzadians in disguise?" Gonzales asked.

"We're sure," Bilal said. "And in any case, it's only a small community, and they don't go anywhere near Little Diomede."

He returned to his seat and leaned backward in his chair, crossing his legs casually.

"So what's your plan?" Gonzales asked. "You've sent in two Seal teams and lost them both. If you keep doing what you've been doing, you're going to run out of Seals."

"I agree," Bilal said. "That's the reason for this meeting. We want to send in the Angels."

"Recon Team Angel?" Gonzales asked.

"The same," Bilal said.

"Children," Russell said, shaking his head.

"There would be Bzadians sitting in these chairs by now if not for those 'children,'" Whitehead said.

"You are aware that the Angel and Demon programs were shut down?" Gonzales asked. She leaned forward on the table and pressed her fingertips together.

"I think that is common knowledge," Bilal said, still apparently relaxed. "But the personnel are still in barracks at Fort Carson. They could be reactivated in a matter of days."

"And why do you think a bunch of kids might succeed, where highly trained Special Forces operatives have failed?" Gonzales asked.

"If it's holes in the ice, polar bears, or the abominable snowman, then they might not," Bilal said. "But if it's enemy activity, then they just might. That's what they do. Go behind enemy lines and pass themselves off as Bzadians."

"And this is our only option?" Gonzales asked.

"No, not our only option," Russell said.

"So what's your plan B?" Gonzales asked.

"More Seals," Bilal said.

"Find another option," Gonzales said. "The backlash against the Angels after the last debacle is not going away in a hurry. I'd never get this past the oversight committee."

"Helluva way to run a war," Whitehead said. "Command by committee."

Gonzales ignored him.

"In that case, we'll have to wait for the storm to pass to get satellite and aerial recon again," Bilal said. "And if that means we wake up in a few days' time with aliens on our doorstep, I want it on the record that you refused to reactivate the Angels."

"The Angels are off the table," Gonzales said. "They're not even trained for this kind of arctic stuff." She studied her notes for a moment. "How long before we get a break in the weather?"

"There'll be a short window tomorrow," Russell said. "We'll get some satellite data."

"What are you looking for?" Gonzales asked.

"Anything," Bilal said. "Anything that gives us reason to believe that a million Bzadians are heading in our direction."

Bilal held the elevator door for Gonzales when they finished. The others were staying for another meeting.

The elevator, although ornate, was armored. It was the only entrance to the underground bunker.

"Convincing enough for you?" Gonzales asked when the heavy sheet-metal doors had closed, cutting off all sight and sound of the command center.

"You almost had *me* fooled," Bilal said.

"When do the Angels go in?" she asked.

"They're already on their way," he said.

2. ABOVE THE ICE

THE COLD WAS STARTLING, EVEN THROUGH THE ARMORED, thermally heated combat suit. Price knew part of that was the adjustment period, as the thermals sensed the rapid temperature drop and slowly warmed to compensate. Part of it was psychological. Just looking around at this desert of sea ice—feeling the spray of ice particles that clattered against the suit, hearing the low throbbing moan of the arctic wind—was enough to cause an involuntary shiver no matter what the temperature inside the suit.

Price's leg itched. The new one. Grown for her by human scientists using Bzadian technology. According to Monster, she was part Bzadian now, and no amount of arguing that it was her own cells they had cloned would convince him otherwise.

Or maybe he just liked to tease.

It was not long after dawn. At this time of year, in this part of the world, the sun could not be bothered to make an entrance until well after ten in the morning. It would hover tiredly above the horizon for a paltry eight hours, then sink, as if exhausted, below the ice.

That gave them only a few hours to reach their mission objective. It was too dangerous to move out on the ice floes in the darkness, even with night-vision goggles. And overnight the temperature dropped to even more dangerous lows.

"Comm check," Price said. She watched the sail of the submarine disappear down the hole in the ice as the five other Angels sounded off, two to six. Two was Sergeant Panyoczki: Monster. She was glad he was here, and not only for his soldiering skills. He was also someone she trusted, absolutely, without question. But more than that. He was someone she cared deeply about. Whatever they faced out here, they would face it together.

It had taken the submarine over four hours to find the lead. A fracture between two floes, where the water had not had time to refreeze and was covered by only a thin crust.

The winter ice in the turbulent Bering Strait has a life and a geography all of its own, due to the constant buffeting of the currents that run through the narrow passage between Russia and Alaska, bringing with them the outflow of sea ice from the Arctic Ocean. Great floes collide with each other, erupting into ridges.

For years the currents had prevented the strait from freezing, but a relatively recent change in the local climate had led to the accumulation of more and more sea ice, "drift ice," latching on to land-fixed "fast ice" and gradually spreading until a bridge of ice connected the two continents, with the Diomede Islands, Big and Little, at its center.

The submarine had located numerous leads in the ice canopy above, but most were too small, unstable, or in the wrong location. Once the right lead had been found, the submarine had surfaced at speed, using the top of its sail as a battering ram to smash its way through a few inches of ice.

But the submarine was gone now as Price sensed, rather than saw, its gray bulk slip away beneath the ice. On the surface of the water, delicate petals of frost flowers were already starting to form. Pretty, fractal shapes, like miniature white ferns, spreading and branching off, again and again. Within minutes, the water would wear a white coat of frost, and within the hour it would probably be strong enough to walk on.

"Oscar Mike in five mikes," Price said. "Check your battery levels."

Batteries could behave strangely in these temperatures, and a dead or low battery meant no thermals, and that meant death in this bitter and frigid world. They each carried a spare battery for that reason, and there were more on the equipment sled.

"Rope up," Monster said.

The ropes were lightweight nylon cords, thin but immensely strong. They had to be.

"We're sheltered here," Price said, clipping her rope on and checking that it was secured properly. "You'd better prepare yourselves for what we're going to hit once we get out of this lead."

"I can hardly wait," the Tsar said. He smiled his confident, charming smile. Another good addition to the team. He had proved that on Operation Magnum. He was still a bit full of himself, but that had diminished as he had gotten to know them better.

PFC Emile Attaya was the next in line in front of Price, and she double-checked the carabiner clips at his end. Emile was a good-looking Lebanese kid who smiled constantly and seemed to burn energy the way other people breathed air. Having Emile around was like having a new puppy in the house, and although it was protocol, nobody, not even the commanders back at Fort Carson, called him by his surname. He was always just "Emile." Like Monster, English was not his first language. But unlike Monster, he spoke it well, with merely a trace of an accent.

"We should have brought parasails," Emile said. "We could have used the wind and sailed there."

"If it was blowing in the right direction," Wall said. "Which it's not."

Spec. Hayden Wall. The other new Angel. He talked constantly and was generally moaning about something. He did it with the broad *a* and missing *r* of the native New Englander. His dour moping was a complete contrast from Emile's infectious enthusiasm and quick smile.

"Or bobsleds," Emile said. "We could have had dogs and they could have pulled us along."

"Somebody find his off button," Barnard said, but she smiled as she said it. Even cynical, sarcastic Barnard was not immune to Emile's puppy dog charm.

Price took an ice ax from the equipment sled and slipped the loop over her wrist. The others followed suit. Watching each of them as they did so, she thought about the faith they were putting in her as leader of the mission. She hoped it wasn't misplaced.

She shouldn't even be here. With a new leg and the intense trauma, both physical and psychological, from the disastrous Operation Magnum, she could have turned the mission down and nobody would have blamed her. But she had said yes and told anyone who asked that it was because she didn't feel her fight was finished, that she didn't want to let down her comrades, that she felt she had something to offer. She had a thousand reasons.

But the truth was that six months lying in a hospital bed plus another six months of rehab had bored her senseless. Fort Carson had bored her with its regimented mealtimes and mindless routines. She needed the buzz, the thrill, the coil-gun jumping in her arms, adrenaline coursing through her body. Sometimes it seemed she only felt alive when she was in imminent danger of death. But she couldn't tell that to anyone. Not even Monster. If the counselors back at Carson heard her say that, they would never let her out of their sight.

Someday the war would be over, one way or another, and she would have to deal with it. But that day was a long way off, and by then she might not even be alive to worry about it.

"Weapons check," she said. She checked her own, hitting the release that would spring the coil-gun over her shoulder and into her arms.

"Okay, Angels," she said. "Listen up. You are probably wondering what we are doing here."

"Yeah, bro," Wall said. "I am wondering why I am freezing my ass off in the middle of nowhere when there are warm bunks and hot pizza back at base." He seemed to be having a problem with his weapon release.

"Don't worry about it, Wall," the Tsar said, moving over to give him a hand. "It's just typical ACOG. They send us out on these missions but everything is so top secret that we don't know whether we're wiping our butts or blowing our noses until we see the color of the tissue."

"And I don't care how warm the bunks are at Fort Carson," Barnard said. "I'd rather be out here doing something than sitting around doing nothing."

She wasn't the only one, Price thought.

"Okay," Price said. "This is a straightforward reconnaissance mission. We are to avoid contact. In any case, ACOG tells us there's no enemy activity within fifty klicks."

"Except for a million Pukes lined up on Russia's Chukchi shore, waiting to have a go at us," Wall muttered.

"That's the point, Wall," Barnard said. "They're fifty klicks away. They're not here."

The Tsar stepped back so Wall could test his gun again. It released with no problem, jumping straight into his hands. He tried it three more times to be sure.

"Little Diomede Island is packed with so many sensors that they can hear a snowflake freeze," Price said. "And those sensors tell us that the Pukes are still sitting on their backsides over in Russia. All we have to do is stroll over to the island, get eyes on the control station, observe, and report."

"Report on what?" the Tsar asked.

"There are two operators on that station," Price said. "Specialist Gabrielle Bowden and Specialist Nikolas Able. We need to know that they're both okay and that everything is as it should be."

"Maybe we should have just phoned and asked them," Wall said.

Price ignored him. "Once ACOG are satisfied that everything is aboveboard, we get the hell out, as quickly as we can."

"And if we run into any real Pukes?" Wall asked.

"Then we'll waste them all," Emile said. "Bring it on."

"He's kinda cute," Barnard said. "Reminds me of Wilton."

Wilton had been one of the original members of the team. He had fought with them at Uluru and on Operation Magnum. She hadn't liked him much. Not at the start. But he had a way of growing on people, and she missed him.

"Emile, our orders are to avoid engagement," Price said. "Don't go all Chuck Norris on me."

"Gonna be a walk in the park," the Tsar said.

"Some park," Wall said. "Where's the grass, the lake, and the pigeons?"

"I think this place is awesome!" Emile said, gesturing around at the translucent blue and white walls of the lead.

Price wasn't sure what was worse, Wall's constant griping or Emile's manic energy.

"All right, Angels. We are Oscar Mike," Price said.

"Checking your ropes, my dudes, and maintain each two-meter separations," Monster said.

Price hid a smile. For two years now she had worked with Monster. His Bzadian was flawless, but he still couldn't speak English worth a damn.

She had warned them the wind would get worse when they got higher, but even she wasn't prepared for it. A furious gust hit them as they emerged from the shelter of the lead, threatening to throw them back where they came from. They crouched, on all fours, heads into the wind, and dug their axes deeply into the ice.

"Booyah, my first real mission," Emile squawked on the comm.

"No, it's not," Price said. "We're not officially here. The Angels have been stood down, remember? This mission doesn't exist."

"At least we get real bullets," the Tsar said. "Not like Magnum when they would only give us puffer rounds."

"Puffers would do no good here," Barnard said.

She was right. The compacted powder of puffer rounds exploded into a cloud when it hit body armor. The target breathed it in and was unconscious within seconds. But puffers were useless against an enemy wearing full face masks—a necessity in this frigid air.

"Move 'em out, Angels," Price called after the worst of the squall subsided.

The Tsar was on point. He stood and began to move, leaning almost horizontally into the wind. Price kept an eye on Wall and Emile. They were unknowns. They had the best scores of all the trainee Angels, but that meant nothing when you got into the field.

Wall in particular had only one year of training, but his skill with a rifle would rival that of the legendary Blake Wilton. Even so, Wall was only on the mission because two more experienced Angels had been injured in training and one had mysteriously disappeared from Fort Carson.

Price's leg itched again, left side, just below the knee.

Some of the ridges and hummocks they climbed, some they avoided. The flat areas in the center of floes were the easiest, but they were also where the wind was the strongest.

Already, Price was starting to wonder if the two missing Seal teams had simply fallen through gaps in the ice. That would explain the screams and the sudden loss of radio contact. But it wouldn't explain Legrand, the station commander who had died in mysterious circumstances.

"We could walk past a Puke patrol in this weather and never even see them," the Tsar said.

"We're not likely to run into any Pukes here," Barnard said. "We're south of the islands. The direct route between Russia and Alaska is to the north. This route would be much longer and the ice here is too rough for tanks."

"Why?" the Tsar asked.

"There's more movement in the ice floes," Barnard said. "Because it's warmer here than up north."

"Yeah, bro, this is real toasty," Wall said.

"Anything else to complain about, Wall?" Barnard asked. "Don't hold back; let's get it all out there."

"Well, now that you mention it," Wall said, "I can't understand why they're making us walk. Haven't they heard of snowmobiles?"

"Or how about a chauffeur-driven limousine?" Barnard said. "Take you right up to the front door and lay out the red carpet for you."

"I was just saying," Wall said, "this is the thirties, not the sixteenth century."

"Snowmobiles make noise and heat," the Tsar said. "You want to advertise that we are coming?"

"Why not?" Wall asked. "The LT said there are no Pukes for fifty klicks."

"Wall," Monster said.

"Yeah?"

"Keep mouth shut," Monster said.

"Amen to that," the Tsar said.

They passed an upside-down V made from two giant slabs of ice, both oddly straight and rectangular. Not long after that, a narrow track dropped into a deep gulley—a huge scar between two floes that had iced over and was gradually healing. Here the going was much easier, as the walls protected them from the wind and the flying snow. A hundred meters later, they emerged onto a flat sheet of ice where the going was smooth, although the wind was cruel.

It was some time after that when Price realized that the ground beneath her feet was vibrating. At first she thought it was the wind or the judder of the equipment sled over the rough ice, but it quickly became clear that the ice itself was moving. The vibrations rapidly progressed to a shaking that made it difficult to walk; then a sudden sideways lurch in the seemingly solid ice beneath their feet threw them to the ground.

Price started to get up, but Monster called, "Wait."

There was another jerk and another. For a few minutes the ice went crazy, shaking like an earthquake.

As harsh as it had been, at least the Australian desert stayed steady under your feet, Price thought, embedding her ax into the ice and gripping it tightly. On Operation Magnum they had been on T-boards or motorbikes most of the way. On this mission it seemed the enemy would be the least of their problems.

"What's going on?" the Tsar asked.

"Ice quake," Barnard said. "It's not a glacier we're on; it's a sea. A bunch of ice floes all bumping and scraping against each other."

"That nothing," Monster said. "Will get much worse."

"Okay, everybody, just relax. Stay where you are," Price said. "We'll be Oscar Mike again as soon as we are sure this has settled down."

■ ■ ■

The flat plain took them to a ridge that stretched as far as they could see in either direction. Two ice floes had rammed into each other here and the compressed ice had pushed up. It was not a smooth shape, but a rough jumble of ice pieces. There was no alternative but to climb it.

The equipment sled was going to be the biggest problem. It would have to be carried. That meant unroping.

Monster took one end by himself. Price and the Tsar were about to take one runner each at the front end when Wall stepped in front. "I'll take it, bro," he said.

Price stepped back, grateful for Wall and the Tsar to be doing the carrying. The rehab had been intense, but she still didn't feel as strong as before. Monster said it was just confidence, and maybe he was right, but either way she was happy not to put her new leg and her rehabbed muscles to such an arduous test.

Wall was surprisingly strong. Not bulky like Monster, but a sinewy strength. He trudged steadily up over the hummock. He didn't appear to notice or mind the lashing of the wind.

Behind them, Monster, carrying the entire back end by himself, seemed happy enough, and somehow they got the sled to the top. They stopped there briefly before beginning the climb down the other side, resting the sled often as they found their footing.

At the base of the ridge, they set off again across smooth, clear ice that was like glass beneath their feet. A brief lull in the storm revealed two dark shapes in the distance, one huge, the other glowing with artificial light.

The glowing one was their destination. Little Diomede. Ice-covered and climbing up out of the sea of white that surrounded it, it was the peak of some underwater mountain. It dominated the area, along with its larger brother, Big Diomede.

There was something majestic, riveting, about these snow-covered, jagged rocky peaks.

The wind came back up and with it great flurries of snow and ice. The islands disappeared as if they were no more than a mirage. The conditions were approaching whiteout, and Price knew they would have to stop soon. It would be too dangerous to continue, a fact that became very obvious when the Tsar stumbled, yelling, his arms windmilling. Monster must have known immediately what was happening and yanked on the rope. Price was jerked backward and sat down on her backside, hard. So did Wall in front of her, and it rippled up the line to the Tsar.

When Price went forward to see, the Tsar was sitting with his legs dangling over the edge of a crevasse.

It was wide, at least four meters across. If Monster hadn't reacted quickly, then the Tsar might have gone straight in, pulling the rest of them after him. The mission could be over in a second, and no one would ever know their fate. Maybe the mystery of the missing Seals really was as simple as that.

At the bottom of the crevasse, nearly two meters down, was a dark river of ocean. The crevasse was new, probably formed in the recent ice quake.

"Okay, Monster," Price said. "How do we get across?"

Monster had served alongside their last lieutenant, Ryan

Chisnall, in the Great Ice War of 2028. He was the only Angel with arctic experience.

"Can we use the ladders?" the Tsar asked.

"Is too wide for ladder," Monster said. "Would not be stable enough. Not in such winds."

"So what, then?" Price asked.

"If we had snowmobiles, we could try to jump it," Emile said.

"And if we had a magic wand, we could make it disappear," Barnard said. "But we don't have that either."

"And if the Bzadians hadn't invaded, I'd be chatting up girls in the school cafeteria right now," Wall said. "Instead of freezing my nuts off here with you Rambo wannabes."

"Shoulda, woulda, coulda," Price said. "We'll split up. Monster, Barnard, and Wall go half a klick north. The rest of us will go half a klick south. Constant radio contact. If we lose contact, return to this point. There'll be a way around or across."

She was right. Price and her team had gone barely twenty meters when Monster's voice came on the comm.

"Angel One, this is Angel Two. How copy?"

"Solid copy, Angel Two," Price said. "What have you got?"

"Bridge," Monster said.

It was a bridge of ice. Part of the wall on their side had sheared off, creating a sloping ramp across to the other side.

Monster went first, easing himself over the side of the crevasse.

He stood on the base of the bridge and jumped up and down a couple of times, testing it.

"Is good," he said, with a thumbs-up at Price.

"If it can take his weight, it'll hold anybody's," Barnard said.

Monster dropped to his hands and knees and crawled out onto the shaft of ice. Still it seemed solid, the broken ice welded at either end by the cold.

"Oscar Kilo," he said, then moved away from the edge, using his ax to anchor himself in case any of the others slipped.

They got the sled across by lowering it on ropes to the bridge, where Monster simply hauled it up to the other side.

Price, now last in the team, eased over the edge of the crevasse and found her footing at the base of the bridge. Her new leg began to twinge and spasm. It did that sometimes, for no good reason. As if she didn't have enough problems to deal with. She stretched it out, which seemed to help, and began to crawl across.

The next spasm made her body shake, but she realized with horror that this was not her new leg playing games. A massive vibration in the ice had made the whole ice bridge tremble.

"Here we go again," Barnard said.

"Hurry!" Monster shouted.

Price was halfway across when the ice began to shake uncontrollably. She buried her ax in the bridge to stop herself from slipping sideways, then wrenched it out again as she felt the rope around her waist tighten.

She slid forward as the rest of the Angels hauled on the rope. Ice was splintering and cracking all around her as the great ice floes moved. Price screamed as the bridge dropped away, the shaft of ice shattered by the unimaginable pressure from either side.

She fell into the crevasse, landing on the rubble of the ice bridge. For a moment the rubble floated on the surface of the water; then the crushed pieces of ice gave way. But before she could fall through, the rope snapped tight, slamming her into the icy wall of the crevasse. She grabbed the rope with both hands and jammed her knees up against her chest to keep her feet out of the water. The impact swung her around, away from the wall. The far wall, which had been four or more meters away, was now less than half that distance and closing rapidly.

"Get me out of here!" she screamed, but already she was rising, sliding up the smooth ice of the crevasse wall.

"Get your feet up! Get your feet up!" Wall yelled as she made it to the top.

Price spun her hips around, lifting her feet up out of the crevasse just as there was a massive rumble and a crunch of ice from behind her.

The world shook with the thunderclap of a thousand explosions.

She rolled over and saw that the crevasse was gone. The ice sheets had rammed together and only a long crack in the ice remained of what had been an impassable chasm a few seconds earlier.

"We should have waited," the Tsar said. "We would have been able to just step across."

"That wouldn't have been nearly as much fun," Emile said.

The others all laughed, and Price laughed with them. But Emile was right.

She bit her lip to stop herself from whooping with exhilaration.

"There it is," the Tsar said.

It had taken them an hour to travel less than a hundred meters over rugged and broken ice, but it had brought them to a wide, flat area. Spirits were good. Their progress was slow but steady, and as the lights of Little Diomede came into view again, Price felt a surge of confidence. It didn't look that far, and with the flatter ice ahead of them, they should make good time. The ice here was strange, like nothing they had seen before. Some odd quirk of the weather and the geology of the ice had created a series of rounded hillocks, giant ice pimples stretching in every direction as far as they could see.

"Do people actually live on that rock?" Emile asked, staring at the vague light in the distance.

"Somebody's gotta do it," the Tsar said.

"It's, like, in the middle of nowhere," Emile said. "What do they do for fun?"

"Scan for Pukes and play Scrabble," Barnard said. "And I'm joking about the Scrabble."

"I'd be bored out of my mind in three minutes," Emile said.

"No surprises there," the Tsar said.

"Has it occurred to anyone that we look like Pukes?" Wall

asked. "I mean, am I the only one thinking this through? Little Diomede is full of sensitive scanners. Their whole mission is to watch out for enemy forces in the vicinity and yet we're expecting to march right up to it?"

"As I said, our mission is to observe and report," Price said. "Their equipment can pick up vehicles and equipment from klicks away, but it won't pick up foot mobiles in these conditions unless they're really close. We'll keep well out of range."

"And if we don't see anything suspicious?" Wall asked.

"In that case I may go in myself and check it out from the inside," Price said.

"Using your invisibility cloak," Wall said.

"Something like that," Price said.

"They don't call her the Phantom for nothing," the Tsar said.

"I'll believe that when I see it," Wall said.

"Monster has seen it, and Monster still doesn't believe it," Monster said. "She like ghost."

"For the record, Wall, you need to watch your attitude," Barnard said.

"My attitude is doing just fine, bro," Wall said. "Thanks for asking."

"I'll remember that if I ever have to pull you out of a crevasse," Barnard said.

"What if they do see her?" Wall asked. "What are they going to think about a Puke creeping around?"

"If I get caught, my orders are to get them to contact ACOG, who will verify my identity," Price said.

"And if they shoot first and ask questions later?" Wall asked.

"I didn't say it wouldn't be risky," Price said.

"If you want a safe job, try Burger King," Barnard said.

Wall snorted and turned away, muttering under his breath. Price couldn't hear what he said and couldn't be bothered finding out.

"What happens if the station really is attacked by Pukes?" Emile asked. "Do they just sit there and wait to get blown to pieces? Seriously, if they want to invade, first thing the Pukes are gonna do is pound the guacamole out of that place, right?"

"Any sign of trouble and the operators bug out," Barnard said.

"How?" Emile asked.

"Hovercraft," Barnard said. "They also have an airstrip, but you couldn't rely on that this time of year, in case of a blizzard. Like this one."

"Enough idle chitchat, Angels," Price said. "It's time to check in with HQ."

"We'll have to get out of the wind," the Tsar said. "The satellite dish needs to be steady."

"There's no shelter here," Barnard said. "These hills are too rounded."

"Then we'll make our own shelter," Price said. "Monster?"

Monster took a snow shovel from the sled and dug quickly into the leeside of the nearest hillock. He scooped out a shallow cave, dumping snow on either side as additional protection from the wind.

"Strange," Barnard said.

"What?" Price asked.

"This hill is made of snow," Barnard said. "Not ice."

"What does that mean?" Price asked. It must have meant something or Barnard wouldn't have said it. Barnard was the exception to the rule that you didn't have to be smart to be an intelligence officer. She was the smartest person Price knew. It was her idea to create the tsunami that destroyed the Wivenhoe Dam on Operation Magnum, and whatever your opinion on the outcome of that, it was very smart thinking.

"It doesn't snow much here," Barnard said.

"So where'd all this snow come from?"

"I don't know," Barnard said. "And how did it get dumped in this big pile?"

"Anything on the scope?" Price asked, suddenly concerned and unsure why.

"Nothing," the Tsar said. "But the feed is so poor that we could be standing next to a Bzadian battle tank and not even see it on the scope."

The handheld scopes depended on a feed from all-seeing satellite eyes high above them. But in these conditions those eyes were almost blind.

As soon as the snow cave was big enough for all of them, Monster strapped the shovel back onto the sled. In the concave shape he had created, the wind's absence was a welcome relief.

"Emile, you take guard," Price said.

The Tsar handed the scope to Emile, who studied the screen

carefully. Retrieving the satellite radio unit from the equipment sled, the Tsar opened the cover of the radio and pressed a few buttons. A small dish emerged, unfolded, and automatically oriented itself to the right point in the sky. He checked a few things, then activated the set and plugged it into his comm unit, switching it so they all could hear.

"Heaven, this is Angel One. How copy?" Price asked.

The voice came back almost immediately. "Solid copy, Angel One. This is Heaven."

"Heaven, we are in position at designated OP: grid reference, Charlie November, four, three, five, niner, three, one, over."

"Good work, Angel One. What is your visibility rating? Over."

"Tango two at best," Price said.

There was a short silence; then the voice on the other end said, "How you doing, Price?"

"Good, Wilton," Price said with a grin. "How 'bout you?"

"I'm fine," Wilton said, his voice thin and crisp through the radio. "How's the arctic?"

"Arctic? This is the subarctic," Price said. "The arctic circle is eighty klicks thataway."

"I'm glad they didn't send us to the arctic," Wall said. "It'd be cold and miserable *there*."

"I wish I was there with you," Wilton said.

"No, you don't," Barnard said.

"Ignore her. It's much nicer than you'd think," Price said.

"Nice?" Wilton asked.

"Sun's out, the water is cool, we're all in our swimsuits, drinking ice-cold beers around the pool," Price said, wiping rime from her face mask and stretching her new leg to stop it from cramping up.

"Now I know you're lying," Wilton said. "You ain't old enough to drink beer."

That brought laughter from the team.

"We have eyes on the island," Price said.

"Any sign of enemy activity?" Wilton asked.

"Negative on that," Price said.

"Confirming no sign of enemy activity," Wilton said, reverting to formal radio procedures. "Next check-in at thirteen-thirty mission time."

"See you then," Price said.

The Tsar unplugged and packed up the transmitter.

"Okay, Angels, we are Oscar Mike," Price said.

"LT!" Emile said.

"Azoh!" the Tsar said.

Price spun around. The mission had barely begun. And it was already over.

3. HEAT

IT WAS TOO WARM IN THE OFFICE, THOUGH THE TEMPERA-ture hadn't changed.

Blake Wilton was uncomfortable and sweating lightly. Perhaps it was some kind of reaction to knowing that his friends were camped out in the frozen subarctic wilderness and wild weather of the Bering Strait. The air-conditioning for his office was controlled from his computer, and he lowered it a couple of degrees, feeling the first cold blush steal into the room.

Technically, he shouldn't even be here.

He had been forced out of Recon Team Angel when he had grown past the height limitation, against all predictions of the geneticists. They had removed the bumps on his skull, recolored his skin, and stitched up his tongue, which still felt strange when he ate or tried to speak Bzadian.

He had been training for the last six months as a gunner with the Canadian Land Force Command, 2nd Spitfire Battalion. Not twenty-four hours ago he had been out on the ice in a small two-man hovercraft, conducting live firing exercises against robotic targets.

He had been called to Virginia without warning or explanation, given a quiet office well away from anyone else, and only instructed at the last minute what he was doing there. Liaison officer for a vital recon mission.

No matter how harsh the conditions the Angels were facing, he wished he were there with them. Doing something more constructive than simply being the radio contact for his old buddies.

The operation was top secret. The participation of the Angels was to be denied if he was questioned. They didn't exist, he didn't exist, and none of them were involved in this mission.

He wrote up his contact notes. That took less than ten minutes. He fiddled with the computer for a few minutes, doing nothing really, then stood up, intending to go to McDonald's for an early dinner. It was only one o'clock on the ice, but it was already after five p.m. here, and his stomach was growling.

That was one thing he really liked about the Pentagon. There was a big food court with every kind of fast food imaginable, from KFC to Dunkin' Donuts.

He particularly liked the shakes at Mickey D's, although they didn't taste quite as good when you only had one tongue.

Even as he thought that, he remembered his friends stuck on the ice, and it seemed wrong. In any case, he never got out of the office. The door opened and Daniel Bilal entered.

Bilal was someone *important.* He was in *military intelligence,* but that was all Wilton knew. He didn't seem to have any rank, at least none that was publically displayed. But he had the power to get Wilton pulled from his hovercraft crew and flown secretly to Virginia.

Bilal was small, black, and dressed casually, as if he had no time for the uniforms and suits that made up Washington. He wore a light gray sports jacket over a T-shirt with a picture of *The Cat in the Hat.*

"You had your first contact?" he asked. It was a question, but Wilton was quite sure that Bilal already knew the answer to it. Bilal seemed to know the answer to everything.

"Yes, right on schedule," Wilton said. "They are on the ground and moving toward the first observation point."

"Good," Bilal said. "What time is the next check-in?"

"In about half an hour. That's thirteen-thirty, mission time," Wilton said, trying his best to sound professional and official.

"I'll sit in on that one," Bilal said, checking his watch. "I'll see you in twenty minutes."

"Sir . . . ," Wilton began, unsure how to frame his question.

"Yes, Blake," Bilal said.

"It's just that I don't understand," Wilton said. "I thought the Angel program was shut down."

"That's what we wanted you to think," Bilal said. "That's what we want everyone to think."

"Why?" Wilton asked.

"Because that's what we want the Bzadians to think," Bilal said.

"But we, I mean they, are not really trained for this kind of mission," Wilton said.

"We know that," Bilal said. "But Angels have certain special qualifications that could prove to be more important than cold weather training. The first teams we sent in were arctic specialists and that didn't seem to help them any."

"Teams?" Wilton asked.

"Two Seal teams," Bilal said.

"What happened to them?" Wilton asked.

"We don't know," Bilal said, shrugging. "Bad luck or bad timing. Or . . ."

"Or what?" Wilton asked.

"Or perhaps someone knew they were coming," Bilal said.

As Wilton was pondering the implications of that, his personal phone rang. He queried Bilal with a glance. Bilal nodded.

It was Corporal Courtney Fox, one of the communications operators at Fort Carson, the Team Angel base of operations.

"Hi, Courtney. How's everyone back at Carson?" Wilton asked, not so much to exchange pleasantries as because Courtney needed a few seconds of his voice to establish vocal ID. It felt good to talk to someone from Fort Carson. Recon Team Angel had been the only place he had felt at home. Like he had belonged. Hearing Courtney's voice reminded him how much he missed it.

"We're all good, Blake. Somehow it's not the same without you around, though," Courtney said.

"You're just saying that," Wilton said. "Do you have a voice match yet? Or do you need me to keep talking?"

"Just came through," Courtney said with a pleasant laugh. "Hey, I have an incoming audio call for you. Do you want me to route it through?"

"Who is it?" Wilton asked.

"She hasn't identified herself, but she asked for you by name and gave all the correct security codes," Courtney said.

"Put it through," Wilton said.

"See you, Blake. Come back and visit," Courtney said.

There was a slight click and the sound of her breathing disappeared.

"Hello. Who is this?" Wilton asked.

"Can you talk freely?"

It was not Price.

The woman's voice was not one he recognized. Her voice had a flat, robotic sound.

"Not really," Wilton said, with a glance at Bilal.

"Okay. Don't say anything. Memorize this phone number, but don't write it down." She gave the number. "Call me back. Make sure you can't be overheard."

"Call who back?" Wilton asked.

"It's Ryan," she said.

"Who?" Wilton asked.

"Chisnall," she said.

4. TANK

PRICE STARED INTO A FOREST OF COIL-GUN MUZZLES. AT the squad of Bzadian soldiers, eyes steady behind the sights of those guns, despite the howling, buffeting wind. They had approached from the rear of the hillock, out of sight, any sounds they made lost in the noise of the wind. The Angels' shelter had become a trap. For a brief instant, Price thought of resisting. They could go for their guns, put up a fight, maybe have a chance. Part of her wanted the fight, but another part of her brain said no. They were outnumbered, and the enemy soldiers already had the drop on them. It would be a slaughter, even if they did manage to take some of the Bzadians with them.

She flicked her comm onto a Bzadian frequency. "Who are you?" she asked in Bzadian. There was no response. She tried two other frequencies, with no more success. Slowly, she raised her hands to the back of her neck, the Bzadian sign of surrender.

One by one, the enemy soldiers stripped them of their weapons and motioned them to move.

They didn't have to go far. It was a short walk between a few of the odd rounded hillocks to one that appeared like all the others, except for the low tunnel dug into the side of it.

Three of the Bzadians dropped to their knees and crawled into the tunnel, while the rest kept their guns close at the Angels' backs. One of the Bzadians, whose uniform markings indicated a squad leader, pointed at Price, then pointed to the tunnel.

After a little hesitation, Price dropped to her hands and knees and led the Angels in, shuffling along the ice through the narrow opening. For now they had to seem cooperative. They had to act like Bzadians, just as they had at Uluru.

The hillock was not a mound of snow or ice. To her shock, Price found herself climbing up through a hatch into the main cabin of a Bzadian battle tank. How many other tanks were there? Price tried to guess at the number of mounds they had seen, and couldn't.

A row of fold-down seats, transportation seats for infantry, lined the outer wall, and without speaking, their captors indicated that they should sit and remove their helmets.

"What's going on?" Price asked as soon as her helmet was

off, with as much indignation as she could fake. Still there was silence from the Bzadians.

The Bzadian squad leader removed his helmet and tucked it under one arm. He was thin, with a hooked nose. He walked along the row of Angels, examining all of them. Price waited. Best to let him make the first move. She looked around, gauging her surroundings. Searching for opportunities to escape.

There were no exits from the cabin except for the hatch in the floor, although on one side was a small rounded door. It was slightly ajar. Inside was a bathroom with a Bzadian-style toilet and a showerhead in the ceiling. All the comforts of home. The Bzadian crews lived in the tank when going into combat. Sleeping, bathing, toileting, all without having to leave the vehicle. So where were they? The tank was empty except for the three soldiers who had preceded them inside.

It was warm. There was a faintly artificial smell, as if the air had been processed and filtered, which was probably true. It would be scrubbed of carbon dioxide and recirculated, to avoid pumping the warm air outside, where it could be picked up by thermal detectors. As the shock of the capture started to wear off, other questions raised themselves in Price's mind. How could a tank be *here,* so close to the supposedly highly sensitive sensors of Little Diomede?

"Who are you and what are you doing here?" the squad leader asked finally, addressing Price.

"I am Priaz," Price said, with even more indignation. "We are scouts from the second regiment, first infantry division. Why have you detained us?"

The squad leader waved his hands in front of his face, a token apology. But still a good sign, Price thought.

"I am Zim," he said. "We were told that second regiment is still at Chukchi."

"Your information is wrong," Price said. "Battle plans have changed. Were you not informed?"

"How could I be informed with the strict radio silence?" Zim asked, but he appeared somewhat satisfied with her answer. "What are you doing in our sector?"

"We did not know we were in your sector," Price said, thinking quickly. "We were patrolling our own sector and were caught in the blizzard. We had to deviate around a huge fissure in the ice. My team was almost at the end of their endurance, so we were taking shelter, gathering our strength. That was when you found us."

The Angels did their best to act like soldiers who had been tabbing through an ice field for hours and were almost at the end of their tether. It wasn't difficult.

"Check our ID tubes," Price said, pulling hers off her shoulder. Zim took it and collected those from the other Angels, handing them to one of the soldiers who went to verify them in a tube-reader at the main control panel.

"And this radio equipment?" Zim asked. "And the sled you were pulling? It looks human to me."

Their comm set was sitting on the floor of the tank in a pool of water, formed from the melting ice.

Price glanced around at the other Angels as she carefully formulated what she would say next. "I agree. It looks human.

We found the sled and the radio in the lee of a ridge, not far from here. For all we know, it may be broadcasting your location to the scumbugz."

One of the soldiers was examining the unit. "Perhaps from the human infiltrators we intercepted yesterday," he said.

Price carefully avoided any expression. The "human infiltrators" could only be one of the Seal teams.

"We captured their equipment with them," Zim said.

"And you didn't think to search for spares?" Price asked. "Or other teams?"

Zim shrugged. The soldier with the ID tubes returned them to Zim and nodded.

The guns that had been trained on them were lowered, holstered.

Price casually glanced at Monster and the Tsar. Not all of the Bzadian squad had followed them into the tank. Some had remained outside, probably guarding the area. There were just five Bzadians and six Angels. If her team could overpower the Bzadians before they drew their weapons again, the Angels should be able to take control of the situation.

"So what now?" Price asked casually, conversationally. "How do we get back to our unit?"

"I am not sure," Zim said. "I don't know how you got here, but you shouldn't be in this area. My commander is on his way and he will sort it out."

"Good," Price said. "The sooner the better."

Down the row from her, the Tsar stretched his arms, then his legs. Wall shifted forward slightly on his seat.

"May I use your bathroom?" Price asked. "We have been in these suits for hours."

Zim looked carefully at her before replying. "Of course," he said.

[1720 HOURS LOCAL TIME]
[Office FC7001, Third Level, West Quarter, Pentagon, Virginia]

"WILTON?" IT WAS A MALE VOICE THIS TIME, WITHOUT the artificial, robotic quality. And it did sound like Chisnall.

"Who is this really?" Wilton asked.

He was sitting in the central courtyard of the Pentagon. A grassy, tree-covered park with five paths converging on a central fountain that, for some reason, was known as the Hot Dog Stand. It was a tall cascading water feature topped by a statue of an owl. The sound of the water blanketed out other sounds, which was why he had picked this place. For all he knew, his office was bugged.

The weather was cold enough to drive everyone else indoors, which also made this a great place for a private conversation.

"It's Ryan," the voice said.

"Uh-uh, no way," Wilton said. "I saw you go over the dam."

"In the desert, on the way to Uluru," the voice said, "someone asked you if you were religious. Do you remember?"

"What did I say?" Wilton asked.

"That when you were young, you prayed every night for God to make you a Christian, but he never did."

"*Ryan?*" Wilton asked. Nobody could know that except one of the five other original Angels. Two of those were in the Bering Strait. One was in prison. The other was killed in the Australian desert. That left only Ryan Chisnall.

"How have you been, Blake?" Chisnall asked.

"Good," Wilton said. "How about you?"

"I'm okay," Chisnall said.

"Where are you?" Wilton asked.

"Australia, but you can tell no one," Chisnall said. "The Bzadians have spies in ACOG and it is vital that no one knows I am alive."

"What about Price and Monster?"

"You can tell Price and Monster, and Barnard and the Tsar," Chisnall said. "But make it clear to them how important it is to keep it to themselves. My life depends on it."

"Okay, I will," Wilton said.

"Where are the Angels?"

"They're . . . um—" Wilton broke off, coughing to clear a sudden choking in his throat. His eyes were full of tears, and he wasn't really sure why.

"Are you crying, Blake?" Chisnall asked.

"Yeah, whatever," Wilton said, wiping his eyes. "Over you? Barely noticed you were gone."

"So where are the Angels?" Chisnall asked.

"They're not here right now," Wilton said.

"On a mission?" Chisnall asked.

"I can't say," Wilton said.

"Fair enough," Chisnall said. "Listen carefully, I don't have much time. I am working with a group of Bzadians who are opposed to the war. I won't go into the details at the moment."

"Seriously?" Wilton asked. "There are Pukes against the war?"

"Seriously. But I need some help. I need to contact Barnard. I can't say why. I tried to get her at Fort Carson, but they wouldn't put me through. Nor to Price or Monster."

"They wouldn't be able to," Wilton said.

"So I asked for you, and they said you didn't work there anymore," Chisnall said.

"Yeah, they kicked me out," Wilton said. "I was too good-looking. Never liked the place much anyway."

Chisnall laughed. "Kept growing, did you?"

"Just a little," Wilton said.

"What are you doing now?" Chisnall asked.

"Gunner on a fast-attack hovercraft," Wilton said.

"Sounds cool," Chisnall said.

"It is," Wilton said. "Much more fun than tabbing around the desert with a bunch of whiny Angels."

"Okay, so how do I get hold of Barnard?" Chisnall asked.

"I should be able to relay a message," Wilton said.

"No, I need to talk to her directly," Chisnall said.

"I'll see what I can arrange," Wilton said.

"Okay, thanks," Chisnall said. "Give her this number and get her to call me."

There was a short silence on the line and Wilton thought

Chisnall had gone. That made his heart race. It was as if by hanging up the phone, he would discover that this was all part of a dream, just a figment of his imagination. That Chisnall was not really alive.

"Hey, Chisnall," he said.

"Yeah?"

"These Pukes that you're working with, would they be willing to help us?" Wilton asked.

"Maybe. Depends what it is," Chisnall said.

Wilton hesitated, wondering if he was giving too much away. He didn't know who else might be listening at Chisnall's end.

"You said there are spies in ACOG. What did you mean?" he asked. "Are they traitors? Like Brogan?"

"You mean from Uluru?" Chisnall asked.

"Yeah, like from Uluru, or whatever," Wilton said.

"I don't know," Chisnall said.

"Can you ask someone?" Wilton asked.

"The people I am working with wouldn't know," Chisnall said. "Uluru was top secret. Most Bzadians don't even know the program existed."

"Shame," Wilton said. "I don't know who to trust nowadays."

"Trust no one," Chisnall said.

"There are some soldiers," Wilton said, "who . . . I mean . . . It could be super important. For Price and the others."

There was a silence at the other end and again Wilton thought the connection had been broken.

"These soldiers, do you have access to their personnel files?"

"I can try to get it," Wilton said.

"Dig around in their history, see if everything adds up. Or . . ." Chisnall's voice trailed off.

"Or what?"

"You could show their photos to Brogan. See if she recognizes them. If they are from Uluru, then she just might."

"You think she'd help?"

"Maybe not. But show her the photos anyway. Watch her reaction."

"I'll try that," Wilton said.

"I gotta go," Chisnall said. "Get Barnard to call me as soon as possible."

"Solid copy," Wilton said.

"Hey, Wilton."

"Yeah?"

"It's been good to hear your voice."

"You too, Ryan."

When he hung up the phone, Wilton found his eyes watering up again. He had lived with the certainty of Chisnall's death for over a year. The truth was almost too much to deal with.

The tears flowed freely. But they were good tears.

The shower nozzle unscrewed silently. It was a metal pipe with a ball-shaped showerhead on the end, which unscrewed as well, leaving Price with a heavy pipe about ten centimeters long. It fitted neatly into the sleeve of her tunic, when she unclipped the cuff. She hid the showerhead behind the spherical toilet bowl and closed the cover. The toilet made a whooshing sound.

She left her cuff loose and checked that the metal pipe would slip easily down into her hand when she wanted it to, then opened the door and stepped out into the main cabin of the tank. She should have been afraid. But she wasn't. Mostly there was a strange exhilaration. A sense of imminent danger and action.

"My turn," Monster said, standing and stepping toward her.

She let the pipe slip down just into her hand, so the end of it touched her palm. The Tsar and Barnard tensed, ever so slightly.

The Bzadian soldiers seemed unaware of the shift in posture of the Angels. Zim glanced at Monster, then turned back to the computer screen he was working on.

Price let the pipe slip lower, until the end of it was in her hand, hiding it behind her leg.

"Stop what you are doing!"

The voice came from the center of the cabin, from the hatch. Price turned to see a Bzadian, in a colonel's uniform, climbing up through the hatchway.

That changed the odds, but not much. She took a firm grip of the end of the pipe.

"Sit down!" the colonel said. The gun in his hand changed the odds a lot more. It was aimed directly between her eyes.

All Price could see was the gun. Monster paused, halfway to the bathroom, watching her for a cue. She shook her head.

By now the other Bzadians had guns in their hands and any chance was gone.

Why hadn't she been quicker?

"All of you, sit down," the colonel ordered, indicating the infantry transport seats around the outer wall of the tank. Price eased the pipe back into her sleeve and, with a quick shake of her head at the others, went to sit down.

The colonel climbed up, followed by a very hard-faced soldier, a female, who towered at least a head above the others. An insignia on her breastplate marked her as one of the elite Vaza corps, bodyguards who protected senior Bzadian officers. Her jaw was wide and her nose was crooked, broken a few times and never set properly. That was a Bzadian badge of courage and toughness. If not for the shape of her armor, Price would have mistaken her for a male.

The colonel was less rough-hewn, almost effeminate in his features. He wore glasses, which was highly unusual for a Bzadian. He took off his helmet and put away his sidearm as he walked along in front of the Angels, stopping before Price. He removed his glasses, then sniffed the air a few times. There was a sense of indifference about him. A sense that he was wasting his valuable time dealing with such a trivial matter.

He replaced his glasses, and without warning, his right hand struck like a snake. He grabbed Price's face, squeezing her cheeks together, forcing her to open her mouth as she struggled in the steely strength of his grip. He examined her tongue before releasing her.

"I am Colonel Nokz'z," he said. He wiped his hand on his uniform with an expression of distaste. "You are the leader?"

"Yes, I am, and I demand to be returned to my unit immediately," Price said. She added an extra buzz after the last word, the Bzadian way of showing annoyance.

"Your unit?" Nokz'z asked.

"Second regiment, first infantry division," Price said.

"Why are they not in cuffs?" Nokz'z asked, with a glance at Zim.

The guns aimed at the Angels suddenly became a lot more steady, the focus of those holding them a lot more intense. The colonel's bodyguard also unholstered her weapon and aimed it at Price.

"This is an outrage!" Price said. She tried to remember how Chisnall had managed to seem so convincing in the Australian desert.

"What is the need to cuff them?" Zim asked.

Nokz'z did not seem to hear either of them. "Secure these scumbugz."

"Scumbugz?" Zim queried.

"Scumbugz," Nokz'z said, still without addressing Price. "They are humans. I can smell them. They are the ones they call Angels."

"I don't know what you are talking about," Price said.

"Our intelligence said that the Angels were shut down," Zim said.

"Let us find out," Nokz'z said. He took a small electronic

device from a pocket and held it in front of Price. A green flash illuminated her face.

He walked to a nearby computer and pressed buttons. Nothing happened at first; then up on the screen came a recognizable picture of Price running through one of the corridors at Uluru. It was taken from a security camera, so it was from above, but her face was clear.

He sniffed again and turned to Zim. "I told you I could smell them. This one was at Uluru."

"Someone who looks like me," Price tried, but it sounded desperate, even to her.

"Facial recognition algorithms cannot be so easily fooled," Nokz'z said. He glanced at Zim. "Cuff them."

The Bzadians first removed the battery packs that powered the Angels' combat suits, and the spares. That was a clever move, Price thought. It trapped them in the tank as securely as if they were in an iron cage. Without the warmth of the powered thermal suits, they would quickly freeze to death outside.

The battery packs, along with their coil-guns, grenades, and other equipment, were placed in equipment lockers, next to the driver's control panel, well out of reach.

Their helmets were taken and placed on high racks. Another lock on the door of the cage. They were going nowhere without helmets.

She was made to face the wall and, when she did, a gun was placed on the back of her head to ensure she didn't resist. A flexible plastic collar was placed around her neck. On either side of the collar was a wrist loop.

The soldier who grasped her right arm stopped, unclipped her cuff, and extracted the shower pipe. He handed it to Zim.

"Whatever would you need that for?" Nokz'z asked.

Price didn't answer.

Once her arms were secured by the wrist loops, Price was made to sit. The neckcuff was clipped to a bracket on the top of the seat back, at neck height. It was ruthless, simple, and startlingly effective. Any movement tightened the collar, choking her. Price found that she had to sit straight, as if at attention. Even slouching was enough to put pressure on the cuff and cut off her air supply.

Barnard was next to be cuffed, scowling at the two soldiers who did it.

Emile was last in line. With the curve in the wall of the tank, Price could see his face clearly. He was staring at her.

Price glanced around the cabin. Her eye fell on the equipment locker. Their guns and grenades were there, so close, but so far away. But if someone was quick . . .

She looked back at Emile, then flicked her eyes to the locker. Emile queried her with a raised eyebrow.

"*Puke spray,*" Price mouthed.

Emile nodded and glanced over at the locker.

Half of their grenades were explosive; the rest were Puke spray. Price had inadvertently invented those during Operation Magnum, when she had shot a hole in a can of the spray. The idea had since been developed into a standard weapon carried by all Special Forces teams.

If Emile could get to one of the Puke spray grenades and

set it off inside the tank, it would immobilize the Bzadians on board, with little effect on the Angels if they held their breath.

Monster was looking at her, too, and shaking his head minutely. *No, don't risk it,* was the clear message.

But they had to do something.

The Bzadians cuffed Wall and the Tsar and then moved to Monster.

Monster made them nervous. That was clear from how they kept a good distance from him and from the steady way the coil-gun was trained on him as one of the soldiers moved in closer to cuff him.

"Turn around," Nokz'z said.

Monster turned to face the wall. The eyes of everyone in the tank were on him. All guns were on him.

Emile was still watching her. She flicked her eyes one more time to the lockers.

Two Bzadians grasped Monster's arms and started to raise them toward the neckcuff. Monster offered no resistance.

"Dingo," Price said. The team's action word. Ever since Uluru.

There was a blur of movement and Emile leaped out of his seat.

The gun that had been covering Monster flicked toward Emile. Too late, the soldier realized that was a mistake. Monster twisted his wrists, latching on to the arms of his captors and pulling them into him even as he thrust himself backward, using them as a kind of shield, ramming them into the soldier behind. The Vaza, the colonel's bodyguard, sensing that the real danger came from Monster, not Emile, was turning her weapon but could not get a clean shot. In a blur of movement, Emile raced around the inside of the tank, a miniature human tornado, pinballing off the walls.

Guns tried to track him and arms stretched out for him, but he was far too fast for them. He made it to the lockers and grabbed a grenade, reached for the pin, then clearly changed his mind with a quick shake of his head at Price. Already, guns were turning toward him, but he ducked under their aim, sliding across the floor to the hatch, and disappearing out of sight.

Why hadn't he pulled the pin? Why had he just made a run for it? Why? It was the wrong grenade, Price decided. Half of the grenades in that locker were explosive ones. Emile had grabbed the wrong one. An explosive grenade in a confined area like this tank would kill everyone inside.

Monster was wrestling with two of the Bzadians, but it wasn't a fair fight. Two on one. He tied them in knots and dumped them on top of the Vaza. The soldiers on the other side of the cabin were trying to get a clean shot at him and one of them took the chance. Monster was flung backward by the impact of the bullet but was quickly on his feet, deep cracks spreading across the armored plates of his combat suit. Another shot and he would be dead. The crash of the gunshot was still ringing in Price's ears as, with an apologetic glance behind, Monster dived headfirst into the open hatch.

The Bzadians recovered quickly. Zim was down the hatch and in the tunnel.

The Vaza was about to follow him when she stopped at an order from Nokz'z.

"No," Nokz'z said. "Stay here, Vaza. I would not want to lose you."

"They will get away," the Vaza said.

"Away to where?" Nokz'z asked. "They have no thermals and no helmets. They have no weapons apart from one grenade. Let them go. We might recover the bodies later." He made a small shrug. "Or not."

5. ARCTIC TEARS

MONSTER RAN INTO THE TEETH OF THE GALE. EMILE RAN just in front of him. It was barely running. It was hardly walking. It was a stumbling, drunken lurch, fighting for every footstep. Two Bzadians had been standing guard outside the entrance to the tunnel, but they had been looking the wrong way. Emile had burst past them, ducking and dodging off into the snowstorm. They had raised their weapons to fire, but then Monster had been on them, bashing their helmets together and leaving them stunned, lying on the ice. Monster glanced at their helmets and batteries but shots from the tunnel behind them kicked up snow at their heels.

Now Monster and Emile ran. The cold was ferocious; ice

spicules beat against their unheated armor and cut their un-protected faces.

The cuts did not worry Monster. The cold here was a bet-ter bandage than any gauze. The blood froze, sealing the cut as soon as it was made. He saw Emile wiping ice from his face, and grabbed his hand to stop him.

The ice was painful, but it was also protection, forming a solid barrier and shielding his face from more of the sharp fly-ing particles.

Monster instinctively kept his head down and a hand in front of his face to protect his eyes. Without goggles or a mask, it was impossible to see, and he blinked constantly to prevent the fluids around his eyeballs from freezing.

Even the body armor offered scant protection. It blocked the wind but not the cold. The thermal lining inside was sup-posed to do that, but unpowered it offered no more warmth than a thin blanket.

Monster ignored the cold, concentrating instead on the greater danger, which would come from behind. Already, he heard the crack of coil-gun fire, but in this blizzard, he knew they were shooting at shadows.

Emile turned and pulled the pin on the grenade that he was still carrying, hurling it in the direction of the gunfire. A mo-ment later came the thump of an explosion, but the firing from behind them intensified.

A waste of a grenade, Monster thought, but he understood why Emile had done it. He was running for his life and get-ting shot at. It wasn't a nice feeling the first time someone was shooting at you, trying to kill you. Come to think of it, it was never a nice feeling getting shot at. The grenade didn't worry him. What worried him was running out on his friends. Had he made the right decision? He had seen the question in Emile's eyes. Seen the brief nod from Price. He had understood what Price wanted Emile to do. But it was an act of desperation.

There was a plan to the universe. He truly believed that. Ever since Uluru. There had to be, otherwise none of this made any kind of sense. And even if he couldn't see the plan, couldn't understand the plan, if his part in that plan ended here, then that was just how things were. But not Price. Please, not Price. She would die, too, after torture by the PGZ. That was like a kick to the stomach, because there was nothing he could do about that.

Around him the landscape was flat and featureless, except for the dome-like hills that were Bzadian tanks.

He steered them on a diagonal course, which was easier than heading straight into the wind.

The first fifty meters were the hardest. Every step was a scream of pain, both from tortured muscles fighting their way into the blizzard and from the burn of ice on his face. Worse was the cold that seeped through his combat suit. That was not the sharp bite of the wind, but a constant ache that became an intense throbbing before it began to fade.

That was a relief, but it meant his skin was going numb. Frostnip could quickly turn to frostbite. That would be followed by the gradual lowering of his core body temperature, leading to hypothermia. Violent shivering would be followed by stumbling and mental confusion, leading to a stupor that was the first stage of death.

He ignored the cold. He ignored the pain. He ignored the fear. He knew that as bad as it was for him, for Emile it must be much worse. He was younger and smaller. Yet there was no bleat of a complaint.

The lights of Little Diomede, the smaller of the two islands, were a beacon in the white desert, a dull glow through a hazy gauze curtain. When Monster looked up, which wasn't often, it was to make sure that those lights were still ahead of him.

He was concentrating so intently on the simple act of putting one foot in front of the other that he almost fell into the crevasse.

It was Emile, behind him, who saw it first and grabbed his arm. Monster stopped with one foot out over the void.

It was a fissure in the ice. Not as wide as the crevasse they had recently crossed, but wide nevertheless. It ran from north to south, separating the two islands.

Emile was saying something to him, but he couldn't hear it. The words were caught by the wind and swept away into the storm.

He bent down so Emile could put his lips next to his ear.

"We gotta go back," Emile said.

"We can't go back," Monster said.

"We gotta!" Emile said. "We gotta go back for the others."

"We cannot," Monster said. "The Pukes will be looking for us. Must keep going."

"I didn't escape just to save my own skin!" Emile shouted. "I'm not running out on the others."

Monster grasped him by the arm, so tightly even through the armor of his combat suit that Emile winced. Monster eased his grip and took a deep breath.

"We not running out," Monster said. "We go back, we all die."

"We can't leave them," Emile cried. "It's my fault we got caught!"

Monster shook his head. "Not your fault."

"I had the scope," Emile said. "I should have seen the Pukes coming."

"Were you watching the scope?" Monster asked.

"Yes. I mean, I think so."

"Then not your fault," Monster said. "Scope not work too good in these conditions."

"But still . . ."

"Not your fault," Monster said for a third time. "If we can make it to Little Diomede, we can alert ACOG, then try to save others."

"Little Diomede?" Emile asked. "You think we can make it that far?"

"I think we can try," Monster said.

Their options were extremely limited. Little Diomede was their only chance and that was hundreds of meters away, across a rugged landscape that would be challenging even in good weather. In this blizzard it was next to impossible. And what if the station had been taken over by Bzadians? He put that thought out of his mind. Little Diomede had to be a place of safety. It had to be.

He looked down into the fissure. It was not deep, little more than a meter, and the ice at the bottom seemed solid. Better still, the drop on their side, although steep, was not sheer.

Monster pointed down into the fissure and, although Emile looked doubtful, he nodded.

If they broke through the thin ice at the bottom into the sea below, at least the end would be swift.

Emile, being lighter, went first, slithering over the edge and sliding down into the cleft. When the ice took Emile's weight, Monster followed suit. The ice cracked as he landed, but it did not break. They crouched, out of the wind, except for the occasional swirl that curled over the lip and eddied around them.

"Which way?" Emile asked. Out of the wind, they could hear each other without shouting.

"To the north," Monster said, hoping that was the right direction. With the random zigzag patterns of the fissures, either way could be the right way to go. Or neither.

He slapped at the ice on his face, feeling it crack, then break into pieces and fall away. Emile did the same and kept pummeling at his face even after all the ice was gone, slapping at the skin until it was red and raw, unable to feel the blows through numb, dead skin.

Monster stopped him. "You got it all," he said.

■ ■ ■

The depth of the channel shielded them from the wind, but it had its own hazards, the least of which was the movement of the walls. This was not a pathway through the ice, but a gap between two constantly moving ice floes. At times the walls ground closer, threatening to crush them, and at other times, for no obvious reason, they shifted farther away, exposing black seawater a few centimeters below their feet. Monster and Emile stepped carefully and made it past those sections without a sudden, and deadly, dip in the sea.

"Talk to me," Monster said after Emile stumbled for the first time on a perfectly smooth patch of ice. The sound of the wind above them seemed to be easing and, when he looked up, the skies were starting to clear. That was good and bad. The snowstorm, as painful as it was, was their ally, hiding them from their pursuers. If the Bzadians found them in this trench across the ice, they would have nowhere to run. Nowhere to hide.

"Talk about what?" Emile asked. His voice was unsteady and the words had to find their way out through a rigid jaw.

"Anything," Monster said. "Monster want to hear your voice."

"I didn't know you cared," Emile said.

"Why you join Angels?" Monster asked.

"I'm starting to wonder that myself," Emile said.

"But really," Monster said.

There was silence for a moment. Silence except for the noises of the ice shifting and cracking on either side. It was a bizarre sound, a mixture of creaks, hollow booms, and something else that reminded Monster of the laser gun sound effects from a science-fiction movie.

"My parents didn't want me to," Emile said eventually, reluctantly.

"Parents?" Monster asked.

"Yup," Emile said. "When a man and a woman love each other very much and the man . . ."

"Ha-ha, funny guy," Monster said. "You know mostly Angels are orphans."

"I must have annoyed them so much that they let me in anyway," Emile said. "I wanted to be an Angel ever since I heard about them."

"You want to be Angel?" Monster asked.

"Yup," Emile said. "Didn't you?"

"Cheese and rice, my dude, no," Monster said. "I was picked out of paintball team. That's how most of us are chosen. I don't even know it is test, until recruiter showed up at my home."

"Well, I knew," Emile said. "There was a guy in my camp who was selected but didn't make the grade. He told me all about it. I joined a paintball team the next day and made sure I was the star player."

"You have death wish?" Monster asked.

"Just wanted to do something to help," Emile said. "And I thought it would be cool. Refugee camp was kinda boring."

"This is true," Monster said.

"How many Angel missions have you been on?" Emile asked.

"Too many," Monster said. *And too many friends have not come home.*

"What were they like?" Emile asked.

"Warm," Monster said.

"No kidding," Emile said. "You served with Ryan Chisnall, didn't you?"

Monster waited awhile before answering. "Ryan was my friend," he said.

"The other Angels talk about him as if he was some kind of superhero," Emile said.

"Not true also," Monster said. "He is just a regular guy. If not for war, he wouldn't even make captain of football team or class president. War brings out best in some people."

"You miss him, don't you?" Emile asked.

Monster didn't answer. All Angel missions were voluntary, and he had volunteered for this one. Part of it was Price, of course. But there was something more. On some deep level, he wanted revenge, for Chisnall and Hunter, and everyone else who had suffered at the hands of the aliens. Revenge, as someone once said, was like biting a dog because the dog bit you, but that didn't stop him from wanting to hurt those who had caused such pain.

Emile stumbled and fell and was slow getting up. Monster grabbed him by an arm and helped him to his feet. "Sing," Monster said.

"Nah," Emile said. "It's hard enough talking."

"Sing, and that is order," Monster said. "So I know you not hypothermic."

"Yeah, and if I'm getting hypothermic, what are you going to do about it, Sergeant Monster?" Emile asked. "Give me a nice warm bath or a hot cup of tea and put me to bed?"

"No, Emile," Monster said. "We keep walking."

"Pity. I like warm baths," Emile said. "And hot tea."

"So sing," Monster said.

"Sing what?"

"You choose."

It took a few moments, and his voice was quavering with the cold, but he did. He sang in Lebanese in a soft, high, melodic voice, a song with strange warbling notes. It reminded Monster of a young Bzadian they had once met in the sands of the Australian desert.

They came to a gap in the ice and stopped while they tried to work out how to get past it. A place where an undersea current bubbled up through the ice, creating a kind of blowhole and preventing the water from freezing.

It wasn't wide, but with stiff, frozen muscles, they had no way to leap across. They were already reduced to a kind of hobbling shuffle.

In the end they managed to sidle past it, although the blasts of water soaked their boots and their armor up to their knees as they did so. That quickly froze, creating a clear sheet of armor that weighed them down and made it even more difficult to walk.

"I can't hear your voice," Monster said when it had been silent for a little too long.

"I'm sorry, Sergeant Monster," Emile said.

"That's okay, but keep talking," Monster said.

"I mean, I'm sorry for all this. This is my fault. I was stupid," Emile said.

"Nothing to be sorry for," Monster said. "You got us out of there. You gave us chance. Chance to alert ACOG and chance to rescue the others."

"I wanted to be a hero," Emile said. "Like you and Lieutenant Price and Lieutenant Chisnall."

Monster swallowed rapidly several times, choking down a spew of hurt, anger, and grief. There were droplets of ice forming around his eyes, tears that froze as soon as they were formed.

"Emile, you are hero," he said, when he could.

The ice beneath his feet was dark and uneven and Monster was surprised to find he was walking on rime-coated rocks.

A few paces farther on, Emile stumbled and fell. He got up slowly, and Monster realized that neither of them had been speaking. Somehow he had forgotten about that. His mind seemed a little foggy, and he knew it was very important to keep talking, but he was not sure why.

"Emile," he said with a thick tongue through lips that seemed like blocks of ice.

There was no answer.

"Emile!" Monster said, and when that got no response, he caught up with him and placed a hand on his shoulder. Emile looked at him dully, through eyes that did not seem to recognize him. He shook off Monster's hand and continued to stumble on.

Monster trudged along after him, not sure why, or where they were going, but knowing that it was vital to keep moving.

They encountered another patch of rocks covered with thin ice. They were slippery and treacherous. Why there would be rocks here in the middle of an ice field, Monster couldn't understand, although something about it caused a tickle at the back of his memory. Why was he even in an ice field?

Emile had sat down, Monster saw, and that seemed like a good idea. He was so cold and so tired. Emile leaned against one of the walls of ice that surrounded them. Where was Price? Monster wondered. She was supposed to be in charge of this mission, but he couldn't see her anywhere. Where was Chisnall? His friend. Why wasn't he leading the mission?

He went to sit down next to Emile and that was when he remembered. Chisnall was dead. His friend was gone. He had died fighting the Bzadians. Price was dead, too, or soon would be if he didn't do something about it.

He loved her in a way that had taken him by surprise. When Price had been terribly wounded on the last mission, it was as though he, too, had been injured. He had helped nurse her back to health; he remembered that. The long hours of rehab, building up the muscles in her new leg. But for what? So she could die in a Bzadian prison cell?

He could not let that happen. He could not stop, no matter how tired he was.

He shook Emile's shoulder a couple of times and when that got no response, he grabbed the smaller soldier by the arms and hoisted him up in a firefighter's lift.

Emile was light, even with his armor, but Monster was so tired and just one step seemed like an impossible task. He managed it, though. After that the second didn't seem as hard, although he couldn't understand why he was doing this, or who it was he was carrying.

He put one foot in front of the other and thought that if he could keep doing that, then he would be all right. They would be all right.

The sky was clear and the sun low on the horizon, a bright red disk that lit up clouds in shudders of orange and streaks of deep dark blue.

Ice under his feet turned to snow-covered rock, which began to rise up, steeper and steeper until it was too hard to climb.

Perhaps if he dropped his pack. It was a heavy pack. He let it slide off his shoulders and was surprised to see a body fall to the ground. He had been carrying someone. But who? And why? Somehow that didn't seem important. It was so hot here. Why hadn't he noticed that before? He was sweating. He had to get cool. He reached for the releases on his armor but his fingers were frozen into claws and he couldn't get the clasps open.

He took one more step, then felt the ground coming up to meet him. The snow was surprisingly hard.

He tried again to take off his armor, to cool himself down, but it would not come off and so he stopped struggling. It was the struggle that was making him hot, he decided. Better to rest.

And although nothing made sense anymore, about why he was here, or why it was so hot, he did understand in some deep place that his body was shutting down. And it made him wonder: Was this really what the universe had in store for him?

All he could think was that it was a silly way to die.

Such a silly way to die.

6. NOKZ'Z

"I AM SORRY ABOUT YOUR FRIENDS," COLONEL NOKZ'Z SAID in perfect English, walking down the row of Angels, neckcuffed and restrained. "They were foolish to go out in those conditions without proper equipment."

Price's heart was thudding in her chest. She had given the order that had started the chain of events that had led to Emile and Monster running out into the storm. It had been her decision. Her call. Had she made a fatal mistake?

It was worth the risk, surely? It might have worked. But things hadn't gone as planned. There was only one explanation for what had happened. Emile had grabbed the wrong grenade. He had taken an explosive one and realized just in time. If that had gone off inside the tank, they would have all been dead.

"They'll be back to kick your Puke ass," the Tsar said.

"They won't be kicking anyone's 'Puke ass,'" Nokz'z said. "They wouldn't have lasted thirty minutes."

Price stared at him, afraid he was right but willing it not to be true.

"Pukes, scumbugz," Nokz'z said, shaking his head. "These are the names we have for each other. Is it not enough that we have to kill each other? Could we not at least be civil about it?"

"Yeah, that would make all the difference," Barnard said.

Price caught Barnard staring at her, although the other girl quickly looked away, with an expression of pity. *Don't pity me,* Price wanted to scream. Monster was not dead. Neither was Emile. They couldn't be.

Price forced herself to remain still, unemotional, fighting the urge to shout and throw herself against the neck restraint. She couldn't lose him, not now. The last year, stuck at Fort Carson, watching the progress of the war but unable to assist, had seemed like a prison sentence. But it was a prison she had shared with Monster. He had been by her side almost every day in the hospital for the six months it had taken her to grow a new leg. And he had trained with her every day after that as she had built up her strength.

But he was gone. And no matter how much she tried to deny it, she knew it was probably true.

First Hunter, then Chisnall, now Monster and Emile.

Emile. Cheeky and quick, both in mind and movement. He hadn't even had a chance to prove himself. To fight.

Monster and Emile. Were their deaths her fault? Should she have waited for a better opportunity? Was her decision influenced by the thrill and the heat of the moment, rather than cold logic? It was one thing to seek the adrenaline buzz of living on the edge of death; it was another thing altogether when it caused the deaths of people you cared about.

Nokz'z completed his inspection.

"So young," Nokz'z said. "So very young. This is what humans resort to."

"Shove it," Price said, still barely containing her emotions.

"Shove it," Nokz'z said to the Vaza. "You try to have a conversation and this is the response. It is like talking to a monkey."

"Shove it up your—" the Tsar began.

Nokz'z cut him off. "Bzadian teenagers of your age are in school," he said. "They are listening to music, hanging out with their friends. I have a child not much younger than you. True, he does his military training, but he is not on the front lines. Especially not in these conditions." He tutted quietly. "Humans ask too much of their young."

Price remained silent. Nokz'z had a gentle, melodic way of speaking. Yet she sensed something else behind the words: something dark and malodorous. Something rotten.

"Perhaps this is good for you," Nokz'z said, just as pleasantly. "You are removed from the battle. You are my prisoners and will be treated well. No longer will you have to endure such hardships or risk death. You will see out the war in comfort." He stopped, apparently thinking. "Unless the PGZ want you, and I suspect they will. They will want to know all about your Angel program. That might not be very pleasant for you."

"We'll take our chances," Barnard said.

Nokz'z turned to the Vaza.

"It might be a kindness if I let them follow their friends," he said with a slight frown. "Out into the blizzard without face masks or thermals. Perhaps that would be preferable to what the PGZ might have in store for them." He shrugged. "But then I would not be doing my duty."

The Vaza looked at Price as though she would be very happy to see Price get tortured at the hands of the PGZ.

"But then again," Nokz'z said, "with the end of the war in sight, perhaps it does not really matter. There is little they could tell the PGZ that would be of any consequence."

"The war is not over yet, you Puke freakazoid," Wall said.

"Still, the grunting of primitives," Nokz'z said. "I have captured you, behind my lines, in our uniforms. Still, I have treated you fairly and with respect. Yet you insult me. If I was in your position, I would be doing everything I could to cooperate with my captors, not to abuse them."

"Perhaps you're right. Let's swap positions and find out," Barnard said.

Nokz'z laughed. "Ah, this one has a sense of humor!" He walked in front of her. "The war is not over. But it soon will be. Let me tell you what is going to happen. The skies are clear. It is the eye of the storm. But it will not last long, and when it is over, my tanks will continue their advance. We cannot be seen. Your army will have no warning. Once we establish a beach-head in Alaska, we will set up landing strips and start flying in equipment and supplies. What will happen in America has already happened in Europe and Asia. Or do you still think there is some miracle awaiting your species?"

"I think the real question is whether we pack you Pukes up in rocket ships and send you back where you came from, or make Australia into a giant prison," Price said.

Nokz'z smiled again. "Bravado. It is such a delightful human trait. We Bzadians don't have it—did you know that? I shall miss it. In the meantime, make yourselves as comfortable as you can. As soon as the storm returns, we will bring up transporters to take you to our base at Chukchi. From there it will be a quick plane trip to New Bzadia." He paused, thinking. "Do you have any idea how beautiful this planet of yours is? On my planet people travel thousands of miles to see a glimpse of blue water or a patch of green forest. Most of our water is underground. Your planet has it in abundance, yet you do not appreciate it. It really is a wonderful world, and when the war is over, I will spend my time traveling it, drinking in its beauty."

"Hard to do that if you're dead," the Tsar said.

Nokz'z just smiled.

"We know what we've got," Price said. "And we're not going to let you take it away from us."

"You are wrong on both counts," Nokz'z said. "If you really did appreciate this beautiful planet, you wouldn't treat it the way you have."

"That's bull," the Tsar said.

"You call *us* the invaders," Nokz'z said. "But it is *you* who are the invaders. On Bzadia we lived in harmony with the other creatures of our world. What do you humans do? You kill, cook, and eat them. You wipe out entire species. And those you don't eat, you fence off into game parks and reserves. Cramming them into smaller and smaller areas. If insects inconvenience you, you spray them with poison. You are monsters, bullies, terrorizing your own world, but you have finally met your match."

"Ignore him," Price said. "He's crazy. You can't reason with a crazy person."

"That, my young friend, is the one thing we both agree on," Nokz'z said.

After some quiet discussion with the squad leader, Nokz'z and his Vaza slipped down the hatch and away.

"There's something not quite right with that dude," Wall said. He spoke in a low voice so that the soldiers on the other side of the tank could not hear him.

"That is an understatement," Barnard said. "Don't you know who that was?"

"Nope," Price said.

"Colonel Nokz'z. The Butcher of Jakarta," Barnard said.

"The Indonesian massacre?" Wall asked.

"He was a major back then," Barnard said.

"That's the same guy?" Wall asked.

"I think so," Barnard said.

"You really think Monster will be back to kick his ass?" the Tsar asked.

Price was silent.

"Monster's not coming back," Wall said. "Neither is Emile."

"Until we see the bodies, there's always hope," Price said.

"You're dreaming," Wall said. "Nokz'z is right. They didn't have a chance out there."

"Shut up, Wall," Barnard said.

"I'm just saying," Wall said.

"Well, don't," Barnard said.

"So what's the plan, Skipper?" Wall asked.

"How the hell should I know?" Price snapped.

"You're the LT," Wall said. "You're supposed to have a plan."

"What's your problem, Wall?" Barnard asked. "Can't take the pressure?"

"Pressure I can handle, bro," Wall said. "Incompetence, not so much."

"Be careful," the Tsar said. "Or it may not be the Pukes you have to worry about."

"And I'm not your 'bro,'" Barnard said.

"Damn right you're not," Wall said. "Not even close."

"Your brother was on Operation Magnum, wasn't he?" Price asked softly.

"He was," Wall said. "And he didn't come home, thanks to that all-American hero Ryan Chisnall."

"Be very careful what you say," the Tsar said. "Ryan was our friend."

"What are you going to do?" Wall asked. "Come over here and beat me up? Have you noticed that you're chained up like a dog?"

"Your brother's death had nothing to do with Chisnall," Barnard said.

"Right. I've heard that one before," Wall said. "Chisnall did what he had to do."

"No, I mean your brother—" Barnard began.

"Leave it, Barnard," Price said. "Wall, Chisnall made some hard decisions on that mission. One day you might have to make some hard decisions of your own. You'll find out it's not easy."

"I'll be certain to make the right ones," Wall said.

"Jeez, Price," the Tsar said. "I don't care about his brother. When we get out of here, I'm going to smack him one."

"*If* we get out of here," Wall said.

"Easy, everyone," Price said. "Wall, you lost someone you loved. Do you think you're the only one rowing that boat?"

Wall stared at her. Price lowered her eyes so he wouldn't see the tears that were starting to form.

It was her fault. She had ordered Emile into something rash. Monster knew that. He could have, he should have, done nothing. But Monster would never leave a person in need. So her decision had sent them both to their deaths.

"Let's concentrate on fighting the Pukes, not each other," she said in a barely controlled voice.

"Can't fight them with our arms stuck around our necks," Wall said.

"That's my point," Price said. "We have to escape before the transport arrives to take us away. Otherwise our next stop is some PGZ prison cell, and there's no going home from that."

7. SILENT ANGELS

THE TIME FOR THE SCHEDULED RADIO CALL HAD COME and gone. Even if the Angels had been delayed in reaching the next checkpoint, they should have checked in by now.

Bilal had arrived in time for the call and sat with Wilton in front of the silent screen. He had shut the door behind him and the room felt like a tomb. Soundproofing on all the walls sucked up their voices, giving their words a flat, dead sound.

Wilton was aware of his hands starting to shake, and he clenched them so Bilal wouldn't notice.

"Maybe they've broken their radio," Wilton said.

"Perhaps," Bilal said. "I believe we currently have satellite coverage of the area. Does that show anything?"

Wilton hooked into the satellite feed and examined the area the Angels had last reported in from. There was nothing visible. Many eyes would be watching this feed, he knew, and no one was reporting anything. *So where were the Angels?*

"Tell me about your friends," Bilal said.

"Tell you what, sir?" Wilton said.

"The team leader, Price, what is she like?"

"Tough as nails." Wilton laughed, although the humor quickly faded as he thought again about the missed check-in. "I mean I think she had a tough childhood. Got beat up a bit. Made her hard. And not just hard. It taught her to be invisible. We call her the Phantom because she has this ability not to get noticed."

"So tell me something I can't read in her personnel file," Bilal said.

"Like what?"

"Anything," Bilal said. "I want to get to know these kids."

"Confidentially?"

"Of course."

"She's going out . . . She's in a relationship with Monster."

"Sergeant Panyoczki?"

"She thinks no one knows, but it's pretty obvious," Wilton said.

"Does it affect her work? Her decision-making?"

"I doubt it, but I haven't been on a mission with her since Magnum, so I can't really say."

"What about Panyoczki?" Bilal asked. "What's he like?"

"Um . . ."

"Be honest," Bilal said.

"Well, he's this big, funny, crude dude. Loves life. Nothing fazes him. You feel it'd take a nuclear bomb to kill him. But . . ."

"But?"

"He went a bit loopy after Uluru. All touchy-feely, spouting about the universe and all sorts of New Age crap. I don't really understand him anymore."

"What about Barnard?" Bilal asked.

"She scares the hell out of me." Wilton laughed.

"Because?"

"She doesn't think much of people who aren't as smart as she is," Wilton said. "And that's basically everyone. I'm always afraid I'm going to say the wrong thing around her and she's going to give me that look." He stopped and stared at his hands.

"What look?" Bilal asked.

"This look," Wilton said, and showed him.

Bilal laughed again. "I think I know what you mean. How about Nikolaev?"

"Who?"

"Dimitri Nikolaev."

"Oh, the Tsar," Wilton said. "He's fun to be around. I like him a lot. I didn't always, though."

"Why not?" Bilal said.

Wilton considered that. "I guess when he first came onto our team he was kinda up himself. He'd been on some important mission in Japan and he was supposed to be a real hero."

"Did you think he was a hero?" Bilal asked.

"Not really," Wilton said. "He seemed to love himself a little too much. I thought Price was a hero for what she did at Uluru, and Chisnall was, well, Chisnall. But he came right, the Tsar. He fitted in all right."

"Emile?" Bilal asked.

"Don't really know him," Wilton said. "He came on the team after I left. I mean I saw him at Fort Carson, but I didn't get to spend much time with him."

"So no reason to think that any of them might be playing for the other team?" Bilal asked.

"The other team?" Wilton asked.

"The Bzadians," Bilal said.

Wilton was shocked. "No, sir. Not Price, Monster, Barnard, or Tsar. Definitely not. And Wall's brother was killed by the Pukes. He hates them more than anyone. I don't know about Emile, but after the thing with Brogan, I think they were real careful about who got to be an Angel."

"I thought so," Bilal said. "But I had to check. Something has gone wrong out there."

"That doesn't mean there's a traitor. Perhaps they just can't get reception," Wilton said.

"I'd think that, too, if it wasn't for what happened to the two Seal teams," Bilal said. "We have to face the fact that whatever happened to the Seals has happened to the Angels." He shook his head in frustration. "This is going to be difficult to explain to ACOG, considering the Angels officially weren't even there in the first place."

Wilton stared at him.

"They were friends of mine," Wilton said, then corrected himself. "They *are* friends of mine."

Bilal evaluated him and Wilton felt uncomfortable under his gaze.

"You wish you were back with them?" Bilal asked.

Wilton shrugged. He did. Being in the Angels was the one place that had truly felt like a home. Like he was part of a family. But he wasn't about to say that to a stranger. In any case, he sensed that this stranger already knew more about him, and the rest of the Angels, than he knew himself.

"I'm sorry about your friends," Bilal said, and Wilton felt that he truly was. "Maybe they will still get in contact. They have only missed one radio call."

It was clear that he didn't think this was likely.

"Stay here for the rest of the week, just in case," Bilal continued. "Then we will return you to your unit. For now you can go back to your hotel, if you wish, but make sure the radio is routed to your phone."

"I'd like to go to Kansas," Wilton said. "If that's okay."

"Kansas?" Bilal asked.

"Fort Leavenworth," Wilton said. "I want to visit Holly Brogan. Do you think you could arrange that?"

"Can I ask why?" Bilal asked.

"She was a Bzadian mole," Wilton said. "If there are more like her, she might know about them."

Bilal stared at him. Wilton again had the extremely uncomfortable feeling that the contents of his thoughts were like an open book to this man.

"You think one of the operators on Little Diomede is a traitor," Bilal said.

"Both of them, for all I know," Wilton said. "But I don't really know anything. I'm just hoping that Brogan might be able to throw some light."

"She has steadfastly refused to speak to anyone," Bilal said. "What makes you think she'll speak to you?"

"She might," Wilton said. "We served together. It's worth a try."

"She's in maximum security," Bilal said. "I'll have to arrange clearance. When do you want to go?"

"Today. I'll route the radio through to my phone like you said," Wilton said. "One more thing."

"Yes?" Bilal asked.

"I want to show her photos of the staff on Little Diomede Island," Wilton said.

"I'll arrange access to their personnel files," Bilal said.

It was later, on the plane, that Wilton realized something odd. Bilal had asked him directly about each of the Angel team. Except one. Hayden Wall.

8. IVRULIK

THE CEILING WAS MADE OF ROUGH WOOD AND CAULKED with something black and sticky, possibly tar. It was supported by crossbeams that were rough-hewn logs. Propping up the crossbeams were huge bones, so large that they must have come from dinosaurs.

Whales. That was the thought that came to him. They were whale bones.

It was cold. Very cold. He was shivering uncontrollably.

Someone brought a ladle to his lips and a warm broth trickled into his mouth. It tasted of oil and fish, but he swallowed it greedily, for the warmth if nothing else.

Another ladle and again he sucked it down eagerly.

He felt warm skin against his own.

Then he slept.

9. BROGAN

FROM THE AIR, THE UNITED STATES DISCIPLINARY BAR-racks at Fort Leavenworth is an odd collection of geometric shapes, like a child's puzzle waiting to be assembled. It is surrounded on two sides by dense forest and ringed by two separate security fences that even extend across the rooftop of the entrance building. At night, those fences are lit up like Christmas tree lights, a string of bright baubles that radiate out across the ground on both sides.

Wilton approached the main entrance with more than a little nervousness.

Getting in meant getting a high-level security clearance, and doing that without setting off alarm bells meant going right to the top. Fortunately, Bilal's friend was connected in very high places. The guards even saluted. Wilton returned the salute lazily, as if he were a little bored by the whole thing, when in fact his heart was pounding as much as it had sliding down a rock in the Australian desert or racing T-boards around the Brisbane River. Nobody questioned why a seventeen-year-old kid would have top security access. Nor should they.

The visitors' center was part of the entrance building, with separate doors for visitors and inmates.

He was escorted by two guards and left to wait at a plain wooden table for over twenty minutes before a door on the other side of the room opened and the prisoner was shown in.

There were no bars. There were no armed guards inside the room. But there didn't need to be. He was separated from Brogan by a thick piece of bulletproof glass. It was not particularly clean and when he caught the light at the right angle, he could see palm prints, fingerprints, even here and there the imprint of lips.

He stood as she entered. "Hey, Brogan," he said.

It was strange seeing her. Strange and unsettling. As though she were a pet dog that was wagging its tail but might turn vicious without provocation.

She wore a gray prison T-shirt and loose-fitting dark blue pants. Prison pajamas. It was after nine, local time. She had been getting ready for bed. Her head still had the distinctive Bzadian bumps and her skin was still the same gray-green shade. She was human but, appropriately for a traitor, had the appearance of an alien.

Her hair was cut short, in a buzz cut. Maybe that was a prison regulation. It looked hard. She looked hard. She said nothing, but crossed the room in three quick steps, coming right up to the glass and peering through it as if unsure that he was real.

She pressed a hand against the glass, and after a moment he did, too, touching hands through three centimeters of glass.

When she moved away, she was crying, silently. The tears softened her.

"You okay?" he asked.

She nodded, then shook her head. She remained standing close to the glass wall.

"It's been a long time since I've seen a friendly face," she said. "I seldom get to see anyone. They keep me in solitary confinement."

Solitary confinement. That was something they shared, but for different reasons. Since he'd left the Angels, his whole life felt like solitary confinement. He didn't say so. His problems were pretty minor compared to hers.

He stared at her for a while, then said, "I ain't your friend, Holly."

"In here, you're as good as it gets," Brogan said.

"You want to talk about friends?" Wilton asked. "Hunter was a friend of mine. Remember him? He was the one you killed. With a snake. A snake!"

"Hunter treated you like crap," Brogan said. "Don't delude yourself."

"He didn't mean any of it," Wilton said. "We were friends."

"Yeah, and some of those people you blew up inside Uluru, they were my friends," Brogan said. "War's a bitch."

"You're a—" Wilton shut his mouth.

"I'm a bitch?" Brogan asked. "That what you were going to say, Wilton?"

Wilton forced himself to be calm. There was no point in being confrontational if he wanted her help. "Ryan would have done anything for you," he said. "He didn't deserve what you did to him."

"So he can come here and tell me that himself," Brogan said. "Instead of sending his boy."

Something must have shown on Wilton's face, because Brogan said, "What is it? What happened to Chisnall?"

Wilton considered that carefully. Chisnall's "death" had occurred on a top-secret mission. He wasn't allowed to tell her about that. Chisnall's "resurrection" was even more secret, and he certainly wasn't going to reveal it to a traitor.

"I need your help," Wilton said. He took out his smartpad and opened a folder of images.

"What happened to Ryan?" Brogan asked.

"That's classified," Wilton said. "Will you help me?"

"I'm the enemy, remember?" Brogan said. "Why would I help you?"

"You helped us before," Wilton said. "At Uluru. You helped us save those children. You're not a Puke, Holly. You're human."

"I helped you save those kids because they were like brothers and sisters to me," Brogan said. "I didn't switch sides."

"But you are human," Wilton said.

"Genetically maybe." Brogan laughed. "Nice job on the skin recoloring, by the way. I almost didn't recognize you without your alien disguise."

"There are others like you, aren't there?" Wilton asked.

"I wouldn't know," Brogan said. "And if I did, I wouldn't tell you. What happened to Chisnall?"

He ignored her question. "How many are there?" he asked.

"I don't know," Brogan said. "I'm seventeen. And I'm never getting out of here. You understand that? This is my life, for the rest of my life. If I ever do get out, I'll be some little old, twisted-back, gray-haired granny."

"I guess Hunter was lucky, then," Wilton said. "His hair ain't never going gray."

"That's unfair," Brogan said.

"Who's this dude?" Wilton asked, twisting his smartpad around to show her a photo of Jared Legrand, the deceased commander on Little Diomede.

"Tell me about Ryan," Brogan said.

"Have you seen this guy before?" Wilton asked.

"What the hell happened to Ryan?" Brogan shouted, stepping closer and hammering on the glass.

An orange light in the corner began to flash.

Wilton stayed where he was. He remained calm. He suspected that if the watching guards got too concerned, they would rush in and the meeting would be over.

She pulled away, retreating to the far wall and curling into a ball, crying.

"Brogan . . . ," Wilton began.

"Where's Ryan?" Brogan yelled back at him.

"He never came back from the last operation," Wilton said. "Ryan's dead."

After a while, she got up, quite calmly, and stood back at the glass wall. Her eyes were red but the tears had stopped.

"I thought so," she said. "I knew so. I felt it." She stared him in the eye. "How? Where?"

"That's classified," Wilton said. "But I saw him die."

There was a long period of silence.

Brogan broke it with a cough, to cover her emotion, Wilton thought.

She gestured at the smartpad, just a flick of one finger. "I never saw him before in my life," she said.

She was telling the truth, Wilton decided, and she had no reason to lie. He had shown her Legrand's photo to test her reaction.

"What about this chick?" He showed her a photograph of Gabrielle Bowden, one of the remaining station operators on Little Diomede.

There was no hint of recognition in Brogan's eye.

"Is she from Uluru?" Wilton asked.

"Not as far as I know," she said, tears staining her cheeks.

"What about this one?" Wilton asked, showing a photo of Nikolas Able, the second station operator.

There was a slight widening of her eyes and a drawing in of breath.

"You recognize him, don't you? From Uluru," he said.

After a moment, she nodded.

"Thanks, Brogan," Wilton said, rising. "Take care."

"I was only doing my duty," Brogan said. "You would have done the same."

"I'm real sorry about Chisnall," Wilton said.

"So am I," Brogan said.

Wilton was halfway to the door when Brogan said, "He's Fezerker."

He stopped. "What do you mean, 'Fezerker'?"

"Just what I said," Brogan said.

"Fezerkers are teams of Pukes," Wilton said. "Roaming around behind our lines."

"That's what you were supposed to think," Brogan said. "Fezerkers are humans. Like me. That's what Uluru was all about. Wilton, I'm Fezerker."

Wilton stood still, in shock. "Uluru?" he managed.

Brogan shrugged. "Long before Uluru," she said. "The Fezerker program goes back to before the first ships."

Wilton's breath caught in his throat. Could that be true? Had the Bzadians been infiltrating human society all that time?

"How do we find them?" Wilton asked. "There must be some way of identifying them. Blood tests? DNA analysis?"

"That wouldn't help," Brogan said. "We are humans, remember. Our DNA is identical to yours."

"So how?" he asked.

She shook her head. "I've got nothing more for you, Blake," she said. "I just betrayed my own people. From now on it's up to you."

He considered that, then turned back toward the door.

"Hey, Wilton." She stood and moved to the heavy glass barrier that separated them, pressing her body against it. This time the warning light did not flash. He did the same and they embraced, two lost souls, separated by an impassable barrier of bulletproof glass. It was probably the closest she had got to human contact in a very long time.

"Good night, Brogan," he said.

10. FEZERKER

THE NECKCUFFS WERE STARTING TO GET EXTREMELY uncomfortable. Part of that was the unnatural position of having her wrists held at neck height for a long time.

"At least Emile's gone to a better place," Wall said. "And Monster is now one with the universe."

"You getting religious on us?" Barnard asked.

"Emile was a Christian," Wall said. "He told me."

"So he's sitting nice and warm up in heaven, chatting to God and laughing his head off at us stuck down here in the middle of this frozen hellhole," the Tsar said.

"If there was a God, do you think he'd let all this happen?"

Price asked. "Millions of lives lost, the human race on the verge of extinction."

"Maybe God's a Bzadian," Barnard said.

"God's a sniper," the Tsar said.

The others all stared at him.

"How's that again?" Barnard asked.

"If there is a God," the Tsar said, "I reckon he's sitting up there in heaven with an M110 sniper rifle and a long-range scope. We're all marching past below, and he's just picking off random targets. Bam, you get cancer. Bam, you die in a car crash. Bam, you freeze to death in the Bering Strait."

"Maybe we should find something else to talk about," Barnard said with a quick glance at Price.

"I'm sorry I got you guys into this," Price said.

"You didn't get us into this," Barnard said. "We volunteered."

"What were you thinking?" Price said.

"I had my reasons," Barnard said. "I guess you did too."

"A moment of madness," Price said. "I'm not a hero, like the Tsar." The words tasted bitter in her mouth and she regretted saying them immediately.

"What are you saying?" the Tsar asked.

"You're a hero. The Hero of Hokkaido," Price said. "Heroes always volunteer."

"Just shows how little you know about me," the Tsar said.

"Why, then?" Price asked.

"Ask Barnard," the Tsar said. "She always thinks she's got me figured out."

"You don't want to know what I think," Barnard said.

"I do," Wall said.

"Feel free," the Tsar said.

Barnard looked at the Tsar for a long time.

"All right," she said. "You were the leader of the Hokkaido mission. Rescued a bunch of soldiers from right under the noses of the enemy, but it cost the lives of your team. They made you a hero for it, and you were proud to wear that badge, until you met Ryan Chisnall. He's a real hero. You're not. But they called you a hero, so ever since, you've been trying to earn it."

The Tsar stared at her.

"How'd I do?" Barnard asked.

The Tsar still said nothing.

"Is she always like this?" Wall asked.

"Most of the time," Price said. Barnard could be brutal, but she was seldom wrong.

"Where's the crew?" Barnard asked.

"What crew?" the Tsar asked.

"The tank crew?" Barnard asked. "These guys are combat soldiers, not a tank crew. So where's the crew?"

"I don't know," Price said. "I've been wondering that."

The center hatch opened and Nokz'z reappeared, followed, as always, by the big Vaza. He did not speak, but moved straight to Barnard, scanning her face with a flash of green light while the Vaza held a pistol close to Barnard's head. Nokz'z checked the screen and seemed happy with what he saw, although he did not share his thoughts with the Angels. He repeated the procedure with the Tsar, with exactly the same result and a slight shake of his head, then moved in front of Wall, who snarled at him.

The green light highlighted Wall's features and Nokz'z stared at him for a few seconds longer before turning his attention to the screen. His eyes widened.

"Hold him," he said, and the Vaza put away her gun, clamping Wall's head in a steely grip, with arms that looked as though they could pop his skull like a pea.

Nokz'z held the device much closer, directly in front of Wall's eye, and the flash this time lit up only his eyeball. A retinal scan for sure. Why? Price couldn't imagine.

Nokz'z took the device back over to the control panel and spent some time on a computer. He had a low conversation with someone, although Price could not hear what he was saying. Eventually, he walked back to Wall.

He spoke to him quickly in a strange language, Bzadian for sure with all the low buzzing sounds, but not one that Price knew or had ever heard spoken before.

Wall stared at him.

"Tell him to get stuffed," the Tsar said.

After a while, Wall spoke, but to Price's surprise, he spoke in the same strange Bzadian language.

Nokz'z nodded to the Vaza, who moved quickly across to Wall and undid the neckcuff.

Wall stood, rubbing his hands where the nylon had bit into them.

"What's going on?" Price asked. "What did he say to you? Why did he release you?"

"I told him I was Fezerker," Wall said.

"And he believed you?" Barnard asked.

"Yes," Wall said.

"Why?" the Tsar asked.

"Because it's true," Wall said, and added, "bro."

BOOK 2—DIOMEDE

11. THE BRIEFCASE

THE MAN WITH THE OLIVE-GREEN BRIEFCASE HAD PERFECT credentials. Nobody recognized him, but that wasn't unusual at a busy place like the Pentagon.

It was just after ten a.m. in Virginia. Although security was extremely tight, thousands of people went in and out of the Pentagon each day, through five separate entrances, and it was impossible to know all of them. This man was very ordinary, with no distinctive features that might stick in the mind of an alert security guard.

He smiled a little at the PFPA officers manning the security checkpoint, as he had the previous day. Just a little. Any more and it might stick in their minds. The briefcase he was carrying went through the usual X-rays and explosive detectors without setting off any alarms. A bomb dog sniffed at it and glanced away incuriously.

The next stage of security was a visual inspection, and on opening the briefcase, the PFPA officer found only official documents and two sandwiches in a plastic Tupperware container.

The man came in and out of the Pentagon regularly. He was part of the furniture, a nondescript part of the background hustle and bustle of people coming and going. If the security guards on any of the days had observed his wristwatch, a stylish black and bronze TAG Heuer, they would have noticed that it was not working. They might have thought that was unusual for such an expensive watch.

12. NUKILIK

THERE WAS A FACE ABOVE HIM, HUMAN, MALE, PERHAPS in his twenties. The face was broad and flat, giving him an Asian appearance.

He spoke, but the words made no sense. It was not a language that Monster knew.

Monster shook his head. He was still shivering, but not as violently.

"I don't understand," he said in English.

"You speak English, demon?" The man seemed surprised.

"I am no Demon," Monster said. "I am Angel." *How did this man know about Recon Team Demon?*

The man looked at the lumps on Monster's forehead and almost laughed. "I see no halo," he said.

The man did not know about the Demons, or the Angels, Monster realized. He meant something else.

"I am human," Monster said.

"That does not appear to be true either," the man said.

"It is true," Monster said. "I wear a disguise."

The man said nothing, but his eyebrows rose slightly.

"There was another with me," Monster said, trying to stop his teeth from chattering.

The man shook his head and glanced away at something Monster couldn't see.

"Is he okay?" Monster asked.

The man shook his head again. "The other boy was much smaller than you, and not as strong. He was already gone when we found you. It was touch and go, even for you."

Monster closed his eyes and lay still, racked every few seconds by bouts of shivering.

It was Emile's first mission. It was supposed to have been a simple reconnaissance task. But the fun-loving little Lebanese kid, the new puppy in the team, was not going home. Emile had risked, and lost, his life to save the other Angels, even though he barely knew them. He had wanted to be a hero, and he had paid the ultimate price for his dreams.

"When I found you, you were lying on top of him, trying to protect him from the cold," the man said.

Monster could not remember that. Perhaps he had just fallen on top of Emile. He did not say so. Either way it had made no difference. He sat up, pulling the furs around his shoulders for warmth. He was naked. "Who are you?" he asked.

"I am Nukilik," the man said. "Of the Inupiat."

"My name is Janos," Monster said. "But everyone call me Monster."

Nukilik smiled briefly at the nickname.

"Where are we?" Monster asked.

"Imaqliq," Nukilik said.

"Big Diomede?" Monster asked. "But it is deserted."

"Not as deserted as you might think." Nukilik smiled. "Now tell me how a demon was freezing to death on our island. Be careful with your answer or you may yet end up at the bottom of the Bering Sea."

"I told you, I am no demon," Monster said, still unsure what Nukilik meant. "I am human."

"Yet you come in the guise of a demon," Nukilik said.

"If you mean Bzadian, then you are right," Monster said. "I am a recon soldier. I am disguised as Bzadian so that I can move behind enemy lines."

"I see no enemy here," Nukilik said.

"They are here," Monster said. "Hundreds of Bzadian tanks. I saw them."

The good nature on Nukilik's face changed to a flinty hardness. "Again," he said.

"They use snowstorms for cover, creeping toward Alaska," Monster said.

"If you are human, then your story makes sense," Nukilik said. "Or this could be just some kind of trickery. Are you a demon?"

"Nukilik, I am not demon, also not alien. I am human,"

Monster said. "So was my . . . friend. Our skin was colored, our tongues split, and lumps added to our heads." He touched the bony protrusions on his skull. Strange how natural they had become to him. As if they were normal.

There were sounds from the far side of the room and a woman appeared from a trapdoor in the floor. She had the same broad face and smiling eyes as Nukilik. A baby was strapped to her chest in some kind of fur swaddling clothes. She seemed cold, and every few minutes she shivered violently.

A dog was at her side, a malamute, unrestrained. It sniffed at Monster and growled.

"He says his name is Monster," Nukilik said.

The woman shrugged and shivered once more.

"This is Corazon," Nukilik said. "My wife."

"Hello," Monster said. Corazon stared at him without emotion.

"He says he is human," Nukilik said.

Corazon shrugged. "As a demon would say."

Nukilik wrinkled his nose. "I have tested him."

"What test?" Monster asked.

"I asked you three times." Nukilik smiled. "An evil spirit may answer twice, but on the third time will leave, or refuse to answer."

"It was test?" Monster asked.

"One of them," Corazon said, with a glance at the malamute. "Asungaq was another. He does not like demons."

Asungaq barked, a strange sound halfway between a woof and the howl of a wolf.

Monster said, "I think he does not like me also."

"Your throat is in one piece," Nukilik said. "He likes you. It was Asungaq that found you in the snow."

Asungaq barked again, as if agreeing.

"Then please help me," Monster said. "I must contact my people and warn them of invasion. Do you have radio?"

"No. We do not use them, for fear of discovery," Nukilik said.

"Do you have way of communicating with mainland?" Monster asked.

"Yes," Nukilik said. "A boat."

"What about the phone?" Corazon asked.

"There is phone?" Monster asked.

Nukilik looked surprised. He nodded. "This island used to be Russian. They ran cables to the island and installed phones. They still work, but they connect to the Russian phone system."

"You can call anywhere in the world through it," Corazon said. "I called my mother once."

"You called your—" Nukilik broke off with a narrow sideways glance at his wife, and a short heated discussion followed in their own language.

"Where is nearest phone?" Monster asked during a break in the argument.

"There is an abandoned Russian guard post, about a kilometer away," Corazon said.

"Can you take me?" Monster asked.

Nukilik shook his head. "We are still bringing your body heat back up. You cannot go out in the cold so soon."

"It cannot wait," Monster said.

He pulled the covers around him. Muscles in his shoulders seemed to have a life of their own, jerking in short spasms. He felt weak and nauseous but managed to raise himself to his feet.

"Please, may I have my clothes?" he said.

13. MONSTER CALLS

PRICE HADN'T SLEPT. HER EYES HAD CLOSED AT TIMES, and she had dozed, but if she slumped down in the neckcuffs, it tightened them around her neck, and that was a terrifying way to wake up. Her hands looked white, and her arms ached, a consequence of having them cuffed to her neck all night. She also needed to pee but doubted the Bzadians would again agree to that request.

Wall had disappeared last night with Nokz'z and the Vaza. Where to, Price did not know, but she bet their night's sleep was more comfortable than hers. She looked around at the others. They both looked awake and as exhausted as she felt.

"I've been thinking about it all night. It doesn't make any

sense," the Tsar said. "Wall's human. And his brother was killed by Pukes. How could he be Fezerker?"

"If he was Fezerker, then so was his brother," Barnard said. "If it even was his real brother."

"Wall doesn't blame the Pukes for his brother's death," Price said. "He blames Chisnall."

Price felt sick. She should have seen this coming. Or at least been prepared for it. Just as Chisnall had been betrayed by Brogan, she had been betrayed by one of her team.

"So what do we do now?" the Tsar asked.

"Same plan as before," Price said. "Try to get out of here before we end up in some PGZ prison cell."

She stopped speaking as the Vaza climbed up into the tank followed by Wall. Wall moved to the lockers and took out the Angels' radio.

"It was a tragedy," Wall said. "Five Angels, lost in a crevasse, and me the only survivor. I will have to let ACOG know the sad news."

"So you can go back and carry on betraying your own species," Barnard said, her face twisted into a sneer.

"So I can betray *your* species," Wall said with a smile.

"Do not talk to them," the Vaza said. Her voice was a rasp, as though there was something wrong with her throat. She turned to Zim. "Nokz'z wants them ready to move at first light."

Zim nodded.

"Vaza," Price said.

The Vaza turned slowly to look at her.

Price stared her down. The Vaza moved across and stood

right in front of Price, folding her arms, which were thick and well muscled.

"I just wanted to see what the best of the Bzadian Army looked like," Price said.

The Vaza snorted. "Now you have seen."

"I am an adolescent of my kind," Price said. "Little more than a child. Yet if it were not for these cuffs, I would beat you senseless. Your species is pathetic. You are pathetic."

She waited for a reaction from the big Bzadian. Maybe if she got her angry enough, it would create an opportunity.

The Vaza took a deep breath. "You are deluded," she said. "Our armies have bested yours whenever they have met."

"You win because of superior technology," Price said. "But that is changing. Eventually, it will come down to people. Like you and me. And I wanted to be sure that I could beat you in a fight, one on one."

The Vaza snorted again.

"If a child can beat you, and you are the best of your army, then it may be time for you to start looking for another planet," Price said.

"Perhaps you think I will let you out of your restraints so that we can have some kind of contest to see who is stronger," the Vaza said.

She lashed out suddenly with the back of her hand, striking Price across the face. Blood poured from Price's nose, down into her mouth.

"Perhaps you think I am stupid," the Vaza said.

"You are wasting your time with her." Wall said. "She is

nothing. She is merely filling a role, because they have no one else stupid enough to do it." He moved to Barnard, staring at her, his face centimeters from hers. "This one you should be careful of. She is smart. Smarter than most scumbugz, although that is not saying much. And this one"—he stood in front of the Tsar—"this one is a trickster. He will try to fool you."

The Tsar muttered something, but so quietly that not even Price could hear it.

"What was that?" Wall laughed. "Are you trying to trick me?"

"It is for your ears only," the Tsar said. "Not for that . . . thing." His eyes took in the Vaza, who seemed unperturbed by his insult.

"I am sure you can share it," Wall said.

The Tsar shook his head.

"Then whisper in my ear, this big secret of yours," Wall said, bending his head closer to the Tsar's, being careful to stay out of range of the Tsar's head, in case he tried to headbutt him.

He was right to be careful, but wrong about where the danger lay. The Tsar's head didn't move. It was his foot that lashed out, kicking the radio out of Wall's hand. It smashed onto the floor, and the Tsar's heel came down on top of it with a crunch.

The Vaza's gun was already in her hand, but Wall was in her line of fire. His fist connected with the Tsar's cheek, drawing blood. The Tsar lifted his feet, wrapping them around Wall, drawing him in closer. Now he tried to headbutt him. Wall grappled with him, eventually stunning the Angel with a sideways elbow to the head. The Tsar slumped in his seat, dazed.

Wall picked up the radio, examined it, then tossed it angrily across the room. "It doesn't change a thing," he said.

The Tsar lifted his head and smiled at him.

"Make sure they are ready," the Vaza said to Zim. "And if the leader speaks again, get a needle from your medical kit and sew her mouth shut."

[MISSION DAY 2, FEBRUARY 17, 2033]
[1130 hours local time]
[Office FC7001, Third Level, West Quarter, Pentagon, Virginia]

WILTON'S PHONE RANG. HIS FIRST THOUGHT WAS THAT IT was Chisnall, but the screen showed that it was Fort Carson again. He flipped it open.

"You're a popular boy nowadays," Courtney's voice said. "I have another call for you."

"Who is it this time?" Wilton asked. "The same girl as yesterday?"

"Is she your new girlfriend, Blake?" Courtney asked.

"Nope. I'm still waiting for you to say yes," Wilton said.

"Can't say yes if I've never been asked," Courtney said. "But that would be against regulations."

"Yes, what a shame," Wilton said.

"Not that I'm a stickler for regulations," Courtney said.

"So who is on the phone?" Wilton asked, a little flustered.

"He didn't say," she said. "But from the way he talks, I'd guess it's Sergeant Panyoczki."

Wilton's breath caught in his throat. He forced himself to stay calm and to keep his voice low. "Put it through," he said.

"Wilton?"

"Yes?"

"My dude, it is Monster here."

It was Monster's voice, no question.

"What's going on?" Wilton asked. "You missed your check-in."

"We were captured by Pukes," Monster said. "I manage to make the getaway."

"And the others?"

"They not so lucky," Monster said. "Still captured. Listen. Big invasion coming. There is large concentration of Puke tanks south of the little island."

"Tanks!" Wilton said. "You're sure?"

"We went inside one," Monster said.

"But south of the island!" Wilton said. "They should be to the north. Where exactly did you see them?"

"At location of our last check-in," Monster said.

Wilton copied the reference into his smartpad. "They thought they'd sneak around the back door while we were busy watching the front. I'll pass this on to ACOG. What about Price and the others—are they at this grid reference?"

"I think so," Monster said. "All except Emile."

"Where's Emile?" Wilton asked, and when Monster didn't

answer, he didn't press him. There was no need. The unspoken answer was clear. "You've got to get them out," Wilton said. "When ACOG hears about this, they're going to blow the Puke out of the whole place."

"I know," Monster said.

"Can I reach you?" Wilton asked.

"You can try," Monster said. "It's a landline, and I don't know number. But maybe you can trace the call back. If I am near phone, I will answer."

Wilton didn't need to trace the call; the numbers were showing on his screen. He wrote them down.

"Monster," Wilton said. "I need to tell you something. I went to visit Holly Brogan."

He waited for a reaction, expecting an explosion, but all Monster asked was, "Why?"

"I thought she might be able to give us some information," Wilton said. "I showed her the photos of the crew on Little Diomede. She recognized one of them."

"You are sure?"

"Positive. The man, Nikolas Able. He's . . . like Brogan."

"Traitor!" Monster said.

"Fezerker," Wilton said, and explained.

"What about the woman?" Monster asked.

"I don't know. Brogan didn't recognize her."

There was silence on the end of the phone, and Wilton wished he had more to offer.

"Thanks, Wilton," Monster said.

"One more thing," Wilton said.

"Yeah?"

"When you see Barnard, give her this number, tell her to call it as soon as possible," Wilton said, and read out the number that Chisnall had given him.

"We are in middle of mission," Monster said. "Can it wait?"

"No, it's important," Wilton said. "And it's top secret. You can't tell anyone. Except the Angels."

"What is it?" Monster asked.

Wilton paused, hesitant to say the words out loud in case they turned out not to be true. "Chisnall's alive."

14. TANKS

"YOU'RE SURE IT WAS PANYOCZKI?" BILAL ASKED. HE WAS sitting opposite Wilton, whose office door was shut.

"It was Monster," Wilton said. "I'd know his voice anywhere."

"Any chance he was under duress?" Bilal asked.

"I don't think so, no," Wilton said. "I know him really well."

"And he's going to call back with more information?"

Wilton nodded. "He's going to try to rescue the other Angels."

"That's understandable," Bilal said. "Bring up the coordinates."

Wilton already had a satellite photograph of the area on his screen. He spun it around so they both could see it.

"South of the Diomede Islands," Bilal said. "That's either very clever, or very stupid. It's the last way we'd expect them to come, but that's for a very good reason. You'd be lucky to get a squadron of tanks through there."

"This is a live view of the area," Wilton said.

"It looks clear," Bilal said. "Is Panyoczki saying that an entire army of enemy tanks is hiding down there somewhere?"

"Yeah," Wilton said. "Check out this photo. It is from a few days ago, the same area." He brought up the photo on the screen, then flicked back and forth between the two. The difference was immediately clear. On the older one the ice was perfectly flat, apart from long ridges and fissures. On the current photo there was a strange pattern to the ice, a kind of dimpling created by low, rounded shadows.

"And that's not just mounds of ice?" Bilal asked.

"That's what I thought you'd ask," Wilton said. "Here is the same area going back over the last month, whenever we could get a clear shot of it."

No shadows were visible on any of the photographs that he rapidly flicked through.

"And here is the same area, this time last year," Wilton said.

Again, no shadows.

"And Panyoczki confirms that these are tanks."

"He said he was taken inside one," Wilton said.

"Okay," Bilal said. "That's good enough for me. I'll take this to ACOG. Good work, Wilton."

"Thank you, sir," Wilton said. "But there's something else, sir."

Bilal waited, without speaking.

"I showed Brogan the photos of the operators on Little Dio," Wilton said.

"And?"

"She recognized one of them. Able. She knew him from Uluru, sir."

Bilal's only reaction was to shut his eyes, a habit of his, Wilton had noticed, when he was considering the implications of things.

"From Uluru?" Bilal asked eventually.

"According to Brogan, Able is Fezerker. So is she," Wilton said. "Fezerkers aren't teams of Bzadian commandos—they are humans. That's why we've never been able to catch a Fezerker team."

Bilal considered that. "If what you're saying is true, then we have some big problems," he said. "First, what is really going on out there on the ice? Second, what do we do about these Fezerkers? And third . . ." He stopped, shutting his eyes again. "Third, who put them there? Someone must have pulled strings to get a Fezerker agent onto the island."

"That's what I've been trying to figure," Wilton said. "Man, it's like my brain explodes every time I try to think about it."

Bilal smiled briefly. "I know the feeling. But the implications of this are staggering. That aliens have penetrated top levels of our command structure."

"They only arrived twelve years ago," Wilton said. "How'd they do that?"

"That's not quite true," Bilal said. "They've been visiting our planet since the 1950s, possibly even earlier. It is conceivable they were setting up moles, brainwashing humans to their cause and infiltrating the military, even back then."

"So anyone could be a mole," Wilton said.

"Trust no one," Bilal said, echoing the words that Chisnall had said to him.

"No one?" Wilton asked.

"No one," Bilal said.

"What about you, sir?" Wilton asked.

Bilal smiled. "I guess for now, we'll have to trust each other. But no one else. I'm going to need someone to do some digging around. Someone I can trust. And for the time being that means you."

"What kind of digging around?" Wilton asked.

He'd never thought of himself as being an investigator, but it sounded like fun. Like being a private detective. He imagined himself creeping through darkened corridors, sliding through air-conditioning ducts, bugging offices.

"Computer stuff," Bilal said.

"Oh, okay," Wilton said.

"I'll arrange security clearance for you," Bilal said. "The highest level. I want you to track the chain of command that put a Fezerker on that island. It won't be obvious; they will have covered their tracks. But if you get the names of those directly involved, and the names of their associates, that will be a starting point."

"Then what, sir?" Wilton asked.

"Cross-check those names against other missions. Operation Magnum, for example. Did the Bzadians know we were coming?"

"I don't think so, sir," Wilton said. "But that mission was top secret." He stopped, thinking. "Even so, there was a patrol boat right at the entrance to the river. One we weren't expecting."

"That could be the clue you need," Bilal said. "Assume our mole, or moles, did not have access to the truth about Magnum. But perhaps they issued some kind of general warning, just in case. That will eliminate anyone who knew the truth about the operation. Then look at other operations. See what matches up with the chain of command from Little Diomede. If you find anything, let me know."

"Of course," Wilton said.

"And this information stays between you and me," Bilal said. "We don't want the moles to know we're on to them." He rose and made to leave. He was halfway out of the door when he stopped.

"If we survive this winter," he said, "we might just win this war."

"Sir?" Wilton asked.

"The one thing that has always tipped battles in the Bzadians' favor is their air superiority," Bilal said. "We haven't been able to compete in the air with their Type Ones and Type Twos.

But Boeing is promising delivery of their new F/A XX fighters by June."

"The scramjets? I thought that program was canceled," Wilton said.

"It was delayed," Bilal said. "But it's back on track, and they've been able to incorporate what we've learned from analyzing the Bzadian planes we managed to shoot down. We should have scramjet missiles too. The implications of that are enormous. If we can achieve air superiority, or even air parity, we'd be able to put our carriers back out to sea, instead of skulking in port under heavy SAM cover. We'd be able to start influencing battles again, maybe start taking back some of this planet."

"But first we've got to survive this winter," Wilton said.

"Exactly," Bilal said. "If Panyoczki calls back, I want to know it immediately. I want you glued to my side from now on."

15. LESSONS FOR THE DEAD

THEY DID NOT BURY EMILE. THAT WAS NOT POSSIBLE ON Big Diomede in winter. Instead, the women of the village washed his body and wrapped it in a blanket of caribou hide.

Monster stopped them before they sewed the hide closed over Emile's face. He stood beside the corpse, looking at the face of a young man who had wanted nothing more than to do his bit. To join the Angels and fight Bzadians. He had never got that chance, but he was still a hero. Giving his life in an attempt to save others. The greatest sacrifice.

There was a calmness about Emile's face in death. A kind of serenity, although Monster couldn't shake the feeling that any second that calm would be shattered and Emile would spring back to life with that frenetic, irrepressible energy.

Chisnall had come back to life. Monster accepted Wilton's words without fully understanding them. He had seen his friend surely die. Yet Chisnall was alive. That was all he knew; there had not been time for details.

But it did not ease the pain in his heart. The desire for revenge.

He nodded to one of the women and stepped back while they completed their task.

Then he kneeled beside the body and said brief, inadequate goodbyes before helping Nukilik carry the body out to a storage hut. It would remain there, frozen, until spring. When the ground thawed, they would bury it along with any of their own dead, if ACOG did not claim it first.

The Inupiat had words of their own, uttered by an old man wearing an ornate cloak. His face was weathered to the point of old leather, with deep crevices lining his cheeks and around his eyes. He wore a battered cowboy hat and his arms were covered with bracelets of bone and rawhide. Around his neck was a long rope necklace tied in intricate knots. Although Monster could not understand his words, there was a power to them that filled the small room. There seemed to be a presence, as though the ancestors of these people had come to say farewell to this stranger.

As soon as the ceremony was finished, Monster took Nukilik by the arm.

"We must hurry," he said. "Or there will be more young people dead on these ice floes."

"Patience," Nukilik said.

"Cannot be patient," Monster said. "My friends face death or torture from enemy. Already, they may be in Bzadian prison cells."

"They are not," Nukilik said. "They are still on the ice."

"How can you know this?" Monster asked.

"They cannot move on the ice floes in darkness," Nukilik said. "It is not safe. Not even for demons."

"You are sure?" Monster asked.

"Your friends are safe for the moment," Nukilik said.

"Not if ACOG turns the place to mush," Monster said.

"If that is the will of the gods, then there is nothing you can do about it," Nukilik said. "But if you want our help, then you must do things our way. The *Umialik,* the leader of our village, will not rush into something that might endanger our people."

"Of course," Monster said. "I understand."

"As I understand your anxiety," Nukilik said. "Go back to my home and wait. I will call for you soon."

The Inupiat people called the home an *ivrulik.* Nukilik's *ivrulik,* like all the others, was mostly underground. Monster crawled down through the tunnel, curved to keep the warmth from escaping, and up through the trapdoor into the main room of the home. There were more tunnels leading off this room to other rooms. A roof of log and sod, held up by whale-bone girders, provided insulation and camouflage.

Corazon was waiting for him with a small wooden bowl full of a gelatinous red substance.

He shook his head.

"It is called *Mikigaq,*" Corazon said. "Try some."

"I don't have time for eat," he said.

Not when Price was chained to the interior of a Bzadian tank and ACOG was about to blow the place sky-high. And the others too. He tried to think of the others, but the image that he couldn't shake was of Price, her hands cuffed to her neck, a Bzadian gun in her face.

"You must eat," Corazon said. "When your body shivers, it burns energy. The energy must be replaced."

Monster considered that, then nodded. She was right. He would need his energy if he was going to try to rescue the others.

The food was dark red, soft and sweet. "What is it?" Monster asked.

"Fermented whale meat," Corazon said. "Does that put you off?"

"I eat anything." Monster laughed.

She smiled. "Not quite a burger and fries, I know."

"You have burgers and fries?" Monster asked, looking around at the bare walls.

Corazon shook her head. "No. Not here. But I grew up in Seattle."

"Really?"

"I thought that might surprise you."

"And Nukilik?" Monster asked.

"He grew up here," she said. "He came to live with us as a teenager."

"But now you live here," Monster said.

"Yes. After we married, we returned. These are our ancestral homelands."

"You must love him a lot to come back here," Monster said.

"You have it backward," she said. "It was me who persuaded him to return home. I had always felt this place calling to me. My parents didn't approve."

"You chose to live here?" Monster asked, looking around again.

"As strange as that must seem to you, yes," she said.

"You must find it cold here," Monster said.

"At first," she said. "But now it seems normal."

"Normal?" Monster laughed. "When I first met you, you were shivering almost as badly as me."

She looked away, a little embarrassed. Monster was not sure why.

"Soon you will meet the others," she said. "Can I give you some words of advice?"

"Please," Monster said.

"You will find the conversation a little . . . unusual," she said.

"Unusual how?" Monster asked.

"We are a quiet people and much is said without words," she said. "You must observe carefully. If I widen my eyes or raise my eyebrows, I am agreeing with you. If I wrinkle my nose, that means no. If I am silent, it may be because my spirit is communicating with yours."

The trapdoor in the floor opened and Nukilik entered.

"Come," he said. "The others await."

What appeared to be a small hill was the *qargi*, a communal meeting place. Monster followed Nukilik inside.

A group of men and women were gathered, seated on the

floor in a circle. Monster was surprised to see so many of them, living on this isolated rock in this hostile environment.

The *qargi* was warm from body heat and oil lamps, which also spread a comforting glow throughout the underground chamber. The Inupiat sat around the edge of the room, their backs against the walls.

The old man who had led the funeral rituals was seated at the head of the room. Nukilik introduced him as his father and the *Umialik*. His name, apparently, was Old Joe. Monster wondered if he had ever been known as Young Joe. If he had, it was a long time ago.

The others introduced themselves in turn. A man named Big Billy was huge, especially for an Inupiat. His face was grizzled and scarred. He didn't speak, and Monster was surprised to learn that this was Nukilik's brother. They looked nothing alike.

There was a lot of staring and whispered discussions, and Monster realized that his Bzadian appearance was causing some consternation among the group.

After a brief discussion in their native language, Old Joe addressed Monster. "Welcome to our village," he said.

"You have saved my life and honored life of my friend," Monster said. "I am humbled to be guest."

"My son assures me that you are human," Old Joe said. "Nevertheless, it gives my heart pause to see the face of a demon here inside our *qargi*."

"It is not demons that we fight," Monster said. "The Bzadians are aliens, from a faraway planet."

Old Joe's nose wrinkled in disagreement.

"They are creatures of blood and flesh," Monster said.

"I know you believe this," Old Joe said. "As we have our beliefs."

"Is not belief," Monster said. "Is fact. They are alien."

Old Joe smiled. "You think we are simple people, because we live simply," he said. There was silence in the room except for the sound of the wind rushing overhead.

"I mean no disrespect," Monster said when the silence continued.

"Yet the stench of it fills the room." Big Billy spoke for the first time. His voice was low, like the grinding of gravel beneath the ice. A chorus of murmurs supported him.

Old Joe held up a hand for silence. "Young man, you think you know us, from what your eyes tell you. But your eyes do not tell you what they cannot see. We live here through choice. All of us have lived in the cities of the *naluaqmiut*."

"*Naluaqmiut?*" Monster asked.

"It is a word for people who are not of the Inupiat," Nukilik said.

"We know about central heating and cable television and high-rise buildings and frozen microwave dinners," Old Joe said. "Yet we chose to return here, following the ways of our ancestors, living in sod huts, eating only what we hunt and catch. We have lived in your world. We understand it, and we reject it. You should take pause before you dismiss ours."

"I apologize for any disrespect," Monster said. "And you are right. What I know is what I believe, and what I believe is that the enemy are aliens."

Old Joe's nose wrinkled again. "That is merely the form the demons have taken," he said. "They are pretenders, ancient evil ones from the depths of the Earth. They come to punish the *naluaqmiut* for losing their way."

Around the room eyebrows were raised in agreement.

Monster thought carefully about what to say next. The extended silence seemed natural to the Inupiat and they did not attempt to fill it with words.

"We agree in more ways than we differ," Monster said finally. "I believe universe is strange and complex, with forces interacting in ways we cannot understand. Also, I believe that sometimes things we do have consequences. Wherever they are from, perhaps the arrival of the Bzadians was a message from the universe, a warning for our carelessness. For greed and selfishness."

Now he had raised eyebrows and widened eyes around the room.

"Perhaps we are supposed to learn from this," Monster said. "But we cannot learn if we are gone. There are no lessons for the dead."

Old Joe widened his eyes in agreement. "You are very young," he said. "But you are wiser than most *naluaqmiut*. What is it that you ask of us?"

Monster was certain that Old Joe already knew what he wanted, as did everyone else in the room. But still they needed him to ask formally. Perhaps that, too, was part of their custom.

"The enemy—demon or alien, it makes no difference—is ready to invade the Americas," Monster said. "Thousands of them are waiting just a few kilometers from here. Our commanders know they are there. They will send planes and missiles to smash this fleet. But I have friends, captured by the enemy, who will be killed when this happens."

Big Billy spoke next. He spoke animatedly and angrily in his native language. When he had finished, there was another silence.

"My brother asks why we should help you," Nukilik said. "He says we helped in the Great Ice War and our reward was to be thrown off our island."

"Thrown off?" Monster asked.

Nukilik nodded. "When the war was over, we were forced to leave."

"Yet you are here still," Monster said.

"The pull of the island is strong," Old Joe said.

"Does anyone know you are here?" Monster asked.

"The eyes on Little Diomede must surely see us, but so far they have done nothing," Nukilik said.

"Perhaps now it suits them to have us here," Big Billy growled.

Another long silence followed during which Monster looked around the impassive faces of the Inupiat. He took a deep breath.

"I do not speak for ACOG, not for any other person except myself and my dead friend," Monster said. "You owe me nothing, and have been wronged by our leaders. I understand if you choose not to help. But not far from here, my brothers and sisters face death, or worse. I cannot refuse them. And I will help them even if it means my death."

"And this is what you are asking?" Old Joe asked.

"This is what I am asking," Monster said.

Old Joe said nothing. Monster wondered if there was some truth to the Inupiat beliefs, if somehow their spirits were communicating on some higher plane.

Old Joe sat still, silently for a long time. Monster knew not to break it. Eventually, Old Joe turned to look at Monster. He did not speak, but his eyebrows slowly rose.

One of the Bzadian soldiers moved to the lockers, unlocked it, and withdrew the Angels' helmets and batteries for their thermal suits. They were getting ready to leave.

"Hold your breath," the Tsar said. "I'm gonna fart, and it's gonna be a doozy."

"What are you talking . . ." Price's voice trailed off as the Tsar lifted one foot slightly, revealing the rounded metal shape of a Puke spray grenade. Price stared at it in amazement. How had he got hold of that? She looked away quickly, not wanting the Bzadians to notice. Out of the corner of her eye she saw the Tsar use the heel of his boot to work the pin out of the grenade.

Two of the Bzadian soldiers unholstered their sidearms and aimed them at Price's head while another one unlocked her neckcuff. Behind them Zim was ready with her battery and helmet.

All attention was on her, but that changed in an instant at the sound of the grenade rolling across the floor of the tank. There was a small explosion and a whooshing sound and the cabin of the tank filled instantly with a white mist that smelled vaguely of peppermint. The only other sounds were those of the Bzadian soldiers slumping to the floor.

Price had taken a deep breath and held it tightly, screwing her eyes shut. Her last experience of Puke spray had not been a pleasant one. She scrabbled around on the floor for her helmet, finding it half trapped beneath a body. She freed it and jammed it down over her head. Locking it into place, she heard the hiss as the self-contained oxygen system pressurized. Still she waited for the air inside the suit to clear before taking a breath and opening her eyes.

Already, the air in the battle tank was clearing as the tank's own air filters removed the Puke spray, but Barnard and the Tsar still had their eyes and mouths tightly shut.

She ran across to the far side of the tank and snatched up the other helmets, fitting Barnard's, then the Tsar's. She found the key to the neckcuffs, still in the hand of one of the Bzadians, and freed the Angels.

Price tossed a battery pack to each of the others before slotting her own into place on her hip, feeling the thermal suit come to life around her. She retrieved her gun, attaching it to the holster on her back.

"Good work, Tsar," she said.

"Where the hell did you magic up that grenade?" Barnard asked.

"Wall gave it to me," the Tsar said.

Price stopped what she was doing and stared at him. "Wall gave it to you?"

"When we were fighting," the Tsar said.

"That makes no sense," Price said. "He's on their side."

"Or is he?" the Tsar asked.

"Unless they want us to escape," Barnard said.

"That makes no sense either," Price said. "Why would they want us to escape?"

"I don't know and right now I don't care. Let's just power this thing up and get the heck out of here," the Tsar said, looking at the controls for the tank.

The Bzadian soldiers, lying in various uncomfortable poses on the floor, stared at him but couldn't move any other muscles.

"No," Barnard said. "Bad idea."

"We have one tank," Price said. "They have hundreds; they'll blow us off the ice."

"Well, at least we'll take a few of them with us," the Tsar said. "And when ACOG sees a tank battle, they'll surely know that something ain't quite right down here."

"Very noble of you," Barnard said. "We die to send a message to ACOG."

"No," Price said. "Nobody else dies today."

"Except Pukes," the Tsar said.

"Anyway, we couldn't even shoot back," Barnard said. "This isn't a tank."

"What do you mean?" Price asked.

"It took me a while to realize," Barnard said, "because they are very similar, but this is a SAM battery. They travel with tanks, but they are surface-to-air defense only."

"So we can't shoot back at all?" the Tsar asked.

"Not unless they attack us with planes," Barnard said.

"We could still make a run for it," the Tsar said.

"We would have a better chance if we got out," Price said. "Try to escape across the ice floes on foot."

"And how are we going to let ACOG know about the invasion force?" the Tsar asked. "Isn't that the whole point?"

"If we rig some explosives up on the gun platform," Barnard said, "we might be able to use the explosion as a distraction to help us get away. And it should be a pretty spectacular bang, which will get the ACOG's attention."

"I like it," Price said. "And that way at least we have a chance."

The Tsar started to object, but Price cut him off before he could say anything. "Do it now," she said.

"What this?" Monster asked, picking up a wooden handle that lay next to a pile of small feathered, metal-tipped spears. They were still in the *qargi*. Nukilik had brought in an armload of the spears and the odd handles.

"It is an *atlat*," Nukilik said.

"What is it?" Monster asked. He picked one up and examined it.

"It is used to throw a dart," Nukilik said.

"These spears?" Monster asked.

"Darts," Nukilik corrected him.

"The Bzadians have coil-guns," Monster said. "We have dart throwers?"

"We have rifles too," Nukilik said. "Hunting rifles. But they make noise, and these do not. In the Great Ice War, my brother carried nothing but an *atlat* and a sling of darts. Yet the demons feared him more than anything else. They called him the White Wolf."

"Big Billy was the White Wolf?" Monster put the *atlat* down.

"You have heard of the White Wolf?" Nukilik asked.

"The White Wolf is legend from the Ice War," Monster said. "The stories are so unbelievable, most of us thought they were fantasy."

"Whatever you have heard, double it," Nukilik said. "Then you will be halfway to the truth."

Right on cue, Big Billy entered, at the head of a half-dozen Inupiat men with hunting rifles slung over their shoulders.

"I do not understand how you can kill with a dart," Monster said. "Even your rifles will not penetrate Bzadian body armor. It will absorb two or three shots easily."

Big Billy grunted something and the others laughed.

"We do not aim for the armor, but for the battery pack," Nukilik said. "They are vulnerable, and in this place, killing the thermals in a suit is almost as deadly as killing a person."

Monster thought of Emile and said nothing.

Big Billy spoke in *Inupiaq* to Nukilik, then handed him a bundle of cloth. Nukilik seemed surprised. He shrugged and handed the bundle to Monster. It was heavy.

"This belongs to my father," Nukilik said. "He wants you to take it."

Monster slowly unwrapped the cloth. Inside was an oilskin, and inside that a deadly black shape: a huge pistol—a hand cannon.

"Smith and Wesson, forty-four magnum," Nukilik said.

Monster picked it up, feeling the balance.

Nukilik smiled. "You have made a real impression on my father. This is his most precious treasure. He has never even let me borrow it."

"I will try to make good use of it," Monster said.

Barnard closed the top hatch delicately, clicking it into place with the gentlest of touches.

"Let's get out of here," she said.

"How long have we got to get clear?" Price asked.

"I set the fuse for thirty minutes," Barnard said. "Twenty-nine minutes on my mark . . . now."

Price tapped a button to set a timer on the display inside her mask.

The exit hatch opened without warning and the Vaza stuck her head up through it. She took in the scene in an instant and dived back down out of sight as Price hit the release for her coil-gun.

"Damn," Price said.

"Gotta get after her," the Tsar said, his coil-gun in his hands also. He ran toward the hatch.

"No!" Price said. "She'll be waiting for you. Go down that hatch, you're dead."

16. THE BUNKER

[MISSION DAY 2, FEBRUARY 17, 2033]
[1440 hours local time]
[Operations Command Center, Pentagon, Virginia]

BILAL STOPPED AT THE ELEVATOR THAT WAS THE entrance to the command bunker. Wilton stopped behind him.

Two guards checked his ID card with a handheld scanner, then repeated the same for Wilton, before admitting them. The doors slid open with a slight whoosh and slid shut behind them as soon as they entered.

When the lift opened on the lower level, another guard checked their IDs again.

"Try to look older," was Bilal's only comment.

After the brightly lit corridors outside, the command center was in virtual darkness, or so it seemed until his eyes grew accustomed to the low levels of light, coming mainly from computer screens. Around the walls were an endless series of workstations, all occupied by uniformed officers. The ceiling was high and domed.

In the center of the room was an oval table, littered with coffee cups and small plates of half-eaten sandwiches.

Wilton looked around the faces, recognizing only a few of them. General Harry Whitehead was often seen on the news, commenting on the ups and downs of the war. General Jake Russell was the head of the Bering Strait Defense Force and therefore Wilton's commanding officer. The others he could only identify by the nameplates in front of each chair. Wilton felt awkward and unsure of himself in such company but tried not to show it. What was he doing here with all these high-powered commanders? Then again, he had battled aliens in the corridors of Uluru and the top of the Wivenhoe Dam. Had any of these guys even seen combat against the Bzadians?

"This is Blake," Bilal said, and Wilton noticed that he deliberately omitted his surname. "He is a Bzadian translator. Fluent in all languages and dialects."

Several of those at the table greeted him with a nod, and Wilton returned it, feeling extremely uncomfortable under their gaze and repeating over and over to himself, *Uluru. Wivenhoe.*

"We have a whole roomful of people for that," Russell said. "What's he doing in here?"

"If we pick up any transmissions from the ice, I want to know what they are saying while they are saying it," Bilal said. "Not half an hour later after your roomful of experts have debated the meaning of every syllable."

Russell opened his mouth to argue, then clearly thought the better of it and simply shook his head. Bilal pointed Wilton to a workstation before taking his own seat.

Wilton logged on to the computer, then took his phone out of his pocket and placed it on the desk. He made sure it was switched to silent.

The others at the table waited while Bilal punched up some information on the screen in front of him.

"You all got my report," Bilal said.

"With no evidence to support it," Russell said. "There's no heat showing on the thermals. There's no sign of movement. And it makes no sense, taking the southern route. There are fissures and ridges. At any moment the floes could break apart."

"If my asset says there is a division of Bzadian tanks in that ice field, then they are there," Bilal said. "Or would you rather wait until they were climbing ashore at Alaska before taking any action?"

"That's not the point," a woman in naval uniform said. She was Admiral Lynette Hooper, according to her nameplate. Wilton knew the name. She was in charge of the submarine fleet, and therefore most of the cruise missile capability that the allied forces had left. "If we waste a shipload of missiles turning half of the Bering Sea into ice cubes, and we are wrong, then we might as well lay down some red carpet for the Pukes and say 'Welcome to Washington.'"

"So we drop a nuke in there," Russell said. "Heat of the blast melts the ice and anything that doesn't get destroyed in the initial explosion ends up at the bottom of the Bering Sea."

"Nuclear weapons are not an option," Whitehead said. "They never have been."

"Well, maybe now's the time to rethink that policy," Russell said. "If we lose the Bering Strait, we lose the war."

Wilton looked at him in alarm. Everybody knew that the Pukes had nukes. Apart from their own weapons, they had the nuclear inventory captured from countries like Russia, Britain, and North Korea. The nuclear option was suicide. Everybody knew that!

"We use nukes, the Bzadians will use nukes," Bilal said, echoing Wilton's thoughts. "They won't have to invade America because there won't be anything to invade."

"So goes the theory," Russell said. "So we hold back. I'd rather hand them a nuclear wasteland than give up the entire planet. But I don't think it will come to that. They won't use nukes against our cities, as long as we don't use them against theirs."

"You can't know that," a woman in civilian clothes said. Her nameplate said "Emily Gonzales." There was no indication of what her position was.

"Tactical nukes on the battlefield is one thing. Strategic nukes, wiping each other off the planet, that's a different ball game," Russell said. "Nobody wins."

"And you're prepared to risk nuclear annihilation on your analysis of the way an alien race thinks?" Whitehead said.

Wilton's heart was beating fast and his pulse racing. He was sitting in a room with ACOG commanders who were calmly discussing the end of the world. The destruction of planet Earth.

"Look, they are invading us because they think they can," Russell said. "We have to show them they can't. That if they try to cross the strait, we will nuke it. That if it comes down to losing the Americas, yes, we are prepared to risk nuclear annihilation."

"That's a pretty big bluff," Gonzales said.

"Not really," Russell said. "They know we have thousands of nukes too. All aimed at their major cities. If they retaliate, we retaliate, too, and it's Armageddon."

"So you're prepared to destroy the world?" Bilal asked.

"Rather than hand it over, yes," Russell said.

"Not going to happen," Whitehead said. "The risks are too great. We will stop them in the strait and we will do it without nukes."

Russell started to object, but Whitehead shut him up with a gesture of his hand. "The discussion is over, Russell."

"The oversight committee would never approve it anyway," Gonzales said. "The no-nukes policy has been debated over and over. The answer is always going to be no."

Russell, who had been standing to emphasize his point, sat back down. He glanced over at Wilton and his cheeks were red with anger. Although it was not directed at him, Wilton quickly looked away. *Thank God for sane heads!*

"So is this invasion for real?" Whitehead asked.

"You've seen the evidence," Bilal said, and punched a button that brought up the photos on the main screen. The low shadows were clearly visible.

"Just who or what is this asset of yours?" Gonzales asked.

Wilton held his breath. What would Bilal say? The Angel mission was top secret. But more than that, if there could be Bzadian moles anywhere, then there could be one in this room. If the Bzadians found out that the Angels were active again, their lives would be in even greater danger.

"That information is 'need to know,'" Bilal said.

"In this case, in order to evaluate the information, I think we do need to know," General Whitehead said.

"All that I am prepared to say is that I trust the source," Bilal said.

"We can't ignore this," General Whitehead said. "Put a squadron of drones in the air, armed with hellfires. Hooper, I want your subs at battle stations. We'll skim those drones just above the ice, where the Pukes can't see them, and pop them up in the air right over the target. If there are any Pukes there and they see a bunch of armed aircraft appear above them, it should provoke some kind of reaction."

"And if the Pukes are smarter than that?" Bilal asked. "What if they just sit tight, try to bluff it out?"

"If we don't see any sign of movement, we'll chuck a couple of hellfires at them regardless," Whitehead said. "See if they sit there and take it while we're scratching their asses for them."

There are Angels down there! Wilton wanted to cry out. But he couldn't.

"The moment the Bzadians detect our drones, they're going

to launch air cover from Chukchi," an air force general said. He was Indian and his nameplate identified him as Kamaljeet Hundal. "Type Ones, Twos, whatever they got."

"What's our time window?" Whitehead asked.

"We have a squadron of Taranis UAVs at Tin City Airbase," Hundal said. "Flight time is about twenty minutes. We can take off low and skim the ice out to the target area. The stealth technology in the Taranis is very advanced. The Bzadian radar wouldn't even know they're there until they climb to attack altitude. Their flight time is only about eight minutes, but on top of that is scramble and take-off time. From the time they detect our drones, to the first Bzadian jets reaching the target area, we'd have about fifteen minutes."

"Lynette?" Whitehead asked.

"I can have steel on target inside ten," the admiral said. "As long as we have clear air. Once that storm hits, the Tomahawks are off the table. We'd lose half of them en route."

"Why is that?" Gonzales asked.

"Terrain sensing," Hooper said. "The guidance system on the Tomahawk uses terrain maps for accurate positioning. In whiteout conditions they are blind."

"Weather?" Whitehead asked.

"It's moving through now," a weather officer said. A weather map filled the main screen. "The storm front will start to move over the Diomede Islands in less than an hour and will drift over the target area after that. We only have an hour or so of clear air."

"Then let's roll," Whitehead said. "Hooper, bring your

subs up to missile depth. Hundal, I want those drones ready to launch as soon as possible."

"If they can scramble their jets faster than we think," Hundal said, "they'll knock our Tomahawks out of the sky. Ever since Uluru they've upped the antimissile capability of the Type Ones."

"What do you suggest?" Whitehead asked.

"As soon as the drones start their attack climb, we launch F-35s from Buck Creek. Come in from the north. That'll draw the Bzadian fast movers away from the Tomahawks," Hundal said.

"All of this will be a waste of time if it turns out there's nothing there," Russell said.

"Better safe than sorry," Bilal said.

Wilton stared at his phone, praying for it to ring.

17. MELTING THE ICE

THEY LAY ON THE RIDGELINE, WELL CONCEALED BY jumbled, broken blocks of ice, and waited for the enemy.

The wind was starting to gust, kicking at loose snow on the ground. The sky was impenetrably overcast, and in the distance dark, heavy thunderheads were chewing up and spitting out the scraps of smaller clouds as they approached.

Monster's parka was doubled. Two parkas, one inside the other. The inner one had fur lining, while the outer one had fur on the outside. The hood offered ample protection and warmth to his head. Monster wound a scarf around his face to protect it, although Nukilik and the other Inupiat didn't seem to need to.

There was still no sign of an attack from ACOG. Had the message even got through? Monster had to assume so and that an attack was imminent. For now, every minute they held off was a blessing. One thing was certain: If ACOG were going to attack, it would be before the weather closed in again. Time was running out rapidly, he thought, watching the thunderheads.

Nukilik scrambled up alongside him, careful to keep below the brow of the ridge.

"Any sign?" Monster asked.

"Be patient, the demons will come," Nukilik said.

"Do you really believe they are demons, evil spirits?" Monster asked.

"I believe what my father believes," Nukilik said.

Monster looked at him without comment.

Nukilik laughed. "You can give me all the logic and the science you want. If my father says they are demons, then they are demons. In my culture we respect the wisdom of our elders."

He handed Monster a large, heavy plastic bag. Monster opened it to find it full of powdery granules.

"What is it?"

"De-icer," Nukilik said.

"Where did you get it?" Monster asked.

"Walmart," Nukilik said.

"What is the plan?" Monster asked. "I do not understand."

"It will melt the ice," Nukilik said. "We use it to dig a hole for the demons to fall into. A trick we learned in the last Ice War." He paused and reflected on that. "It was my wife's idea," he said with more than a little pride.

"Is Corazon all right?" Monster asked, scanning the rough white horizon of the ice field.

"She is as strong as a walrus," Nukilik said. "Why do you ask?"

"When I first met her, she was shivering, as if she was sick," Monster said.

Nukilik smiled. "She said you had asked about that."

"But she is fine?"

"Yes, she is well. She was cold because she had shared her warmth with you."

"Shared her warmth?" Monster asked.

"For the first hours, after I brought you in, she lay next to you in the bed," Nukilik said. "To bring up your body temperature."

Monster was silent for a moment. "I had no clothes," he said.

Nukilik laughed again. "Neither did she. That is how it is done. But your virtue is intact. Think of it only as a medical procedure."

"I am not sure what to say," Monster said. "Will you thank her for me?"

"It is not necessary," Nukilik said. "It is what is done." He raised a hand and pointed at the ice field. "There!"

Monster followed his finger. A slight thickening of the

horizon was all he saw, but if Nukilik said something was there, then he believed him. It was approaching from the west, from the direction of the Chukchi Peninsula.

"They are bringing up a transporter to take away your friends," Nukilik said.

Whatever it was drew closer, resolving into a moving cloud of snow. It was definitely a vehicle of some kind, he saw, and he assumed that the snow was being thrown up by its tracks, although as it appeared over a rise in the ground, he saw that was not true.

A nozzle on top of the vehicle was spraying water straight up into the air, the droplets immediately freezing in the subzero air and turning before their eyes to snow, a cloud, which not only helped conceal the transporter from satellite eyes but also fell to earth after the vehicle, covering its tracks.

"That is new trick," Monster said. "They not have this in last Ice War."

"They're learning," Nukilik said.

The vehicle was tracked, like a tank. Monster recognized it from its low profile. It was a Russian DT-30 Vityaz, one of the many human vehicles that the Bzadians had commandeered.

"There's more than one," Nukilik said.

He was right. A second vehicle followed, and another behind that.

"If those are full of troops, then we might be biting off more than we can chew," Nukilik said.

"Monster have big appetite," Monster said.

Nukilik threw back his head in laughter and clapped

Monster on the shoulder. "I think I understand why my father likes you."

The DT-30s passed by, not far from where they were hiding on the ridge. Ugly, squat, articulated vehicles, the front cab about the same size as the trailing cabin. Four small windows across the cab were constantly being cleared by fast-moving wipers. The trailing cabin had no windows.

The transporters veered close to the ridge to avoid a large crack in the ice that was on the verge of becoming a fissure, then disappeared behind the snow-covered battle tanks in a roar of diesel. As soon as they were out of sight, Monster and Nukilik ran down to the tracks, already mostly covered by the freshly created snow. They scattered the granules around them, as though sowing seeds, crushing them into the ice with the soles of their boots.

The ice almost instantly turned to mush under their feet, then to a semi-frozen slush that sloshed around their boots.

"How far down will it go?" Monster asked.

"A half meter, maybe more," Nukilik said. "By then it will have diluted too much. But that's good. We don't want to melt all the way through the ice, because then the liquid will just flow down out into the ocean. But we want it deep enough and wide enough to stop the transporters."

"What if they don't return this way?" Monster asked.

"They will," Nukilik said, gesturing at the large crack in the ice that began a few meters away from them. "There is no other way."

Nukilik walked around the edge of the pool of slush, testing the depth with a stick, occasionally pointing to an area where he wanted more granules.

"Okay, that's enough," Nukilik called. "Let's take our positions."

[MISSION DAY 2, FEBRUARY 17, 2033]
[1520 hours local time]
[Operations Command Center, Pentagon, Virginia]

BEING IN THE COMMAND CENTER WAS MUCH LIKE BEING out in the field, Wilton thought. You spent most of your time waiting.

He was waiting for contact from Monster. He had tried the number that Monster had given him a couple of times, but it still would not connect.

He used the time productively, though, hunting traitors.

He logged on to the main Pentagon system and was amazed to see a host of menus and options that had never existed before. Top security access opened all sorts of doors.

"Ten minutes to launch," a voice called from somewhere in the room, startling him. He glanced around to see a woman moving to the front of the room. He brought up a list of the personnel in the room and identified her. Her name was Cheryl Watson. She was the command coordinator, responsible for relaying information to the decision makers.

Next he brought up the staffing allocations page. Finding

the operational orders that posted the Fezerker agent to Little Diomede was easy. The chain of command that put them there was long, and stretched all the way up to General Russell, who was sitting at a table only a few meters away.

"Five minutes to launch," Watson called.

Wilton glanced over at Russell, trying not to stare. Surely Russell was above suspicion? But Chisnall had said to trust no one.

"We have launch," Watson called out. "Taranis squadron is in the air. Time to target, twenty-three minutes."

"You're sure the enemy radar won't pick them up?" Gonzales asked.

"Sure enough," Hundal said. "They're stealth. Plus they're flying low, hugging the ice. If we're lucky, the enemy won't know they exist until they begin their climb."

Wilton eased his nerves by focusing on his own work.

The list of people who had known about Operation Magnum was small. That list included General Whitehead, ACOG commander; General Elisabeth Iniguez, recently retired; and Daniel Bilal. That put all of them above suspicion.

He started digging into the Uluru operation. The first ever Angel mission. Again, that had achieved complete surprise. Anyone who knew about that was also in the clear.

The man with the olive-green briefcase sat alone in an office on the second floor of the building, the main floor. The office was empty, as he had known it would be. He had unlocked the door using the key card that hung on a lanyard around his neck.

He checked the time, using his phone, not his watch, then retrieved an identical briefcase to the one he had been carrying from under the desk where he had left it the day before. He opened both briefcases, placing them side by side on the desk. The first briefcase contained nothing more than a can of Pepsi.

He opened the plastic lunch container and removed the sandwiches, blowing into the container afterward to remove any crumbs. The bread he discarded into the round, leather-clad bin on the floor under the desk.

The filling, which appeared to be some kind of gelatinous meat, he placed back in the plastic container. Opening the can of Pepsi, he poured it over. An observer would have been surprised to see that the liquid from a perfectly ordinary can of Pepsi was not black, but almost clear, with a light green tinge.

Whatever it was, it was not Pepsi.

As the liquid pooled around the gelatinous substance, it began to dissolve and the combination of the two elements fused into a pale pink color. He stirred it with a metal ballpoint pen. If a bomb-sniffing dog encountered the substance now, it would probably have a heart attack.

The man opened two muesli bars and placed them in the container, allowing them to soak up the liquid, turning them to treat both sides, until the container was empty. He placed the watch on top of the two jellified bars, pressing it down firmly and holding it there until it was dry enough to stick. Replacing the lid of the container, he sealed it with packaging tape. It had taken two minutes.

His hand dipped into a pocket of his jacket and emerged with a phone. He placed it on the desk in front of him.

He waited.

"Price."

The voice on the comm was Wall's.

Price glanced around at the others. The Tsar was still working on the radio. Barnard was sitting silently, thinking. She looked up at Price.

"Talk to him," Barnard said. "See what he wants."

Price nodded. "What do you want, Fezerker?" she asked on the comm.

"Clever move with the grenade," Wall said. "How did you get hold of that?"

Price glanced at the others. *Wall had given Tsar the grenade.* Why would he ask that question?

"It was a magic trick," Price said. "What do you want?"

"You can't go anywhere," Wall said. "You can't do anything. Come out quietly and we'll make sure you get to a nice safe POW camp. I'll personally guarantee that the PGZ won't get their hands on you."

"And why should I believe you?" Price said. "As if the PGZ would listen to you anyway."

"I am Fezerker," Wall said. "Not even the PGZ get to tell us what to do."

Price thought back to Uluru and realized that he was right. Fezerkers outranked everyone, even the dreaded PGZ.

"We don't have a lot of options," Barnard said. "But delay him a few more minutes."

"What are you thinking?" Price asked, and Barnard explained.

"Teranis squadron begin climb to attack altitude in three, two, one," Watson said. "Climbing now."

"How long?" Whitehead asked.

"A few minutes," Hundal said.

"Come on," Wilton said, and then realized he had said it out loud. It earned him a few glances but nothing more. Everybody was just as keyed up as he was.

Out over the ice, the unmanned aircraft were sacrificing ground speed for height, their engines straining to pull the craft up to the altitude from which they could launch their missiles.

"If we don't get some kind of movement on the ground, get those drones out of there, before the Pukes can get within range," Whitehead said. "Have we got air cover up?"

"Yes, sir," Hundal said. "A squadron of F-35s is lifting off as we speak."

Price was the first out. She emerged from the tunnel under the tank and raised her hands to the back of her neck. She kept a close eye on the time, ticking away on the inside of her visor. Barnard and the Tsar followed her out.

Bzadian soldiers surrounded them, guns raised. Nokz'z and the Vaza watched from behind the line of soldiers. Wall too.

A small convoy of vehicles was pulling to a halt behind the soldiers. Low, squat, armored transporters. They looked Russian. Other soldiers disappeared into the tank behind them and then reemerged, dragging out the limp bodies of Zim and the others.

"Get on your knees," the Vaza said.

Price ignored her.

Two minutes.

They were too close to the tank, Price thought. They had to get farther away. She took a step forward, then another. The Tsar and Barnard were right alongside her.

"That's far enough," Nokz'z said. "One more step and I will be forced to—"

He never got to say what he would be forced to do. His voice cut off abruptly and his eyes narrowed; he was clearly listening to something on his radio. His eyes turned upward, as did most of the other Bzadians'. The air of calm vanished, the Angels almost forgotten while he issued urgent orders.

One minute.

Price took another step.

Big Billy had an *atlat* with a dart already hooked onto the end. He had a look in his eyes as though he was never happier than when he was out here on the ice, hunting, especially when the prey was Bzadian. Nukilik also seemed to be in his element, lying between two jagged ends of ice as if he were part of the ice floe.

The other Inupiat were lying along the ridgeline with rifles or standing below it with *atlats* and quivers full of darts. Some of those on the ridge would act as observers for those behind it, indicating with hand signals where to fire the darts.

Monster tried to remain still, although it was uncomfortable on the cold ice. The Inupiat, he saw, were like statues. Movement attracted the eye.

Nukilik eased up alongside him. "We are running out of time," he said.

"Why?" Monster asked.

"Big Billy says he can hear aircraft approaching," Nukilik said.

Monster strained his ears but could hear nothing over the rising howl of the wind.

"He's sure?"

"Big Billy is never wrong," Nukilik said.

"On my mark, hit the deck," Price said.

"Don't dive," the Tsar said. "Fall."

"What?" Barnard asked.

"If you dive, they'll know something is up," the Tsar said. "Act like you're fainting. Collapse to the ground. It will confuse them."

"Whatever you're going to do, you've got three seconds," Price said. "Two . . ."

She let her legs go limp and fell to the ground, feigning unconsciousness. She saw Barnard fall beside her. The Tsar added some theatrics, clutching at his throat as if poisoned.

Several of the soldiers moved toward the fallen Angels. The rest stood where they were, unsure and unmoving.

Price played dead. The timer inside her visor ticked to zero. Nothing happened. Had the timer not worked? That wasn't like Barnard. She was normally so precise. So efficient. So . . .

The thought died as the air around her was ripped apart by thunder and fire.

"These are the snow hills you were talking about," Whitehead said.

"There're a lot of them," Bilal said.

The image from one of the drones was up on the main screen and showed the unusual mounds of ice stretching into the distance.

"Taranis three is picking up foot mobiles," Watson said. "A group of them down by one of the mounds."

The feed came up on the main screen as she spoke.

"What the hell's going on down there?" Whitehead asked. "Get us in closer. We . . . Whoa! What was that? Did we do that?"

A ball of fire had just blossomed in the middle of the screen.

"Negative, sir," Watson said. "We didn't fire anything. But

the operators on Little Diomede are reporting a large explosion to the southwest. That's what we just saw."

Wilton found himself on his feet, staring at the screen, his heart racing. What had happened?

A few people were looking at him and he forced himself to sit back down and act calm.

"I don't know what's going on," Bilal said, "but I don't think those mounds are igloos."

On the large screen, images from the drones showed the ice pack clearly, with the little island to the northeast.

As Wilton watched, pinpoints of light appeared on the screen, making the ice sparkle like a Christmas tree.

"SAM, SAM, SAM," Watson called. "Multiple in-bound surface-to-air missiles from the ice field."

"That's it!" Whitehead said. "That's confirmation. Engage those SAM batteries with the drones and get those cruise missiles in the air."

"We haven't seen a tank yet," Russell said.

"Those SAM batteries are not there guarding empty ice," Whitehead said. "Hooper?"

Admiral Hooper, who was already on the phone to her staff, nodded and gave a thumbs-up. "Missiles away," she said.

From a line of ten submarines, lying south of the ice field, twenty Tomahawk missiles exploded up out of the water, ejected by gas pressure, before rocketing to three hundred meters on the shiny tail of a solid-fuel booster. The wings unfolded and the air scoops deployed as the turbofan engines kicked in.

The Tomahawks plunged to barely ten meters above the

sea, dropping off radar screens, hugging the ocean, then the ice pack, as they raced in to the attack.

"Launch, launch, launch!" Watson called out. "Multiple tangos lifting off from bases across the Chukchi Peninsula."

"It's going to be close," Whitehead said.

The air burned. The armor on Price's body burned. Even the ice burned.

The Bzadians were scattered, blown off their feet, dazed and shocked, or worse.

The Vaza was the only one who had reacted. Knowing something was wrong, she had twisted around in front of Nokz'z, protecting him from the brunt of the explosion. Now she lay unconscious on top of him.

Price pushed herself up off the ice and looked to see if the others were okay. Barnard was already on her feet and collecting coil-guns from the downed Bzadians. The Tsar was sitting back on his haunches, gathering his wits.

Barnard tossed Price a coil-gun, then threw one to the Tsar, who caught it deftly, despite his dazed condition.

"Let's get out of here," Price said. One or two of the Bzadians were already starting to stir. Nokz'z was conscious and struggling to get out from under the weight of the Vaza.

"Give me a hand," Barnard shouted. She had her hands under Wall's shoulders.

"Leave him," Price said.

"No way," Barnard said. "He saved our lives."

"He's Fezerker," Price said.

"Either way, we need him," Barnard said. "We need to get him back to ACOG so they can interrogate him."

"He'll slow us down," Price said, but the Tsar already had Wall's feet and was running with him toward one of the transporters.

The windows of the transporter had been shattered by the explosion and the driver was leaning, unconscious, against the door. Price opened it and hauled him roughly out.

The stunned Bzadians were recovering quickly and coilgun rounds were sparking off the armored sides of the transporter as Price gunned the engine. The tracks of the machine bit into the ice and the machine lurched into a tight turn, away from the smoldering wreckage of the SAM battery.

Price headed west, back along the tracks that the transporters had already made. It was the wrong way to go; they needed to go east, but a high ice ridge to the north and a deep crack in the ice to the south were forcing them into a narrow funnel. Ahead, the ice rose into a low mound, but once past that they could outskirt the crevasse and head east.

Heavy machine-gun bullets were thudding into the transporter, and in her rearview mirrors she could see at least one of the other transporters giving chase. The fifty-caliber top-mounted machine gun was spitting fire in their direction.

"Someone get on the fifty," she yelled.

She pressed the accelerator to the floor and the machine surged forward.

"I have three vehicles heading west at high speed," Watson announced.

"Running like dogs," Russell said.

"Light 'em up," Whitehead said.

Already, hits were coming in from the battlefield. Some of the icebreakers were getting through; others were being shot down by the concentrated surface-to-air defenses of the Bzadian invasion force.

As Wilton watched, an icebreaker landed, disappearing into the ice with what looked like no more than a puff of smoke.

It wasn't smoke; he knew that. It was pulverized ice. That's what the icebreakers did. They didn't have to hit their targets. Their job was to fracture the ice floes, weakening them. A succession of them would turn the floes into crushed ice, dumping anything on them into the sea. There was little to see from above, because all of their energy was directed into the ice itself, fracturing it, weakening it.

Another icebreaker landed, but more and more were exploding in midair above the ice. The Taranis drones were falling from the sky, too, victims of a vicious response from the ice below.

Wilton had seen too much.

He had heard nothing from Monster. That meant the Angels had not got out. They were somewhere down there. Right in the middle of the kill zone.

18. AMBUSH

"ICEBREAKERS!" MONSTER YELLED, PICKING HIMSELF UP from the ground.

The entire ice floe had shuddered as if the world itself were breaking apart. A plume of snow and ice erupted somewhere to the southwest.

"Get down! Here they come," Nukilik said.

The first transporter appeared from behind one of the mounds.

"Any second," Nukilik shouted.

The top-mounted machine gun of the first transporter was firing, spitting a constant stream of high-caliber bullets at the transporter behind it, which was returning fire.

"Why are they shooting at each other?" Nukilik asked.

"Angels!" Monster said.

It had to be. But they were heading right for the trap that he and Nukilik had laid.

He leaped out from behind the safety of the ridge, yelling and screaming at the transporter.

The transporter made no attempt to slow. The tracks of the machine hurled ice in the air. At the last minute, the driver must have realized that something was wrong as the tracks jammed, the DT-30 slewing sideways as it hit the pool of slush.

The nose of the machine completely disappeared, all the way back to the driver's door, water spraying up in all directions. Monster felt a judder through the ice as the vehicle hit a solid wall on the far side of the pool.

The truck and trailer jackknifed vertically, the rear riding up onto the top of the cab and engine. The connecting rods snapped with an explosive crack and the trailer bounced over the front, landing on the other side, first with one track, then the other, sliding a dozen meters before flipping onto its side, wedged against a slab of ice. The second vehicle locked up its tracks and slid across the ice, ramming into the now vertical tracks of the first vehicle and pushing it over onto its roof.

Half a second later, there was a streak of light from the sky: a lightning bolt that struck the ice just a few meters in front of the vehicle. A fountain of pulverized ice shards exploded into the air. If not for the pool of slush stopping the DT-30 in its tracks, it and anyone on it would have been vaporized.

The third vehicle skidded to a halt well clear of the jumble of twisted metal.

Monster was already running, leaping down the slope of the ridge. Nukilik was right behind him.

Price lay on the ice, struggling for breath. She had seen the ice shimmer in front of her as she had driven the machine down the slope and had known that something was wrong. But there was no time to do anything about it, no time to stop, no way to change direction.

The transporter had slammed into a brick wall. At that point things got confused. She remembered hurtling through the windshield, already smashed by the explosion of the SAM battery. She seemed to be flying briefly; then the ice had come up to meet her and there was a moment of blackness.

Now there were vague shapes around her, whirling and turning in the wind. Animals . . . no, humans in animal furs.

Shouts drifted to her as one of the shapes helped the other Angels out of the wreck of the transporter. She strained to catch their words but got only scraps with the wind and the buzzing in her ears.

She tried to get up, but the ice clung to her, refusing to let her go.

One of the fur-clad shapes slid to a halt beside her and she was lifted. She heard gunfire but couldn't tell where it was coming from. Bullets kicked up puffs of ice around her and sparked off the side of the wrecked vehicle behind her.

She glanced up at the roar overhead and caught a glimpse of a blur of black metal. The ice thundered not far away, and she was back on the ground, the man lying across her. He was a native of the area, she realized. An Inupiat.

Some semblance of consciousness was starting to return, and as the man stood, she pushed away his hand and stood on her own, a little wobbly but okay.

The firing had stopped with the explosion of the missile, and the other Angels were already running for the safety of the ice ridge.

The man beside her shouted "Run!" in her ear. Was there something familiar about his voice, or was that her imagination? He pulled her with him, running after the others.

There were more gunshots now, but they didn't seem directed at the Angels. When she glanced around, she saw the Bzadians firing at the ice ridge. As she watched, a barrage of small spears came flying over the ridge.

Then they were climbing up among the jumbled ice rocks of the ridge and over, to cover, to safety.

Wilton could not take his eyes off the main screen, switching between cameras on different drones. The screen was full of smoke, fire, and bursting pinpoints of light. And somewhere beneath that were his friends.

"We are facing intense SAM activity," Hundal said. "Whatever they've got on that ice floe, they sure want to protect it."

"If they want to protect it, then we want to destroy it," Whitehead said.

"The invasion force is much larger than we thought," Russell said. "Based on the SAM activity, it spreads a long way to the south and the west."

The picture on the main screen was not encouraging. The ice floes near the islands were crushed and broken, creating a large dark area amid the white of the sea ice.

But the dimpled effect of the mounds that were the hidden Bzadian tanks spread far to the east and the south.

"If every one of those hills is a Bzadian battle tank, then that's got to be over half the Bzadian Army right there," Whitehead said. "This is the invasion we've been waiting for."

"Most of our Taranis drones are down," Hundal said. "Taken out by SAMs or by the Type Ones. I'm pulling the other ones back."

"How about the Tomahawks?" Whitehead asked.

"A good percentage of the first strike got through," Hooper said. "By the time the second strike got there, the Type Ones were on station and they're knocking them down as fast as we can fire them."

"F-35s coming into range," Hundal said. "That'll draw off the Type Ones for you."

"It had better," Hooper said.

"We either stop this right here, right now, or it's all over," Whitehead said. "As soon as those Type Ones are engaged, I want you to blanket that entire area with the cruise missiles. Smash that ice field to pieces."

"We've already committed over a third of our inventory," Hundal said.

"That won't matter if we can turn this attack around," Russell said.

"Let 'em have it, Jack," Whitehead said quietly.

"Let them have what?" Hooper asked.

"Everything," Whitehead said. "Those tanks are not getting through. Not on my watch. Not this winter."

"Angels, get out of there," Wilton murmured to himself, "before it's too late."

But he had a bad feeling that it was already too late.

Monster helped Wall up a low section of the ridge. The Angels were not in good shape, dazed and bloodied by the crash. Wall seemed to have come off the worst, and the front of his armor was blackened and burned. Monster put his arm under his shoulders and helped him climb.

Roaring over the top of them were the sleek shapes of Bzadian jets. From the way the sky was exploding to the south, Monster could tell that a furious air battle was taking place.

The Bzadian soldiers had stopped firing altogether now and were climbing on board the one functioning transporter. Thin fissures were opening up all around the vehicle, and it took off even as soldiers were still clambering on board. Many clung to handholds on the sides. Some, the unlucky ones, chased after it on foot as it lurched across a gap in the ice and raced to the west.

Monster concentrated on climbing. On the other side of the ridge lay comparative safety. The ice behind them was collapsing, but the thick, compressed ice remained solid. With more and more missiles slamming into the ice floes behind them, it wouldn't last long.

At the top of the ridge, Monster looked back at a loud grinding, cracking sound. The floe behind him disintegrated. No longer a solid sheet of ice, it was merely a loose collection of pieces. The crashed transporters wobbled on an edge, then disappeared into the Bering Sea.

A massive piece of ice with three of the camouflaged Bzadian tanks started to turn turtle, tipping up steeper and steeper until the white hillocks began to slide toward the black surface of the ocean. They disintegrated as they went, no longer mounds, now just low piles of crumbled snow. No sign of any tanks, but there was no time to make sense of what he had seen. Monster all but carried Wall down the far side of the ridge, although Wall pushed him away at the bottom and found his own feet.

Price was heading too far to the north, Monster saw.

"Price!" he shouted, running up behind her, catching her by the arm and pointing. "This way!"

She changed direction as instructed. She flipped up her visor, ignoring the ice that blasted her unprotected skin.

"Who are you?" she asked. "How do you know my name?"

That was when Monster realized that his head was still covered by a hood, and a scarf concealed his face. He pulled the scarf away.

She stared at him, not recognizing him. He pulled back the hood, not minding a sudden flurry of snow that swirled around them both like a miniature tornado.

"Monster?" Her voice was so faint that he had to read the word from her lips. "You're dead."

"Not anymore," he said.

19. DECOY

THE APPLAUSE BEGAN IN A FAR CORNER OF THE ROOM. Wilton didn't see who started it, but it quickly spread.

"That last strike seems to have been conclusive," Hooper said. "While the fighters were engaging our planes, we got almost a full flight of missiles through."

Each Tomahawk carried twenty-four individual warheads, and these were all a variant of the icebreaker. They were scattered over a wide area and the combination of the shattering explosions was too much for the ice pack, now a crazy jigsaw, gradually drifting apart and away to the south where the ice would eventually melt in the warmer waters of the Bering Sea.

"The ice floes have pretty much ceased to exist south of the

Diomede Islands," Watson said. "And the damage extends for over five kilometers south and west. If there are any tanks still in that area, they're floating by themselves on a tiny bit of ice, and they won't last long."

"SAM activity has also completely ceased," Russell said. "I think we're in the clear."

"All right, all right," General Whitehead said, beaming. "Good work today, boys and girls. What were our losses?"

The room went quiet as Hundal read out a report of the F-35 fighters that were lost to the faster, better-armed Bzadian jets.

It was a heavy price.

Whitehead stood up at the head of the table. "During World War Two, Churchill said, 'Never in the field of human conflict was so much owed by so many to so few.' He was referring to the Royal Air Force and how they held the line during the Battle of Britain. Well, it's happened again, ladies and gentlemen. Our gallant aircrews have held the line for us, and although many have paid with their lives, their sacrifice was not in vain. Each year we get stronger. Each year our technology improves to match that of the alien invaders. Another winter without an invasion and I think we will be able to show these Pukes a few new tricks."

This time there were cheers mixed in with the applause.

Wilton did not clap or cheer. His Angel friends had had a big part to play in what had happened. Perhaps Whitehead was right in a way he didn't even know. Never before was so much owed by so many to so few. Six teenagers. Recon Team Angel.

Were they alive or dead? Unless they made contact, he couldn't know. He might never know.

The meeting hall smelled of smoke and rancid fish oil. Price had smelled worse. She followed Monster into the underground room, immensely happy that he was still alive.

The Inupiat filed in slowly and she scanned their faces, smiling at all of them. Grateful for their help. The Inupiat sat around the outside walls, leaving space for the Angels in the center. Price was struck by the quiet camaraderie of the locals. There was an air of success, as though they had just had a fruitful hunt, but none of the whooping and high-fiving that a group of ACOG soldiers would have had after a successful mission. Yet they had taken on a larger force equipped with high-tech firepower, with weapons that had been around for thousands of years, and they had won.

Only when they were all seated around the walls of the room did she turn back to Monster and raise an eyebrow.

"Emile?" she asked.

Monster shook his head.

Price nodded, acting calm, but her emotions were in turmoil. She had already convinced herself that both of them were dead. Then that they had both survived. It was worse somehow to have Emile snatched away a second time.

An old man began to speak in his own language and the room fell silent. The Inupiat listened with heads bowed and without expression. There was a short discussion when he had finished, then most of the Inupiat stood and began to file out until only three remained.

Monster introduced the three as Old Joe, Big Billy, and Nukilik; then he introduced Price and the team.

"Thank you for your help," Price said.

Old Joe nodded but said nothing.

"Where have the others gone?" Monster asked.

"They prepare for a journey," Nukilik said.

"A journey?" Monster asked.

Old Joe nodded slowly. "It is no longer safe for us here. The demons saw us helping you."

"You think they will attack this island?" Monster asked.

"Who can know?" Old Joe said. "We would not take that chance."

"You knew this, yet you helped us anyway," Monster said. "Where will you go?"

"There are many places," Old Joe said. "Our people have lived here for generations. When it is safe, we will be back."

"There are no words to expressing my gratitude," Monster said.

"Words are not necessary," Old Joe said.

Monster smiled, and agreed by raising his eyebrows. He turned to Price.

"I have something to tell you," he said. "But is most secret."

"Wait," Price said, glancing at Wall. "Tell me later."

Monster followed her glance. "You don't trust Wall?"

She shook her head.

"Why?" Monster asked. He had suddenly gone very still.

"He's a traitor," Price said, "like Brogan."

"Fezerker!" Monster said, his hands clenching into fists.

"Brogan was Fezerker too?" Price asked. Monster didn't answer her, but he didn't need to. It all suddenly made sense.

Monster's mouth closed tightly and he took three quick paces to cross the room, standing right in front of Wall. For the second time in her life, Price saw Monster truly angry. The last time had been on the dam at Wivenhoe with a Bzadian named Alizza. That had not ended well for Alizza.

This time his anger was directed at Wall. Price couldn't help but think that a great deal of the frustration and emotion he was feeling came from Emile's death.

"Go easy, Monster," Price said. "He helped us."

"Fezerker," Monster said again.

"What she says is true," Wall said mildly.

Long shadows from the tallow candles made dancing patterns on the faces that surrounded them. Monster's fists clenched and unclenched. The Inupiat watched with interest but made no move to interfere.

"I am Fezerker," Wall said. "I grew up in Uluru, with a friend of yours."

"She no friend of mine." Monster's voice was a low growl.

"You seem proud of this," Price said.

Wall shook his head. "Not proud. Not ashamed. I didn't choose where I was born or how I was raised."

None of us did, Price thought.

"Why did you help us escape?" Barnard asked.

"Believe it or not, I am on your side," Wall said. "I've got something to tell you and you need to listen."

"Shut your mouth, Puke." Monster's fists were raised.

In all the time she had known Monster, Price had never seen this side of him. It was as though all the tension of the last few hours, of the last few years, had boiled up inside him and spilled over. Wall sat calmly, perhaps realizing that doing anything to further inflame Monster might result in him getting torn to shreds.

"Does it even matter?" Barnard asked, clearly trying to ease the situation. "Let's get out of this godforsaken place and get home. Get Wall back to ACOG for interrogation."

"That would be a big mistake," Wall said.

"I'm sure that's what you want us to believe," Price said.

"Let him speak," Barnard said. "It can't hurt."

"Just don't believe anything he says," Price said. "If he's like Brogan, then he's trained to be a fluent liar."

"Talk quick," Monster said.

"There were no tanks," Wall said.

"That's bull," the Tsar said. "We saw them."

"We went inside one," Price said, but she saw that Monster's face was troubled. "Monster?" she asked.

"When we running from the missiles, I look back," Monster said. "Saw some of those 'tanks' fall into sea."

"So what's the problem?" Price asked.

"No tank," Monster said. "Only big pile of snow and ice."

There was silence while they digested that.

"Maybe some of the hillocks were dummies," the Tsar said. "To make the invasion force seem bigger than it really is."

"They all were," Wall said.

"That makes no sense," Price said.

"I told you I had something to say," Wall said. "Feel like listening now?"

"Tell us," Price said.

"The hillocks were dummies," Wall said. "Except for a few unmanned SAM batteries to make it look real. Nokz'z told me."

"Why?" Price asked.

"Decoys," Barnard said.

"Decoys," Wall agreed. "Think about it. The Bzadians know that ACOG have only limited stockpiles of Tomahawks and icebreakers. They wasted most of them blowing up piles of snow and ice, and guess what, Angels, we're the ones who told them to do it."

"Don't say 'we' when you talk about Angels," Monster said. Wall shrugged.

"If this whole thing was a decoy, where is the real attack?" the Tsar asked.

"Nokz'z didn't say," Wall said.

"It would have to be to the north," Barnard said. "Decoy south, strike north."

Old Joe cleared his throat. "Always to the north," he said. "South is no good for tanks."

"All we've got is Wall's word for this," Barnard said.

"What about Little Diomede?" Price asked. "How can they slip past the sensors?"

"One of the techs there is Fezerker," Monster said. "Like Wall."

"How do you know?" Price asked.

"Wilton told me. Brogan told him. The man, Able, he is Fezerker."

"What about the other operator, the woman, Bowden?" Barnard asked.

"Wilton didn't know," Monster said.

"So we can assume that the sensors on Little Dio are out of action," the Tsar said.

"In which case Wall could be telling the truth," Barnard said. "There could be a whole invasion force there and nobody knows."

"If so, we're going to need proof," Price said.

"If we can get into Little Diomede station," the Tsar said. "I may be able to work out what they've done to the sensors."

"No," Monster said. "We must go north, find Puke army."

"I think we need to do both," Price said. "We need eyes on the invasion force, make sure it's there and that it's not just piles of snow. But we also need to take control of Little Diomede. Plus we can use the radio there to alert ACOG of whatever we find."

"Is too risky," Monster said. He kicked at one of Wall's feet. "He is lying. Tricking us. Trying to save his own skin."

Price looked at Wall, trying to see behind the eyes. Who was he? Was anything he said true?

"What's your story, Wall?" Barnard asked. "How can you be a Fezerker and on our side?"

"I was turned," Wall said.

"And you expect us to believe that?" the Tsar asked.

"What about that guy on Operation Magnum? He said he was your brother," Barnard asked. "Was that even true?"

"Darryl, yeah," Wall said. "We had the same mother."

"Really?" Price asked. "Which number was she?"

"I don't know and it doesn't matter," Wall said. "It was Darryl who found out. About our mother. He had this thing about finding out who he really was and where he had come from."

"So how did you end up on our side?" Barnard asked. "Let's see if you can make this convincing."

"Again it was Darryl," Wall said. "They always told us that we were Bzadian, that we just looked like humans, but Darryl wasn't convinced. He said if we came from human mothers, fertilized by human fathers, then we were human."

"But you'd been brainwashed since birth to hate humans," Barnard said.

"And you think most kids are messed up," Wall said. "Try living my life."

"So what happened?" the Tsar asked.

"Holly Brogan happened," Wall said. "After she got caught out, ACOG came down hard on everyone else."

"That's true," Price said. After Uluru, teams of investigators had gone through everyone's background with a fine-tooth comb. Price had been questioned three times, and two of them were very unpleasant experiences.

"So they caught you," the Tsar said.

"No." Wall shook his head. "Darryl gave us up. Volunteered us to be double agents."

"Why?" Barnard asked.

"I told you. He didn't believe what he had been told. He felt we were humans. I wasn't so sure, but even if I had been born a Bzadian, I don't think I would have agreed with this war. Invading a planet and wiping out the inhabitants—that ain't cool."

"So why was your brother on Operation Magnum?" Price asked. "He was an MPC driver."

"Bzadian command wanted him there," Wall said. "They knew something was up, but they didn't know what or where. He fed them false information right up until he was killed."

"Who do you work for at ACOG?" Barnard asked.

"Bilal. Daniel Bilal," Wall said. "Military intelligence."

"Never heard of him," Barnard said.

"That's kind of the point with those MI guys," Wall said.

"Should be easy enough to check out," Price said.

"Please," Wall said.

"Even if it does check out, that doesn't mean we can trust him," Barnard said. "He's already a double agent, why not a triple?"

"Why do you think I'm even here?" Wall said. "Why am I on this mission?"

"What do you mean?" Price asked.

"You didn't think it was strange how all those more qualified people conveniently got out of the way just in time?" Wall asked.

"A little, yeah," Price said. "So what are you doing here?"

"Bilal pulled strings. He wanted me on this mission."

"Why?" Barnard asked.

"In case anything like this happened," Wall said.

"He's lying," Monster said.

"Are you forgetting that I slipped Tsar the grenade? Saved your lives?" Wall asked.

"Unless we were supposed to escape, to tell ACOG about the supposed invasion force," Barnard said.

Wall shook his head. "You were bound for Russia and then to New Bzadia. It wasn't going to be a pleasure cruise."

"You say you can help us," Price asked. "How exactly?"

"I can get you into Little Diomede," Wall said.

20. SNOW ANGELS

MONSTER LED THE ANGELS DOWN THROUGH THE tunnel and up the trapdoor into Nukilik's home. Wall, now roped and bound and guarded by Big Billy, remained at the *qargi*. One look at Big Billy and Price had been happy to leave Wall under his watch.

Monster closed the trapdoor behind them. Whatever he wanted to say, he clearly wanted nobody else to hear.

"What's up?" Price asked.

"Wilton had more news," Monster said.

When Monster didn't continue, the Tsar said, "Well, shoot."

The wind shrieked above them for a moment, drowning out any possibility of conversation.

"He says he has spoken to Ryan," Monster said when the noise died down.

"Chisnall?" Price asked. *Of course, Chisnall. Who else could he mean?* But still she had to ask the question. It gave her breathing space. Thinking space. She needed time to get her head around what Monster had just said.

Monster nodded.

"They got a hotline to heaven now at the Pentagon?" Barnard asked.

"I just tell you what he says," Monster said.

"So he spoke to someone who claimed he was Chisnall," the Tsar said. "We all saw the LT go over the dam. Nobody could have survived that, no matter how lucky they were."

"Wilton believes it," Monster said.

Monster wanted to believe it too. That was obvious. So did Price. But she couldn't bring herself to. She couldn't allow herself to.

"Wilton's never been the sharpest tool in the shed," Barnard said.

"What did this 'Chisnall' want?" Price asked. "Whoever it was, he must have contacted Wilton for a reason."

"According to Wilton, Ryan want to talk to Barnard," Monster said. "He give this phone number." He repeated the number from memory.

"What do you think, LT?" Barnard asked.

"When we get back to Carson, give him a call," Price said. "Ask him some tough questions. See if he can prove he is who he says he is. But I'm with the Tsar. I think it's some kind of trick."

"It cannot wait till Carson," Monster said. "That's what Wilton say. Is urgent."

"He calls while we're in the middle of a top-secret mission," the Tsar said. "That strike anyone else as more than a little suspicious?"

"How would I phone him?" Barnard asked, looking around.

"There is phone at old Russian guard post, about half hour from here," Monster said. "We could use it to contact ACOG too."

"No," Price said. "There's no point in contacting ACOG until we have some kind of proof. And this 'Chisnall' will have to wait."

Monster shrugged.

"So what now?" the Tsar asked.

"Okay, Wall says he can get us into Little Dio," Price said. "He can talk his way in."

"Talk his way in?" Monster asked.

"He speaks some strange Fezerker language," Price said.

"It's the high language," Barnard said. "It's reserved for Bzadian priests, high-ranking officials, and Azoh himself."

"And Fezerkers," Price said.

"As we recently found out." Barnard nodded.

"Do you understand any of it?" the Tsar asked.

Barnard shook her head. "I don't think any humans speak it. Few, if any, have ever heard it spoken."

"But Able will speak that language," the Tsar said. "Do you trust Wall to talk to him?"

"Not enough," Price said. "But I think I know a way that we can use him to get inside, regardless of whose side he is really on."

"What about the recon north?" Barnard asked. "Who's going to do that? We have to know if the invasion is real this time."

"Big Billy is," Price said. "He's going to follow the sensor line. He's taking a dog team and a sled, so they'll be moving quickly. Monster, you go with him. Let us know what you find."

That made her think of Emile. He had wanted to ride with a dog sled. But he would never have that chance.

"I have no radio," Monster said.

"Take Wall's helmet," Price said. "And his spare battery. He can suffer for a while without them. Let us know what you find as soon as you're back in comm range."

Monster nodded and disappeared down the trapdoor.

"Okay, Angels," Price said. "Little Diomede . . ."

"I bet they have a phone," Barnard said.

[OPERATIONS COMMAND CENTER, PENTAGON, VIRGINIA]

ABLE AND BOWDEN WERE TECHNICIANS. WILTON focused his attentions on Able, the one they knew was definitely Fezerker. Able's TDA (temporary duty assignment) had been requested by ACOG, Bering Strait Defense Force, Technical Support Section. An assignment at a place as vital as Little Diomede had to be signed off all the way up the chain of command, right to the highest level, by General Jake Russell himself.

Surely General Russell was above suspicion? Somewhere in that chain of command was the person responsible, but where? Barnard would probably have made short work of this assignment, Wilton thought. But she wasn't here. He was.

He made a list of everyone who had signed off on the order, then tried to give each person a score. The more closely involved in the TDA assignments, the higher the score. If a person was involved in the planning for Uluru or Magnum, he reduced their score, and if they were involved in both, he crossed them off altogether. As far as he knew, the aliens had had no warning on either of those missions. There had been an unexpected patrol boat at the start of Operation Magnum, but if the Bzadians had actually known the place and purpose of that mission, there would have been a lot more than that. The boat was probably just a coincidence.

He managed to cross at least a dozen people off his list, and the rest he sorted from highest to lowest score. That still gave him ten people with a high score, and no way that he could see to choose between them.

One thing concerned him. General Russell was among the ten. As head of defense forces, he had not been involved in the planning for either Uluru or Magnum, as both of those were offensive operations.

There was no real reason to suspect Russell, certainly no more than any of the others on the list. But the others were not sitting in this bunker, commanding the defenses that would decide the fate of the free world.

Even the slightest possibility that Russell was involved made this a game of very high stakes, and Wilton did not enjoy being the person responsible for checking him out.

If only Barnard were here.

Price found Big Billy and Monster in a small hollow, rimmed by spindly scrub, behind the village. It was sheltered from the wind, which made it a good place to muster the dogs. When she got there, Big Billy was walking along the harness lines, checking the ropes. The malamutes snapped and snarled at each other, as if anxious to get going, but leaped and licked when Big Billy passed them. He was the top dog in the team.

The sled was a simple affair, just two wooden runners joined by cross slats. At the back were more slats between two raised handles. Monster was sitting on the sled, trying to make himself comfortable in between a few canvas bundles. From the end of one of the bundles protruded the metallic heads of spears. Monster looked up as Price approached.

"Looks like you got it easy," Price said. "Got the passenger seat."

Monster grinned. "I offered to drive but he laughed."

She stood, watching him, while Big Billy checked the ropes. "Tell me about Emile," she said. "I need to know."

"He didn't make it," Monster said with a short shrug. "No more to know."

"Monster, tell me the truth," she said, putting her hand on his arm.

Monster stared at her hand. He could not meet her eyes. That was not like him.

"You left him on the ice field," Price said.

"I did everything I could," Monster said.

"You saved yourself and left him behind," she said, more bitterly than she intended.

It wasn't Monster she was really angry at. She knew that. But that was how it came out and the words could not be unsaid.

"Emile was not so strong," Monster said.

"Which is why you should have helped him," Price said.

At that moment there was no one in the world she hated more than herself. How could she be so selfish, to be happy that Monster's life had been spared when Emile's had been taken? She hated herself for the way she was feeling. She hated the blackness of her own heart.

"I regret his death," Monster said, head bowed. "He was impetuous. Perhaps if he had waited . . ."

"Waited?" Price let go of his arm and stepped away from him. "Waited for what? What other opportunity would there have been?"

"I not know," Monster said. "Maybe when they take us transporter."

"Speak bloody English," Price snapped. She shut her eyes

and took a deep breath. "You know that Emile acted on my command. So you're saying it was my fault that he died?"

"It is a war," Monster said. "People die."

"So you do think it was my fault? Chisnall would have done better—is that what you're trying to tell me?" she asked, aware that her voice was rising to a high pitch.

He was silent. But by not arguing, wasn't he agreeing with her?

"How dare you?" she said. "You're the one who should have stayed with him, carried him if you had to."

"Then we would have both been dead," Monster said.

A wave of self-loathing swept over Price.

"Get away from me," she said.

"Price—"

"Get away from me."

Big Billy was back behind the sled now. He shouted something in Inupiat and the dogs leaped at their harnesses. The sled began to move and Monster grabbed at one side of the sled to keep his balance. He watched her as they pulled quickly away.

She turned and covered her face with her hands, her whole body shaking.

When she looked back, he was lost in the swirling snow.

The sensor buoy lay on the ice in front of them. A black ball with knobby lumps on all sides, it looked for all the world like a sea mine.

Big Billy stood tall at the back of the sled. Despite the cold, he did not have the hood of his parka up, and instead wore just a woolen hat, from under which his long hair streamed behind. He stood on the back runners of the sled, leaning it into corners. He shouted commands occasionally, guiding the dog team, though they seldom seemed to need instructions, steering instinctively around raised, jagged edges.

The dogs ran with little obvious effort, breath steaming from their mouths. They did not run in a row, or in two lines, as Monster had expected, but in a loose pack, spread out like a fan over a wide area of ice. At the head was Asungaq, Nukilik's dog, clearly the leader of the pack.

Watching Big Billy, Monster knew this was a man truly in his element. He was made for this place as surely as this place was made for him. A wild man, untamed.

Over the flat areas of ice they made good time, sliding along with the wind in their faces and the snow hissing underneath the runners of the sled. But when they came to a ridge, they had to manhandle the sled over it.

On the long stretches of just sitting, Monster's mind turned again and again to Price. He hadn't meant to accuse her of causing Emile's death, but it had come out that way. Somewhere deep inside he felt it was true. They should have waited. Shouldn't they? But who could know? If Emile had done nothing, they could all be dead by now. Or at least in a PGZ cell. Emile had saved them.

Monster tried to stretch out his legs on the sled. There was little room, and to retain his balance he had to wedge himself against the upright struts at the back, jamming his legs against the cross slats between the runners. Another buoy approached. A dark shape in the middle of a flat patch of white.

Big Billy didn't slow and Monster watched it slide past with a strange fascination. Were they registering on the scopes at Little Diomede? A dog team and a single sled. That shouldn't concern them greatly, he hoped. He pondered that as he watched the buoy disappear behind them.

Price was at the rear of the group. Four Angels, with Nukilik leading the way.

The ice between the two islands was a series of undulating crests and irregular blocks, corrugated by the turbulent current between the two islands. It looked like waves frozen in the act of crashing upon a beach.

Wall stumbled along in front of her, his hands still tied behind his back. He fell several times, and without hands to protect himself, each fall was hard. Nor did he have a helmet or visor, just a woolen hat and a scarf to shield his face from the cold. Each time he fell, the Tsar helped him back to his feet. Was Wall with them or against them? His actions said he was on their side, but it would be foolish to trust him, Price thought.

Nukilik led them through a maze of channels between the crests. He knew the location of the sensor buoys between the islands and avoided them. Still, he made them walk in a strange shuffling manner, sliding their feet across the ice to reduce vibration.

They emerged finally at a jumble of huge ice cubes, as though a gigantic ice-maker tray had been emptied and scattered randomly across the ground. Price wondered at the unimaginable forces that must have converged in this spot. There were gaps in and around the odd geometric shapes, offering many places of concealment with a good view of the island, which was less than fifty meters away, over a beach of relatively smooth ice.

The cliffs of Little Diomede were sheer, but softened by clinging sea ice that seemed to reach up out of the ocean, as though trying to drag the island back down into the sea. Across the beach in front of them, a sloping ramp led up to a chunky concrete building.

A security fence skirted around the base of the island, just above the ice line. According to her mission briefing notes, it was covered by cameras and movement detectors, as well as infrared heat sensors, all constantly monitored by computers in the station.

A row of automated heavy machine guns in narrow pillboxes stood like sentries a few meters behind the fence line. They were the last line of defense for the station in the event of an attack, a delay tactic to give the station operators a chance to escape in their hovercraft.

Price crabbed sideways to Nukilik and touched him on the shoulder to get his attention. He nodded and shuffled a heavy canvas sack off his shoulders.

Price took a camo sheet out of a utility pocket. She placed it on the ground and activated it so that it picked up an image of the ice below. She had cut the camo sheet into a kind of rough coat, with holes for her arms. She took off her coil-gun, then put the coat on, tying it in place with thin cord. The last time she had used a camo sheet was in the Australian desert, on the Uluru mission, but she pushed that thought out of her mind. That brought back too many memories.

The camo sheet rendered her virtually invisible. It also blocked much of her heat signature.

From the sack, Nukilik produced the hide of an arctic wolf, complete with head. It belonged to Big Billy. According to Nukilik, he had worn it when he hunted Bzadians in the last Ice War.

Nukilik strapped the hide to her back, fastening it with leather straps. He tied the legs of the hide to her arms and legs. It was far from a perfect disguise, but in these conditions it might just pass.

She crawled across to Barnard.

"All good?" she asked.

Barnard looked at her and nodded without speaking. The Tsar gave her the thumbs-up.

Price dropped to her hands and knees and crept forward, out of the cover of the ice rubble, until she was in view of the station but still partially concealed by the blustering snow and ice. The infrared cameras would have picked her up and she hoped that the camo sheet blocked enough of her heat signature to approximate that of a wolf.

There was no response from the station, but she hadn't expected there to be. Not yet anyway.

She continued on, trying to mimic the movements of a wolf. It wasn't easy. A wolf had four legs and she had hands and knees. She didn't make a beeline for the fence; that would have been too obvious. Instead, she wandered in an aimless pattern, investigating patches of snow, all the time moving closer and closer to where she really wanted to be.

She kept a close eye on the pillboxes that housed the two nearest machine guns. If either of those began to fire, she would have two choices. Drop and play dead or make a run for it. Neither way would help them get inside the station.

Closer now, the fence line barely five meters away. She moved up to it, careful not to touch the wires. The fence was electrified as a deterrent to animals like caribou. Or wolves.

She pawed at the snow outside the fence, as if something was buried there. Shuffling around, she brought her front "paws" up to one of the fence posts. In her right hand was a pair of wire cutters. She waited for a strong gust of wind, a thick flurry of snow, virtual whiteout conditions. Being careful to avoid the electrified strands, she cut one of the wires that led to the sensor on top of the fence post, then loped away as rapidly as she could down the slope.

Able and Bowden would have to do something. At the very least they would have to investigate. Back in the shelter of the huge ice blocks, Nukilik helped her out of the wolf hide and they waited.

They did not have to wait long. A door opened in the squat

building above them and a figure emerged. Price crossed her fingers. *Which one was it?* That would decide how they would play the game that followed. From the height, it was Bowden. Able was much taller. Price sucked in a huge sigh of relief.

Bowden wore a hooded parka and snow goggles. She had an automatic weapon and was scanning the area through its sights as she walked cautiously down the ramp and along the fence line.

"Get ready," Price whispered.

Bowden reached the fence post and began to examine it.

"Okay, go!" Price said.

She stood with the others and opened the visor of her helmet. Icy wind immediately stung her unprotected skin. Barnard and the Tsar also raised their visors and the Tsar pulled the scarf away from Wall's face. It was painful, but it was essential that Bowden get a clear view of their faces.

Their hands were clasped behind their backs as if tied there. Wall's really were tied, but he was the only one.

Nukilik was right behind them, rifle raised. He called out as they emerged from the ice field.

"Hello, soldier!"

Bowden's reaction was instantaneous. She forgot about the faulty sensor and grabbed for her gun. Price tried to imagine what she was seeing. Three soldiers in Bzadian uniform being herded along by an Inupiat with a hunting rifle. Would she take the bait? Bowden lifted her goggles for a clearer view as they got closer.

"Who are you?" she shouted.

"I am Nukilik," he called out as they rapidly crossed the open ground toward her. "Of the Inupiat. I have captured these enemy soldiers scouting around your island."

Bowden kept her gun trained on all of them, clearly nervous and unsure.

As soon as they were close enough, Price said, "Now, Wall."

Wall spoke loudly and rapidly in the "high" language. What he was saying, Price could not know. But it did not matter. What mattered was how Bowden reacted.

Price watched the woman's face closely and saw no spark of understanding. "Barnard?" she asked, needing confirmation of what she had just seen.

"She's clean," Barnard said in English. "She has no idea what Wall said."

If Barnard was sure, then Price was sure.

"What the hell is going on?" Bowden asked. "Where did you find these Pukes?"

"Specialist Gabrielle Bowden, please listen carefully," Price said. "My name is Lieutenant Trianne Price, of Recon Team Angel."

"Angels!" Bowden said, eyes wide.

"Nikolas Able is an enemy agent," Price said. "He has done something to disable the sensor equipment in your station, and as we speak, an enemy invasion force is passing the island to the north."

"That's not possible," Bowden said.

Price understood her difficulty. It was a lot to take in. "It *is* possible and it *is* true," she said. "We have to get into your station and apprehend Able, then try to work out what he has done to the sensors."

"But . . . ," Bowden spluttered.

"Before it is too late," Price said.

It was already too late.

The sled slid to a halt. Monster felt it too. What he had thought was a vibration of the runners was clearly something more. The ice was quivering like it had before the ice quake. That seemed so long ago.

"What is it?" Monster asked.

Big Billy shook his head and put a finger to his lips for silence. He removed his woolen hat, listening. Without speaking, he mushed the dogs and they started again with a jerk, toward a long, high ridgeline. At the base of the ridge, he stopped again, stepped off the sled, and began to climb.

Monster rolled out of the sled. His legs were stiff and sore from sitting on the cart too long, and it took him a few minutes of shaking some feeling back into them before he could scale the jagged surface of the ridge. Near the top, Big Billy had flattened himself on the ice. The entire ridge seemed to be juddering.

Monster crawled up beside Big Billy and eased his head up into a V in between two fractured ice pieces. At first, he could see nothing; the blast from the wind on the other side of the ridge plastered his visor with snow. He wiped it clear.

"Cheese and rice," he said.

Below him, barely visible in the flying ice, was a Bzadian battle tank. It rumbled past right at the base of the ridge, so close that he felt he could touch it. Beyond it was another. And another. As far as he could see through the blizzard, there were tanks—and he could hear them. The sound of engines brought to him on the back of the wind. The roar was constant, the sound of hundreds, perhaps thousands, of engines all melded into one never-ending thunder.

Big Billy tapped him on the shoulder and motioned for him to follow to the west. They crept along just below the top of the ridge. After a hundred or so meters, it stopped abruptly, sheared off at a vast crevasse, two or three meters wide and at least a meter deep. Peering over, Monster saw a metal bridge spanning the crevasse. A momentary lull in the wind revealed a row of bridges stretching into the distance. The bridges were temporary, he realized. Military bridging units with their own armored carriers. As they watched, a battle tank crossed the bridge. Followed by another. Behind that was a line of tanks all waiting to cross.

He unclipped his wrist computer and used the camera function to video the procession. They had to show this to ACOG. The invasion was real. This was no decoy.

"How long do you think before they reach Alaska?" he asked.

"Not long enough," Big Billy said.

"Okay, let's go," Monster said. "We have enough—"

"Get down!" Big Billy shouted, hurling himself back down the slope and dragging Monster with him as the crest of the ridge exploded in red-yellow flames and deadly, jagged shards of flying ice.

The gunshots sounded close by.

Bowden ducked instinctively and spun around, looking for the source of the sound.

Able was half hidden by a large rock to the side of the ramp, his weapon steady on top of it. No one had seen him emerge from the building.

Price checked her team to see if anyone had been hit. They all seemed okay. There was a grunt from behind her and she turned to see Nukilik drop to his knees before pitching forward in the snow, the rifle falling beside him.

A shocked silence spread over them.

"What the hell, Able?" Bowden shouted. "What was that all about? He was human!"

Her own gun was on him now; she seemed to have forgotten the Angels.

"Leading a party of Pukes right up to our front doorstep?" Able asked. "I don't think so."

He began to walk in her direction, his weapon held casually.

"Able's a traitor," Price said quietly.

Bowden glanced at her, then back at Able, trying to process too much information at once, Price thought.

Able was just behind Bowden.

"What were you thinking?" Bowden yelled.

"Shouldn't you be covering these Pukes?" he asked.

"I can't believe you shot that man," Bowden said, but her gun swung back to cover the Angels.

"Bowden, he's a traitor," Price said.

"You can't trust anyone these days," Able said, and now he was right beside Bowden. The snout of his gun came up to her head.

Bowden caught the movement out of the corner of her eye. She turned, then froze, shocked into immobility.

"Sorry, Gabby," Able said, and Price had the feeling that he really meant it as his finger tightened on the trigger.

Monster leaped and fell down the jagged slope of the ridge. As fast as he was, Big Billy was at the bottom before him, yelling to the dogs. They had been lying in a group, huddled for warmth, but at his shouts they jumped to their feet and wrenched at the sled, breaking it free of the grip of the ice.

Monster dived on the front as the sled took off.

From behind them, there was a new noise, the buzz of small engines, and two snowmobiles came flying over the top of the ridge, bouncing and crashing their way down the slope, somehow staying upright as they skipped from block to block. Monster recognized the shape. He had seen these in the last Ice War. Single-man craft with a fixed heavy coil-gun at the front. They were deadly against infantry.

One of the machines let out a burst of machine-gun fire, and Monster heard the bullets sizzling through the air around him.

He rolled over onto his stomach and gripped one of the

stays at the rear of the sled. He pulled the magnum from its holster. He took quick aim and fired. A spark flew off the armored front of one of the snowmobiles.

With shouted commands, Big Billy veered the sled left and right, upsetting the aim of their chasers, then whipped the sled around past a small hillock and into an area of rough ice.

"When I say jump, you jump," Big Billy roared. The dogs seemed connected telepathically to Big Billy's mind, dodging slabs of ice.

"Jump!" Big Billy yelled, and Monster rolled off the side of the sled, sliding in between two ice boulders and slamming into a small wall.

A few seconds later, the first of the snowmobiles roared past him, but the magnum was ready and steady in Monster's hands. He fired at point-blank range. The powerful bullet shredded the rubberized tread of the snowmobile as it passed him. It slid first one way, then the other, going into a speed wobble that could not be corrected. The machine flipped and rolled, and the second snowmobile, close behind, had to swerve violently to avoid it, hitting a wedge of ice and flying into the air. A spray of liquid came from its side as Monster's pistol sounded again, punching through the light armor on the side of the gas tank. At first there was nothing more; then the leaking fuel must have hit the hot exhaust and the flying snowmobile became a ball of flame, a fiery meteor, crashing back to Earth, the rider leaping off it, armor on fire.

The rider landed, rolled, took cover, and without concern for his flaming battle armor began to lay down coil-gun fire toward Monster. Monster ducked behind the low ice wall as bullets found his position. He slid sideways, seeking an angle.

There was no need. The firing stopped abruptly. The Bzadian, focused on Monster, never saw the dark shape that somehow grew out of the ice floe behind him, nor the shiny knife in its hand.

The thunder of gunfire reverberated from the concrete walls of the sensor station and the rocky cliffs around them.

Able lay on his back, Wall on top of him.

Wall had shouted something in the high language; Price had no idea what, but it was enough to make Able pause, and in that half second, when the gun wavered, Wall had hit him, head down, charging at him like a battering ram, knocking him over backward onto the ice. Able's shots had gone wild.

Able pushed Wall off him, but Bowden's boot was on Able's shoulder, pressing him back down, and it was her gun in his face.

"Stay there," she said, "while I figure this out."

Barnard kneeled by Nukilik's side, checking his pulse, feeling for the wound. She looked up at Price and shook her head.

A cold chill moved over Price. This man had tried to help them. His was another death on her conscience. Another face she knew she would see in her dreams until she dreamed no more.

Able shifted around, uncomfortable under Bowden's boot.

"Nothing is what it seems," Price said. "We look like Pukes, but we're not. Your friend looks human, but he's not."

"You're really Angels?" Bowden asked. "Recon Team Angel?"

They all nodded.

"Then what does that make him?" she asked.

"Fezerker," Price said.

Bowden shoved the muzzle of her gun into the temple of the man on the ground as he began to reach for his weapon, lying next to him. She kicked the gun out of reach. "I thought Fezerkers were Pukes," she said.

"So did we all," Barnard said.

"Why would humans betray their own kind?" Bowden asked.

"You should ask him that," Price said.

Barnard took a step toward the hunting rifle that lay next to Nukilik's body. Around it, the snow was turning pink.

"Can I pick up the rifle?" Barnard asked.

"No," Bowden said. "I . . . just . . . I need time to sort this out."

"It's easy," Barnard said. "Able was about to kill you; we saved your life. We're Angels; he's Fezerker. Now can I pick up the rifle?"

Bowden nodded and her gun shifted a little as she did so.

Able spun out from under her boot, pushing the barrel of her rifle away from him. Catlike, he was on his feet, sprinting out of sight among the rocks of the island even as bullets from Bowden's gun kicked up puffs of dust around him.

"Let him go," Price said as Bowden started to run after him.

"Okay, let's get inside," Bowden said. "We'll lock the place down."

"What about him?" Barnard asked, looking at Nukilik.

"Leave him there," Price said, feeling cold and heartless as she said it. "The cold will preserve the body. Once we've sorted out Able, we'll come back and make a more permanent arrangement."

Wall was still lying on the ground at Bowden's feet. Price reached down and grabbed his arm, hauling him to his feet. "Good work," she said.

He nodded.

Price took one last look at Nukilik's body before following Bowden inside. He lay facedown in the snow. The pink snow was spreading out in a random, irregular pattern from either side of his chest. A little like wings.

21. PROOF

WILTON'S PHONE BUZZED.

He checked the screen. It was the operations radio channel that he had routed through to his phone.

"Wilton," he said quietly, not wanting to draw attention.

"Wilton, Wilton." It was Price's voice. She sounded agitated.

"What's going on?" he asked.

"The tanks to the south, they were decoys," Price said. "The real attack is to the north. Do you understand?"

"Got it," Wilton said. "Are you at the sensor station?"

"Yes," Price said. "Bowden is with us. She's cool. Able got away. Bowden is going to contact ACOG directly to confirm."

"Okay," Wilton said. "Tell me how this invasion force has managed to slip past the sensor station. I gotta know, 'cause they're gonna ask me."

"I don't know," Price said. "Bowden and the Tsar are going to see what they can do to figure it out. You must warn ACOG."

"I'm sending the message as we speak," Wilton said, and did so. "Stay on the line."

"Also, see if you can find a man named Daniel Bilal," Price said.

"Bilal? I know him. Why?" Wilton said.

"Ask him about Wall," Price said.

"What about Wall?"

"Just ask him."

On Wilton's screen, a message flashed up from Bilal. *Can you confirm this?*

He quickly typed back. *Angel Team are in Little Diomede Station. They confirm presence of Bzadian forces to the north. The attack to the south was a decoy. They want me to ask you about Wall.*

That got an immediate reaction from Bilal. He looked straight over at Wilton and nodded his head. A second later the message came up on Wilton's screen. *Wall can be trusted.*

"Wall's good," Wilton said on the phone. "Bilal confirms it."

At the table, Bilal stood up to get the attention of the others. He raised his hand.

"I'm afraid I have some bad news," he said. "It appears that the attack to the south was merely a decoy. The real attack, as we originally predicted, is under way right now to the north of the islands."

There was pandemonium for a few minutes, before White-head got out, "Are you sure of this?"

"Positive," Bilal said. "My asset confirms it."

"Your asset confirmed that there were tanks to the south of the islands," Russell said. "Leading us to waste most of our supply of missiles. What confirmation do we have of this new assessment?"

"Eyes on the ground," Bilal said.

"We already have eyes on the ground," Russell said. "Electronic eyes. They have reported nothing."

"Those eyes cannot be trusted," Bilal said.

"What are you saying?" Russell asked.

"That your man on the island, Able, is a traitor," Bilal said.

"And you have proof of this?" Whitehead asked.

"Not yet," Bilal admitted.

"I'm afraid we're going to need a little more than the say-so of some undisclosed spy," Gonzales said.

"I have Gabrielle Bowden on channel seven two," Watson said. "Her vocal patterns are showing stress signals. She says she has Angels in the station with her."

"Recon Team Angel?" Russell asked.

"I think that's what she means, yes, sir," Watson said.

"These are your precious assets?" Whitehead asked, turning abruptly to face Bilal.

"I had no choice," Bilal said.

"The oversight committee will decide that," Whitehead said. "But that can wait. Ask Bowden about this invasion force."

"I already did," Watson said. "Her only information comes

from the Angels. She has no independent confirmation and no Bzadian vehicles are showing on any sensors. But she also told me that Able just tried to kill her."

There was a shocked silence in the room.

"Enough proof?" Bilal asked mildly.

"Bilal, you'll have to bring me something more than this," Whitehead said. "Get back to your Angels. Get us some photographic evidence, something, anything."

Wilton found himself grinding his teeth. *What is wrong with these people?*

"We don't have the time," Bilal said.

"Give me a reason to commit our remaining defenses," Whitehead said. "And you'd better be quick."

Bilal glanced at Wilton but did not message him. There was no need. Wilton had heard it all.

"Gotta get us some proof," Wilton said on the phone. "They're not buying what you're selling."

Monster tried the comm as they came closer to the island and into range.

"Price, can you hear me?"

He got an answer almost immediately. It was Price. She sounded cold and formal.

"Angel Two, this is Angel One. Send traffic, over."

"Many tanks," Monster said. "Big army. Real tanks, not decoys."

"Do you have evidence?" Price asked.

"Got some video," Monster said. "Not wonderful, I think, but clear enough."

"Good work. Approach the station carefully," Price said. "Able is on the loose."

"Okay, we'll be there soon," Monster said.

"One more thing," Price said.

Monster waited.

"I need you to talk to Big Billy," Price said. "I'm afraid it's bad news."

22. ELDERS

"HOLY MOTHER OF GOD!" HOOPER SAID.

The video was grainy and shaky even with processing and stabilizing, but still it was enough to spread a shocked silence across the room.

The line of giant Bzadian bridges stretched into the haze of distance. The rows of battle tanks crossing the bridges were just as shaky and just as terrifying.

The video looped, ending each time with an explosion just in front of the camera lens.

"Bilal, you and your stupid spy games may have just cost us this war," Russell said.

Wilton almost jumped out of his chair with indignation. The Angels were out there in brutal conditions, risking their lives, while these people sat in an air-conditioned room in padded chairs. If not for the Angels, ACOG would never have discovered about Able and the invasion.

"Without my spy games"—Bilal gestured broadly at the screen—"we wouldn't be seeing this right now."

"And we wouldn't have wasted most of our missile inventory on a red herring," Russell said.

"Sorry, Daniel," Whitehead said. "I am shutting you down. As of now. The Angels should never have been there in the first place. They've done enough damage already."

Bilal stared at him, then lowered his eyes and typed slowly on his smartpad.

Sorry, Blake, said the message that flashed up on Wilton's screen. *Nothing more I could do.*

Wilton stared at the message before replying. It wasn't fair, and he wasn't going to enjoy telling the Angels the news.

What about the team? Wilton messaged back.

They're on their own, Bilal messaged. *There is an escape hovercraft on the island. They can use that. If possible, bring Able in for questioning.*

"What is the status of our submarines?" Whitehead asked.

"Heading back to the naval base at Esquimalt, to rearm," Hooper said.

"Sir, if we can't stop the Pukes here, it's all over," Russell said. "We have to think about tactical nukes."

"There is no nuclear option," Whitehead said. "There will be no more discussion about that. What is the status of the ground defense forces?"

Russell took a deep breath and let it out slowly.

"Level One alert, and ready to go," he said.

"Hovercraft teams?"

"First reconnaissance squadron is already out on the ice," Russell said. "First and second assault battalions are waiting for the word."

The reality of another ice war came home to Wilton with that statement. He was part of a hovercraft team. If not for this cushy assignment, he would be among those about to head out on the ice. Maybe not at first, because he was part of a reserve squadron, but undoubtedly sooner or later, he would have been part of the action. He wasn't sure which he preferred. There was something distant and sterile about this room. At least out on the ice he would have felt that he was making a difference.

"Tanks and artillery?" Whitehead asked.

"Second and third battalions are dug in around Wales, Alaska. First battalion is holding back in reserve. They'll hold their fire until the last minute to avoid revealing their positions. Artillery batteries are ready for shoot and scoot."

"Hundal, what can you give me?" Whitehead asked.

"In these conditions, nothing," Hundal said. "Our aircraft can't fly in this weather, but neither can theirs."

"How long before those subs are back on station?" Whitehead asked.

"Four hours there, four hours back, a couple of hours to rearm," Hooper said. "Minimum ten hours. But that's not the problem. You can bet that the Pukes will have a heavy SAM defense. I doubt we'd get enough missiles through to do the kind of damage we need, and that's it. These are our last reserves."

"Okay, we hold the Tomahawks back," Whitehead said. "This is going to be a ground war, not an air war."

And I'm missing it, Wilton thought.

Big Billy stood for a long time over the body of his brother. His lips were moving. The language was ancient and Inupiat. The wind was whipping up into flurries and snow whirled around him, but still he just stood. Alone in his grief.

Barnard stood next to Price. Mourners at this private funeral.

There was no sign of Able, but to be safe, Monster stood guard. He was on the roof, armed with the hunting rifle.

The Tsar was inside, working with Bowden, trying to figure out what was wrong with the sensors.

When Big Billy finished, Price helped him load Nukilik onto the sled.

Asungaq sniffed and pawed at the body of his master as it was carried past him.

"I'm sorry," Price said.

"He is with the elders," Big Billy said. "We have both lost loved ones."

"Yes," Price agreed.

"Your friend Janos, you call him Monster," Big Billy said.

"Yes," Price said, a little uncomfortably.

"He is strong," Big Billy said. "Strong like Nanook, the white bear. And a good fighter."

"Yes," Price said.

"He tried to save your friend," Big Billy said. "Emile."

"He told me," Price said.

"He cannot tell you what he does not know," Big Billy said. She turned to look at him. "What do you mean?"

"Monster was hypothermic," Big Billy said. "He was almost in a coma when my brother found him. He does not remember anything."

"But he said . . . ," Price said.

"He could not know," Big Billy said. "Nukilik told me. He followed the footsteps for over a kilometer, with his dog. Monster carried Emile off the ice pack and halfway around the island. Then he lay down on top of him to shelter him."

"He did that?" Price asked, blinking away sudden tears.

"I don't know how," Big Billy said. "In those conditions. Without furs. Without headgear. I could not have done it."

Price looked up at the big man. She had needed to hear that.

"Thank you," she said.

Big Billy just nodded.

"Please tell Corazon how sorry we are," she said.

What good will our sympathy do? she thought. Corazon, with a young baby, was now without a husband.

"I will tell her," Big Billy said. "But there is something I must do first."

She didn't ask him what he meant. She didn't have to. He slipped on the wolf coat, then loosened a knife at his belt. Price got a glimpse of shiny steel. Then he took a single dart and an *atlat* from the sled, and without another word, the tall Inupiat disappeared into the snow flurries as though he were part of them. The White Wolf was on the hunt.

"He didn't take a gun," Barnard said.

"He doesn't need one," Price said.

Once back inside, they locked the door, and Price went to check on the Tsar. He was lying on the floor with his head inside an inspection panel below the desk. Bowden was leaning over the desk.

She was a compact woman, in her thirties, with close-cropped hair and a firm, almost masculine jaw. She seemed shocked by the events of the last few minutes, but it was clear that her training had kicked in. She was a professional, Price thought, and in the midst of such turmoil, that would get her through.

"Any progress?" Price asked.

"The firmware on one of the circuit boards has been replaced," Bowden said. "The new code has a deliberate bug. It no longer picks up any signals from the sensors, yet if you run diagnostics on it, it checks out fine."

"What can we do?" Price asked.

"We have backups of all the firmware upgrades," Bowden said. "If we revert the firmware using an older backup, we should get a version without the bug."

"How long will it take?" Price asked.

"Not long," Bowden said.

"Great," Price said. She raised an eyebrow at Barnard.

Barnard nodded. "I'll find a phone," she said.

"And somewhere private," Price said, looking at Wall.

"Still don't trust him?" Barnard asked. "He helped us escape, tackled Able, and Bilal vouches for him. You want my opinion? I think he's with us."

"I trust him," Price said. "I just don't trust him this much."

A telephone handset sat in a cradle on the control desk. Barnard took it and they moved through into a rest area behind the main room.

"You know Chisnall better than me," Barnard said. "Give me a thumbs-up or a thumbs-down as soon as you're sure."

"Either way, don't give away any more than you have to," Price said. "Something's fishy about this whole thing."

Barnard picked up the handset and dialed. The phone rang. Price's heart was pounding at the thought that Chisnall might still be alive. Barnard seemed emotionless.

The phone rang. And rang. And rang.

After the buildup, the tension of making the call, the lack of an answer was a painful anticlimax. And in one way, a kind of relief. It would turn out to be a hoax, or a trick; Price was convinced of that. Once they talked to the person, they would know for sure, but until then, she could hang on to the slender hope that Chisnall was still alive.

"We'll try again later," Barnard said.

Price wanted to wait, to hang on longer in the hope of an answer, but the Tsar's voice called out from the main control room.

"Price, I got Wilton on the radio."

Barnard hung up the handset and followed Price into the main room.

"Wilton, it's Price," Price said. "What's happening?"

"You're being shut down," Wilton said. "They want you out of there."

"How can we be shut down?" the Tsar asked. "We're not even here. Not officially."

"They found out about the mission," Wilton said. "They're kinda upset about wasting all their missiles on the decoys."

Price and Monster exchanged glances.

"We just told them what we saw," Price said.

"It doesn't matter," Wilton said. "Mission is over. Nothing I can do about it. The orders are for you to return to base as soon as possible."

"And how do they expect us to do that?" Barnard asked.

"You have permission to use the escape hovercraft," Wilton said. "If possible, they'd like you to bring back Able for interrogation."

"In pieces maybe," Barnard said. "Once Big Billy is through with him."

"Only if you can," Wilton said. "If it were me, I'd get the hell out of there."

"We'll see what we can do," Price said.

"Wilton," Barnard said. "I tried that number you gave

Monster. No answer. Question for you. How sure are you that it was . . . who you said it was?"

"No doubt in my mind," Wilton said. "I know Ryan. It was him."

"Okay," Price said, although still far from convinced.

"Barnard, can you help me with something?" Wilton asked.

"Shoot," she said.

He quickly explained the problem of the temporary duty assignments. She listened patiently.

"What do I do?" he asked. "What would you do?"

"Think like a spy, Wilton," she said.

"What do you mean?" Wilton said.

"Look at it from the traitor's point of view," Barnard said. "If he or she was involved somehow, and he or she wanted to ensure that the right people got the right TDAs, how would they do that without leaving a paper trail?"

"I don't know," Wilton said.

"They'd have to have a cutout," Barnard said. "Someone where all the trails ended cold, with nothing to connect them to the traitor. Perhaps a nonexistent person so there's no one to interrogate. Perhaps a ghost."

"A ghost?" Wilton asked.

"Someone who died, perhaps in the course of duty, just before these assignments were made."

"Say there was a ghost," Wilton said. "How would I link that back to the traitor?"

"They would have to have logged in as the ghost to issue the assignments," Barnard said. "They wouldn't do that from their own computer, because that would leave a trail. But it would have to be a computer in the Pentagon, to have access to that level of security."

"Ummm . . . ," Wilton said.

"Listen, Blake, it's easy," she said. "Find the computer on which the assignments were made. Then access security camera footage from the Pentagon corridors on the day in question. Find out who was using that workstation. If you can, you've got them. But you'd need top security clearance to get access to the security camera footage."

"I kinda have that already," Wilton said. "I'll let you know what I find out."

23. CREDENTIALS

THE MAN WITH THE OLIVE-GREEN BRIEFCASE WALKED casually along the Pentagon's C-ring toward the sloping ramps that had been a part of the design of the building since its origins during World Wars One and Two. There were elevators in one of the newer parts of the Pentagon and one of those led down to a heavily guarded underground level. Here the security was not handled by the PFPA but by military police, and the weapons were not pistols but snub-nosed submachine guns.

Again, the man's credentials were checked and passed scrutiny.

When the elevator doors opened on the lower level, he entered casually and nodded to a few people inside the room as if he knew them. Most of them nodded back, certain that they had met him before somewhere, in a meeting perhaps or at a barbecue.

No one doubted his credentials. If he had made it past all the layers of security that surrounded this room, then he had the right to be there.

He moved to one of the workstations on the outside wall and sat down, placing the briefcase beneath the table. The man dialed a short number on his phone and let it ring six times. He was rewarded by an almost inaudible click from the briefcase. He dialed another number and hung up immediately.

A moment later his phone rang. He answered it, speaking the first words he had spoken since arriving at the Pentagon.

"Certainly, sir," he said. "I will be there immediately."

No one could know that the other end of the line was completely silent.

The man rose and walked toward the exit. He did not make eye contact with anyone. A naval officer, adjutant to Admiral Hooper, noticed that the man had left his briefcase but thought nothing of it.

The door to the bunker slid shut behind the man. He was gone, as if he had never existed.

[1510 HOURS LOCAL TIME]
[Big Diomede Island, Bering Strait]

THEY GATHERED IN THE MAIN CONTROL ROOM. FIERCE gusts of wind hurled snow at the narrow windows. Monster had come down from the roof; there was no longer any point in being up there. He couldn't see past the end of his rifle. Able was still outside, somewhere, with Big Billy hunting him.

"We're out of here," Price said. "Mission's over."

"How do they figure that?" Barnard asked.

"We came here to recon this station, and we've done it," Price said. "Time to go home."

"Thank God," the Tsar said.

"So we can relax in comfort while the Pukes take over the world?" Barnard said. "I can't get behind that."

"There's nothing we can do," Wall said.

Barnard stared at him. "Or is that what you'd like us to think?"

"He's right, Barnard," Price said. "There're only five of us left. We're a recon unit. It's not up to us anymore."

Instead of replying, Barnard twisted around and punched a button on the control panel. Monster's video began playing on a screen above their heads.

"See these," Barnard said. "Bzadian bridgers. If we could take those out somehow, we could stop the whole Bzadian advance in its tracks."

"Only if they run into another crevasse," Wall said.

"They will," Barnard said. "Our last line of defense is a minefield that stretches for kilometers around the western tip of Alaska. Pukes get within spitting distance of the coast and ACOG will blow it, leaving a dirty great channel of water right in their path. The way the currents are around the tip of

Alaska, it could be days before it refreezes strongly enough to take tanks."

"Wouldn't they just bring up reserves from Chukchi?" Price asked.

"Probably," Barnard said. "But that would mean a big delay while they bring them forward. All that time their invasion would be stalled and vulnerable. The weather could change, and who knows what could happen?"

"These bridges are very huge," Monster said. "Heavily armor also. What can we do?"

"The bigger they are, the harder they fall," Barnard said.

"Meaning?" the Tsar asked.

"Monster and Nukilik stopped a Russian transporter with a handful of de-icing crystals," Barnard said. "Who's to say we couldn't do the same for these bridgers? Melt the ice in front of them."

"You'd need a truck-full of the stuff," Price said.

"We have a truck-full of the stuff," Bowden said.

Everybody stared at her.

"We have a small airstrip," Bowden said. "There's a pickup truck in the hangar with a tank of it on the back. We use it for de-icing the runway."

"It's suicide," Wall said. "You're going to drive a truck out on the ice floe? Even if you did, the Puke's would pick it off before it got twenty meters. There're six hundred tanks out there, or had you forgotten that bit?" He saw the looks of the others and protested, "There's no point in committing suicide."

"Are you with us, Wall?" the Tsar asked. "One hundred percent? Now's the time we gotta know. There can't be any doubt."

"I always have been," Wall said.

Price gazed at him, thinking. She turned to Barnard, who nodded.

"I believe him," Barnard said.

She was seldom wrong, Price thought. And that was as good as she was going to get.

"Wall's right," Bowden said. "You'd never make it in the truck. But you could use the hovercraft."

"Is it large enough?" Price asked.

Bowden nodded. "Easily. It's an LCAC troop carrier," Bowden said. "It's rigged for stealth, and it's armed with two heavy machine guns. We have a small forklift tractor too. I'm sure you could find a way to rig the de-icing tank onto the hovercraft."

"In these conditions, we should be able to creep right up to their back door before they even know we're there," Barnard said. "A surprise attack."

"Everybody just slow down," Price said.

As Barnard had been talking, she had felt a familiar feeling. The thrill of the chase, the excitement of the hunt. The thirst for danger. But that was what had got Emile killed. Was she now really thinking about possibly sending the whole team to their deaths?

"You okay, Price?" the Tsar asked.

"We've been ordered home," Price said. "We should go."

"Are you crazy?" Barnard asked. "We have a real chance of doing some damage here."

"And a real chance of all dying and achieving nothing," Price said.

"But—" Barnard began, before Monster cut her off.

"It was not your fault," he said.

As always, he seemed to know what she was thinking.

"Yes, it was," Price said. "I am the one who gave the order. I should have waited."

"And I should have tried harder out on the ice," Monster said. "And the Pukes should not have invaded. It is war. We take our chances. You make impossible decisions in impossible circumstances. You go with gut instinct, and sometimes people die."

"It's not fair," Price said, struggling to restrain her emotions.

"It is not fair," Monster agreed. "It is war."

"I . . . don't know," Price said. "I don't know what to do. I don't know what Ryan would have done."

Monster put his hand on her shoulder.

"Is not up to Ryan," he said. "What is gut instinct telling you?"

Price waited, aware of all the faces watching her.

"That if we don't try, and the Bzadians win, we will always be wondering what would have happened if we did try."

"Then there is answer," Monster said. "I know you guys all thinking I am loopy, but I believe we are here, in this place, right now, for reason. Maybe this is reason."

"We could die doing this," Price said. "Anybody want to opt out, just walk away now."

Nobody moved.

"We could die any day," the Tsar said. "At least today we'll know why."

24. WAR PLANNING

WILTON WAS HUNTING GHOSTS.

If Barnard was right, that would narrow down his list rapidly, but it all depended on finding a person who didn't exist. He kept an ear on the conversations at the big table while he scanned lists of recently deceased soldiers and matched them against security logins.

"All right," Gonzales was saying. "Tell me what's happening here."

Wilton still wasn't sure who she was, but she carried some kind of weight. Although she was clearly new to the room, the others deferred to her.

Russell looked at Whitehead, who nodded.

"Advance reconnaissance units report that the Pukes are advancing exactly as predicted," Russell said. "Standard Bzadian spearhead attack formation. They are heading straight for the town of Wales. They will want to secure an airbase so they can start airlifting in the bulk of the invasion force when the storm finishes."

"Once they have an airbase here, they'll no longer be dependent on the ice coverage in the Bering Strait," Hooper said.

"Any chance they could use the old airport at Wales?" Gonzales asked.

"Unlikely," Whitehead said. "We destroyed the runway pretty thoroughly when we evacuated the town. It'll be quicker for them to ignore it."

"Almost certainly they will just use it as a beachhead," Russell said, "and roll toward Tin City. We're already preparing to evacuate. Our fighters will remain there until the last minute, as it's the closest airbase we have to the strait. But we'll pull them out once the situation becomes untenable. Before the Pukes get their SAMs within range."

"The runway there will be destroyed too?" Gonzales asked.

"Yes, as per our scorched-earth policy," Russell said. "The explosives are already in place."

"But when they rebuild the runways at Tin City or Wales, or both," Gonzales asked, "what then?"

"They'll use the airbase to provide cover for a ground attack, probably on Lost River," Russell said. "What's going to slow them down here is the terrain. There are few roads and the tundra is passable, but it's hilly and rough. It will be slow going;

however, they can keep hopping from airbase to airbase all the way to Canada."

"After that, there will be no holding them back," Whitehead said. "We have to stop them on the ice."

"So tell me about the ice," Gonzales said. "What is our strategy?"

"There is a significant ice ridge to the north," Russell said. "We're designating it the Northern Ridge. It extends from the fast ice around the coastline well up to the north. They'll have to come south of that. They could try to skirt around it, but the ice floes north of it are unstable, and very thin in places."

"How significant is this crevasse to the south?" Whitehead asked.

"It's a major rift in the ice floes," Russell said. "Only happened a few hours ago. It may have had something to do with our bombing to the west. A large chunk of ice broke off from the main ice pack. It split in two, which created this jagged fissure through the center. They could bridge it, but I suspect they will just avoid it. That narrows their approach considerably, but as they usually attack in a tight formation, it probably won't worry them."

"So while they're getting squeezed between this northern ridge and the southern crevasse, we'll be hammering them," Whitehead said.

"Yes, sir," Russell said. "We're deploying mobile antitank units along the Northern Ridge. The geography will give our guys a lot of protection from the tanks, while enabling them to get close enough to engage them. The Bzadian advance will stall until they clear the ridge."

"They'll hit it hard," Whitehead said.

"We anticipate heavy attacks using rotorcraft and snowmobiles," Russell said. "We've deployed three Spitfire squadrons, along with an entire infantry division backed by hovercraft."

"They could bypass the ridge by breaking up their spearhead formation," Hooper said.

"They won't," Russell said. "If they break formation, they expose the support vehicles inside, especially the SAMs and bridgers. If we take out their SAMs, they'll be vulnerable to our cruise missiles. They won't break formation."

"And the minefield?" Whitehead asked.

"Of course," Russell said. "There's a strip of mines from one end of the ice field to the other at the point where the drift ice meets the fast ice. We blow that and they'll have a channel twenty meters wide to cross before they can continue."

"But they'll just bring up bridging units," Gonzales said.

"Correct. It won't stop them, but it will slow them down. It's a war of attrition. If we can do enough damage to their force before they hit dry land, we have a good chance of turning them around."

"Is there any way to stop them completely?" Gonzales asked.

Russell and Hundal looked at each other. "No, ma'am," Hundal said. "Not without a nuclear weapon."

As always, the threat of a nuclear strike made Wilton look up.

"That's not an option," Whitehead said.

"The concentrated nature of the attack makes it ideal for a tactical nuke," Russell said. "If we stop them at the mine barrier and drop a nuclear weapon in the center while they're bringing up their bridgers, we would destroy most of the force, and the damage to the ice would make it impassable for days."

"We have already had this discussion," Whitehead said. "We are not starting a nuclear war."

"Yes, sir. I understand that, sir," Russell said. "I was just answering the lady's question."

"General Russell," Gonzales said. "A direct question. Do you think we can stop them without deploying a nuclear weapon?"

Russell shook his head. "No, ma'am, I do not. We can slow them down. Hold them up at the Northern Ridge and stop them temporarily at the minefield. But apart from that we have about as much chance of stopping this invasion as a tree has of holding back an avalanche."

Wilton was barely listening. His attention was focused on his computer screen. He had found a ghost.

The ghost was a woman. Lieutenant Colonel Francine Bartholomew. A high-ranking officer in the Bering Strait Defense Force. Her plane had gone down in a storm. She had died on December 3. Yet somehow Lieutenant Bartholomew had accessed her computer in the Pentagon on December 15, precisely twelve days later. Not bad for a dead woman, Wilton thought.

The first access time on the fifteenth was at 0943. Her

office was in E-ring, third level. There was a mountain of security footage, but it was all neatly catalogued by date and searchable.

Wilton searched the security video files for that day and waited while the system brought the recording to his screen.

There was light traffic in the corridor that morning, but all of it bypassing the dead woman's office. Wilton scrolled forward through the video, looking for anyone opening the door of the office.

He reached 0943 and stopped. Whoever it was was already in the office by that time. He scrolled back, stopped at 0830, and played from there. A uniformed officer walked casually to the door of Bartholomew's office and swiped a key card, entering with a quick glance around.

The man wore a naval uniform, complete with cap, and kept his face low, so it was not visible to the security cameras.

There was no way to identify him.

Wilton scrolled forward again, waiting to see when the officer came out of the door. That happened at 1010.

Again, the officer kept his head down, but just for a brief flash he glanced up at the security camera, an involuntary reflex. Wilton rewound to that spot and went forward, frame by frame, until he found the clearest shot.

His mouth dropped.

He took screenshots showing the time and date and saved them with the details of the assignments and the information about Bartholomew's death.

Scarcely believing what he was seeing, he logged into the

TDA system to see what duties had been assigned that day at that time.

There was a long list, but Bartholomew's name stood out like a beacon. He clicked on it and brought up the details of her assignments.

There was only one.

It was not Able.

It was for a Special Forces operative named Clordon. Wilton brought up Clordon's details but did not recognize the photo. There was nothing distinctive or memorable about him, and although Wilton had an odd feeling he had seen the man before, he could not place where.

But there seemed to be no correlation with the Fezerkers or with Little Diomede.

Yet there had to be. What was he missing?

He looked again at the screenshot from the security camera. There was no doubt. The face on the camera was that of General Jake Russell, supreme commander of the Bering Strait Defense Force.

Wilton looked up as an aide arrived at the central table, carrying a radio. He handed it to General Russell, who took it, listened, then handed it back.

"You'll excuse me for a brief moment," he said. "We may have a lead on the Fezerker on Little Diomede. I need to talk to one of my investigators."

Wilton looked back at the screen. Had he gotten this all wrong? Was Russell hunting the Fezerkers too? Was the mysterious Mr. Clordon the investigator he mentioned?

The phone on his desk buzzed and the screen lit up. He snatched at it.

"Wilton." It was Price's voice.

"Yeah, how are you guys doing?" he asked.

"We're good. We may have a way to stick a rod in the spokes of the Puke invasion," she said.

"Don't do anything stupid," Wilton said. "One of the guys here keeps muttering about dropping a nuke. I'd get out of there if I were you."

"Talk them out of it, Wilton," she said. "Really bad idea. Let ACOG know what we are doing. It may influence their thinking."

"Okay, shoot," Wilton said, and listened carefully as she explained it.

When she hung up, he sent a message to Bilal, who read it and glanced at Wilton with his lips pursed.

Would Bilal even let the others know? The Angels had been ordered to leave. What would the top dogs think when they found out that the Angels were planning to disobey that order?

His phone rang.

"You somewhere private?" Chisnall asked.

Wilton looked around at the room full of people. "Not really," he said.

"Call me back as soon as you are," Chisnall said.

The elevator was on the far side of the room, which meant skirting around the oval desk in the center. Wilton felt as if all their eyes were on him as he made his way toward the door, although he didn't look at them to make sure.

The security guard pressed the elevator call button for him and Wilton waited patiently. There were no lights at the top of this elevator to let you know whether it was going up or down or what floor it was on. But he could tell from the whirring noises inside the doors when it stopped, and when it started again, he knew it was descending.

Wilton stared straight ahead at the doors as he waited, not making eye contact with the security guard. There was no sound as the elevator stopped. No ding. The noise of the motors stopped and the doors slid quickly open. Stepping inside, he pressed the button. There was only one. The elevator only stopped at two places, so if you were at one, it took you to the other. The doors closed and the whirring of the elevator motors came from above him. The elevator lurched slightly as it began to move.

And then hell came to the Pentagon.

BOOK 3—ICE WAR

25. AFTERMATH

THE BZADIAN EXPLOSIVE WAS VERY POWERFUL. Although the amount was small, it was still enough to kill everybody in the room. Had it been a normal room.

But the command bunker in the basement of the Pentagon had been designed to withstand a direct missile strike, and the moment the chemical reaction began in the bomb, the room responded with its own defenses.

The air pressure in the room was deliberately kept as low as possible. The high domed ceiling, although it looked solid, was a thin metal, little more than tinfoil. Beyond it was a large chamber filled with nothing. Not even air. A vacuum. A sudden pressure change in the bunker, like an explosion, would tear the ceiling from its mountings, sucking most of the air from the bunker up into the vacuum chamber. A pressure wave needs a medium, like water or air, and without either, the energy of the bomb was quickly dissipated. The same switch triggered airbags built into each of the chairs at the oval table, instantly cocooning the occupants in a Kevlar balloon.

The table itself was a partial shield for those on the far side of it.

As the blast of the bomb was sucked up into the vacuum chamber above, the lack of air also suffocated any fire, and in the few seconds while the occupants of the chamber gasped for breath, a network of nozzles opened up from hidden locations in the walls, filling the room with a fine mist of water and extinguishing any remaining flames.

Only then did the automatic systems allow oxygen back into the room.

As instantaneous and as clever as the bombproofing systems were, they were not designed to cope with such a powerful explosive detonating inside the room. Several of the Kevlar cocoons were torn to shreds by the blast, which ripped in and around the chairs themselves.

Adjutants and aides, seated at workstations around the circumference of the room, fared worse, getting slammed into the walls or their computer workstations by the shock wave.

The searing heat, in the seconds before it was stifled by the vacuum and smothered by the watery mist, did even more damage.

Seven people were killed in the Pentagon bunker in that moment, and two more died on the way to hospital. A dozen were severely injured.

26. WILTON

WILTON OPENED HIS EYES AND LOOKED AROUND, TRYING to work out where he was and what he was doing there.

He was in an elevator, or at least the remains of one. It was jammed in the elevator shaft halfway up the doors. The doors were open. That was his first impression. A second glance revealed that they weren't open in the usual way, sliding to each side. They were buckled inward, melded with the metal of the elevator cage. The handrails above him were twisted and warped. The wooden paneling was splintered and smashed.

He cautiously checked his body for injuries, unsure what had happened. Had the elevator malfunctioned somehow?

That wouldn't explain the damage, though.

He found no broken bones, and he seemed to be breathing, although the air was thin and smoky. When he put his hands to his face, they came away bloody, but it was just cuts, he thought. His skull felt intact.

The floor of the elevator was destroyed, twisted, corrugated metal with scraps of burned carpet clinging to it. He crawled toward the narrow gap where the elevator doors had burst inward. Wilton slid down from the cage to a scene of terror and panic. People were on the floor moaning, screaming, or not moving at all.

Giant balloons had sprouted in the center of the room around the main oval table. Some people were already running around, tending to the injured. Small fires were burning here and there around the room, but a soft mist of water was drifting everywhere and the fires were slowly dying away.

Somewhere in the distance, an alarm was blaring.

At his feet, a woman was crawling toward him, her eyes pleading, blood pouring from a deep cut on her arm, which appeared to be broken.

Wilton took one more look around, then breathed deeply and went to work.

[1540 HOURS LOCAL TIME]
[Little Diomede Island, Bering Strait]

"ANY SIGN OF BIG BILLY OR ABLE?" PRICE ASKED.

The Tsar shook his head. He was seated at the control panel monitoring the video feeds from the cameras that surrounded the building. The video cameras were all but useless in the storm, but the infrared would show either of the men as a heat signature.

"Nothing," the Tsar said.

Somewhere out there a deadly game of cat and mouse was being played.

"What would you do, if you were Able?" Price asked.

"Well, he can't stay out there forever," the Tsar said. "Not in these conditions. With the windchill factor, it's well below freezing, and it'll be dark in a couple of hours."

"Maybe that's what he's waiting for," Price said.

"Maybe," the Tsar agreed.

"Can Able get in the building?" Price asked, suddenly worried that Able might already be inside, hiding, waiting for a chance to strike.

"I doubt it," the Tsar said. "There are only two entrances. The main door and the tunnel that leads to the hangar. Bowden locked them both down as soon as we got inside. Besides, all the main areas have movement sensors." He pointed to glowing dots on a screen. "That's Bowden—she went to the armory a few moments ago. Those three are Monster, Wall, and Barnard, out in the hangar."

Wall and Barnard had gone to assist Monster in transferring the de-icing tank from the pickup truck to the hovercraft.

"He's not inside," the Tsar said.

The dot that was Bowden reached the control room and as it did, the door opened. Bowden backed in, her arms full of grenades, claymore mines, even packs of C4.

"Nice," Price said.

Barnard had asked for explosives. She'd be happy with this lot, Price thought.

"What do you use the C4 for?" Price asked.

"Clearing ice mainly," Bowden said.

She helped Bowden lug the cache of explosives through to the hovercraft hangar. The two buildings were joined by an underground tunnel, which reminded Price of the tunnels in the Inupiat homes, although it was a lot larger, with concrete walls and metal staircases at each end.

The hangar itself was a simple metal-framed structure with plasticized sides.

Inside the hangar were three vehicles, the largest of which was the hovercraft. It was armored, the heavy Kevlar plates fixed on odd "stealth" angles to deflect radar. At the back was a large fan to provide propulsion. It was painted white with a variegated gray pattern for camouflage.

Monster was operating a forklift. He was delicately maneuvering the forks under a large plastic tank on the back of a pickup truck with triangular snow treads. Barnard and Wall were up on the tray of the truck with spanners and wrenches.

"How is it going?" Price asked.

"It's a big job," Barnard said. "And once we have this shifted, we still need to rig the nozzle system."

That lay on the ground behind the hovercraft. A wide spray wand with multiple nozzles spread evenly along its length. Long plastic tubes were coiled up on the ground beside it.

"Sure you know what you're doing?" Bowden asked.

"No idea," Wall said. "We're making it up as we go."

"As long as you're having fun," Price said. "We brought you some presents."

They laid the explosives carefully on the floor near the hovercraft.

"Thanks," Barnard said.

"Got a plan for those?" Price asked.

"Never know when a big bang might come in handy," Barnard said, and, unusually for her, she grinned.

"What can I do?" Price asked.

"Nothing," Monster said. "Eat. Get some rest. We going nowhere tonight. But tomorrow is going to be big day."

[MISSION DAY 2, FEBRUARY 17, 2033]
[2145 hours local time]
[ACOG Emergency Operations Center, Raven Rock Mountain Complex, Pennsylvania]

THE INTERROGATION ROOM WAS A BRIGHTLY LIT chamber, somewhere in the depths of the building. Exactly what building it was, Wilton was unsure. He had heard people referring to it as the Rock. It was the backup command and control center for the ACOG military machine, and within an hour of the bombing, all those fit to continue had been bundled onto helicopters and flown here.

But someone had pointed out Wilton as the person who had left the room right before the bombing.

That had painted him a prime suspect.

He had been questioned for an hour, protesting his innocence loudly and vehemently.

Then both the interrogators, hard-faced men in dark suits, had left. For the last twenty minutes he had been alone.

He was supposed to ring Chisnall. In all the shock and disorientation of the bombing, he had not forgotten that. But they had taken his phone. Chisnall would be wondering why he hadn't heard from him, but there was nothing he could do about it.

The doors opened at last and to his surprise, and no little discomfort, it was General Russell who entered, followed by an aide. He did not sit, but stood behind one of the chairs, leaning on it.

"I've been looking for you, son," he said.

Wilton was unsure what to say.

"You were the liaison for the Angels," Russell said.

Wilton nodded.

"Yes," Russell said. "A translator, Bilal said. Seems he likes to play his cards close to his chest."

"I had nothing to do with the bombing," Wilton said.

"Of course not," Russell said. He didn't quite smile; it wasn't a time for that, but his expression was friendly and genuine. "When I heard they were holding you, I told them exactly that."

"Thank you, sir," Wilton said.

"Bilal trusted you, so I trust you," Russell said. "Besides, we think we have the actual bomber on video."

"Is Mr. Bilal all right?" Wilton asked. If Bilal was dead, then who else could he talk to about what he had found out? Certainly not Russell.

"Bilal's in the hospital," Russell said. "He'll be all right. How about you? How are you feeling?"

This was clearly a reference to the bandages on Wilton's face.

"I'm fine, sir," Wilton said. "Just minor cuts. I was very lucky."

"Yes, you were," Russell said. "Are you okay to travel?"

"Certainly, sir," Wilton said.

"Good." Russell nodded at his aide, who handed Wilton some papers.

"With the Angel mission over, there's no need for you to stay," Russell said. "So you've been released back to your unit."

"Thank you, sir," Wilton said.

"Take care, son," Russell said.

27. THE HUNT

PRICE AWOKE TO THE SOUND OF GUNFIRE. OR HAD THAT just been part of a dream?

The lights were low in the sleeping quarters, but she could see Barnard, sound asleep on a bunk on the opposite wall. On the bunk above her, Wall's head was visible.

Was the gunfire real? It hadn't woken the others.

She checked the time on her wrist computer and was angry to see that her one-hour nap had turned into more than six hours of sleep.

She rolled out of the bunk, snatching up her coil-gun on the way to the control room.

The Tsar was in the control chair as he had been earlier. He looked bleary, as though he, too, had dozed off.

"Did you hear those gunshots?" Price asked as she entered.

The Tsar looked up at her in surprise. "Price? You're here?"

"Where else did you think I'd be?" she asked.

"Then who is that in the hangar with Monster?" the Tsar asked, pointing to two glowing dots on the movement sensor.

Price swore. She keyed her comm. "Monster, is Bowden in there with you?"

"No, my dude," came back the reply. "Am alone."

"No, you're not," Price said.

The Tsar was already halfway out of his chair.

"No, stay here," she said. "Wake up the others."

She was already running for the tunnel to the hangar.

Monster circled the hovercraft carefully, the magnum in one hand and a heavy wrench in the other. He could see no one in the hangar, and there was nowhere to hide, except perhaps up on the hovercraft. Was Price sure? He had been busy connecting up the tubing according to Barnard's instructions, and someone could have been sneaking around the hangar behind his back.

He had sent the others off to grab a short sleep. They all needed it. He had been certain that he was alone.

He was about to key the comm and ask the Tsar to check when the sound of running footsteps in the tunnel made him look in that direction.

He froze.

The tunnel emerged into the hangar on the west side of the building. There was no trapdoor, just a guardrail so you couldn't accidentally fall in. At the base of the guardrail were two claymore mines. Armed and ready. Anyone who came up those stairs was going to get their head blown off.

"Price!" he shouted. "Stop!"

Then a locomotive hit him from behind.

The magnum went flying across the floor in one direction, the wrench in another. Monster hit the concrete floor, hard.

Able was tall, not broad but a mass of sinewy strength. Monster had no idea where he had been hiding. Nor did he care. All that mattered was breaking the grip of the man, whose arm was around his neck, cutting off his air. He was pinned to the ground under Able's weight.

He twisted in the man's arms, trying to breathe, to call out to Price, but no air came.

Price stopped halfway up the staircase. *Stop*, Monster had said. He had said that for a reason. But why? She could hear the sounds of a struggle above her. She took another step, peering above her for any sign of danger. There! At the base of the guardrail. The deadly gray shape of a claymore mine, triggered by motion. One step higher and she would have been dead.

Still the sounds of fighting came from above her. She would have to go around.

"Tsar!" she shouted, running back the way she had come. "Open the main hangar doors!"

■ ■ ■

Monster let go of the other man's arm and brought his hands in close to his chest, in the push-up position. He pushed down and inch by painful inch lifted himself, and Able, off the ground. When he reached the full stretch of his arms, he twisted again, dropping one arm so that he and Able crashed to the floor on that side. Able's grip loosened momentarily as they landed, and Monster was ready. He pulled the man's arm away from his neck with both hands and tucked his chin to his chest to stop him from doing it again. Able's arm wrapped across his mouth, but Monster could breathe again, through his nose, sucking in huge lungfuls of air.

A blast of cold air hit him and snow swirled around him. The main hangar doors were slowly starting to open.

He pushed himself over on his back, lying on top of Able, who was refusing to let go. He put his legs flat on the floor on either side of the man, and lifted himself up off the ground, then thrust downward. Being shorter than the tall man, his backside drove into Able's belly, winding him. Able gasped, and in that instant Monster twisted again, breaking free and rolling away from his attacker.

Able was fast, though; he was on his feet like a cat and diving across the floor. *The magnum!* Monster realized. He was after the magnum. Monster got to his feet and began to run, but he was a lifetime too late.

Able got there first. His hand found the magnum, even as he was still sliding across the floor, and it began to swing around toward Monster. The gun came up in agonizingly slow motion. The black hole that was the muzzle looked like the entrance to a tunnel. A very long, dark tunnel. Any second Monster expected to see the flash of light that would lead him to another long dark tunnel from where there was no return.

But the gun didn't fire.

The magnum began to drop again as Able looked down in surprise at the metallic head of an Inupiat dart that was now protruding from his throat.

A dark shadow flitted across the half open doors, silhouetted by the floodlights outside.

The White Wolf had finished his hunt.

28. SPITFIRE

THE SPITFIRE PILOT WAS NOT THERE WHEN WILTON arrived, and after a few minutes of waiting he started going through the precombat checks, as he had been taught. He had about two hours before the mission briefing, and it was a good chance to refamiliarize himself with the craft.

The HC980-LD, Light Attack Craft, known as the Spitfire, was a two-person hovercraft with short stubby wings. It could not fly, but it could jump and even glide for a few meters if the air currents were favorable. The wings also held the craft's main armament, six sidewinder missiles, three on each wing. They were of little use against the armored, spinning hulls of the Bzadian battle tanks, but they were effective against rotorcraft and snowmobiles.

As gunner, he was seated in the front seat. The pilot, slightly elevated for visibility, sat behind. The machine gun was gimbal mounted and controlled by a joystick. He could aim it anywhere from thirty degrees left or right, and up or down about five degrees.

The Spitfire, named after the famous British fighter plane of the 1940s, had defensive armament too. Six contact mines were attached beneath the air cushion and could be dropped in the path of a pursuing vehicle.

The Spitfire was only lightly armored, its main defense being its speed and its ability to jump into the air. If it was weighed down by heavy armor, it would be sluggish and earthbound.

Wilton powered up the control system and ran preflight checks on the missiles and the craft's only other offensive weapon, the forward-mounted machine gun. His hands were shaking slightly, fatigue perhaps, or the after-effects of the explosion. He clenched them together to try to make it stop. He didn't need that if he was going into a battle zone.

It had been a six-hour flight, and he had slept most of the way, but in that sleep had come dreams, always of the same thing. The face in the photograph. Clordon. He awoke in a sweat, the face still vivid in his mind. It wasn't a face you would remember. There was nothing distinctive about it. You could walk past this man in a corridor, then walk past him again a few minutes later and swear you had never seen him before. But major traumatic events have a way of throwing memories into supersharp focus, of highlighting tiny unimportant details that you would never remember otherwise.

And now Wilton was sure he had seen that man somewhere else.

It was the man who had entered the bunker and then left, leaving behind an olive-green briefcase. If Clordon was the bomber and Russell had assigned his TDA, then Russell had to be behind this. His pilot, Captain Adrienne Anderson, arrived just as he was thinking it over.

"Wilton," she said.

It wasn't a question or an order; in fact, Wilton wasn't sure what it was.

"Yes, ma'am," he said.

"You can drop the ma'am straightaway," she said. "It's Captain. Or Captain Anderson if you're feeling extra polite."

"Yes, Captain," Wilton said. "I'm looking forward to serving with you."

"You're looking forward to serving with me?" She clicked her tongue a few times. It was clearly a habit.

"Yes, Captain," Wilton said.

"You know what, Wilton?" she said. "I'm a professional soldier. Not like most of the ACOG conscripts. Eight years in the US military before the Pukes arrived, and seven years of constant fighting since then. You know the problem with that? Most of the people I trained with are dead. They keep sending me replacements with three months' training, and somehow we're supposed to keep each other alive. You gonna keep me alive, Wilton?"

"I hope so, Captain," Wilton said.

"How old are you, Wilton?"

"Seventeen, but I'm—"

She cut him off with a wave of her hand. "I know who you are, and I know the Angel reputation. You're supposed to be good with a gun, but the fact is you're still a kid and you don't belong here."

"Sorry, Captain," Wilton said.

"Me too," she said. "But I'm stuck with you. You do exactly as I say, and maybe we'll both walk away from this."

"Yes, Captain," Wilton said.

"All right," she sighed. "Show me what you know. I'll try to fill in the gaps."

29. ANGELS

THE HOVERCRAFT MOVED SLOWLY AWAY FROM THE island. Monster found an ice ridge and kept close to it, reasoning that it would reduce both radar and the chance of being spotted visually. It also cut down the wind, which kept trying to blow them off course. Not that Price minded the weather. The blizzard was getting worse, and that meant they would be hard to spot and harder to kill.

Added to the hammering winds and the driving snow were sounds of thunder and flashes of lightning from the battle raging between the light, fast ACOG hovercraft and the heavy tanks and rotorcraft of the Bzadians. The battle had started before it was light and was now in full roar.

Barnard had tested the spray nozzles once, pulling a lever

that opened a valve and left a pool of slimy liquid on the floor of the hangar. At first light they had left.

Bowden had stayed, saying she could do more good manning the station than as an extra man on the hovercraft.

"What's our stealth profile?" Price asked.

"We're getting bombarded with radar," the Tsar said. "But according to the indicators, we shouldn't be returning a strong enough signal for them to detect. We're invisible to them at the moment."

"Perfect," Price said. "Let's try to stay that way."

"No problem," Monster said, at the controls.

"Okay, Wall, when we start our run, I want you up on the rear gun," Price said.

"Won't do much good against tanks," Wall said.

"It's not the tanks I'm worried about. They're not effective against small fast targets. But you can bet they'll send their rotorcraft after us. Snowmobiles too."

Wall nodded.

"Barnard, you do what you need to do with the de-icing controls, and I'll take the top gun," Price said.

"The suicide position," Monster commented.

"Someone's got to take it," Price said. "You're our best driver, and I need Tsar on the scopes. Who does that leave?"

"I'm going to test the de-icer," Barnard said. "Can you run her up to thirty klicks?"

"Okay," Monster said, and a moment or two later, "Steady at thirty klicks."

Barnard pulled on some cords that connected to the

de-icing unit. After a few meters she said, "Okay, circle back. I want to see how that worked."

Monster looped the craft back to where they had started the run. Barnard slid over the edge of the rubber cushion and ran to the wet patch on the ice. She checked the time, then plunged an aluminum rod into the water, testing the depth.

The Tsar gave her a hand back up on deck.

"All good?" he asked.

She said nothing, working on some calculations in her head.

Wilton sat silently on a hard, plastic folding seat.

The briefing center was a prefabricated metal hut. A large screen on the wall showed icons representing the various human and Bzadian elements involved in the battle.

This was different from an Angel mission. There was tension and nervousness before those, but it was a different kind of tension. On Angel missions they were undercover, trying their best to avoid conflict, to stay out of harm's way. Here, they were preparing to head into the thick of it. To get right in harm's way.

People were dying out on the ice, and there was a good chance that he could be one of them.

The squadron leader, Major Jaylen Gerrand, waited silently while the rest of the pilots and gunners filed in.

"This is not going our way. It looks like we'll lose the Northern Ridge," Major Gerrand said. "The Pukes have mounted a major offensive; they've committed over two hundred tanks to this, with heavy support from their rotorcraft and snowmobiles.

However, that opens a window of opportunity for us. They had to weaken their defenses to the south. We're going to try to exploit it. Third reserve Viper squadron are going in after their SAM batteries. We're their escort."

"How, sir?" Anderson asked. "We'd have to pass through the front lines. We'd get eaten alive."

"We think the Pukes have pushed too far forward," Gerrand said, pointing to a large jagged line on the screen. "They've ignored this southern crevasse. Our plan is to move the Vipers up the eastern fissure. The ice is nearly two meters high there. We're going to creep along below their radar until we reach the crevasse. Then we'll accelerate to attack speed and pop up behind the main battle lines. We'll still have to contend with their flank guards, but by the time they see us, we'll be past them and in among the SAM batteries. The Vipers will take them out with spiderwebs, while we keep the Puke rotorcraft and snowmobiles off their tails."

"How do we get out?" another pilot asked.

"Any way you can," Gerrand said. "Any further questions?"

There were none.

This was it, Wilton thought. Time to find out if those hours of training against robotic targets had done him any good. He made two stops on his way to his craft. One to use the bathroom. The other to send a quick email to Daniel Bilal.

30. ATTACK RUN

[MISSION DAY 3, FEBRUARY 18, 2033]
[1100 hours local time]
[Forward Operations Base, Tin City, Alaska]

THERE WAS A SLIGHT SHIFTING OF WEIGHT AS THE engine started and the air cushion filled, lifting the craft off the concrete of the landing pad. Ahead and behind, Wilton could see the rest of the squadron rising up.

They began to move in single file, ice flying from beneath their skirts as they slid easily down the ramp and out across the storm-tossed waters of the bay. The ice-covered tundra slipped quickly past and then the white cliffs of the ice floe emerged out of the curtain of snow and flying ice.

Ahead, Wilton saw Gerrand, the squadron leader, disappear into a gaping crack in the cliff face. The fissure. It seemed barely wide enough for his craft, but Anderson maneuvered the little Spitfire expertly into the same gap.

The walls of ice sliding past them were jagged and rough torn. As if someone had taken this huge sheet of ice and snapped it in two like a cookie. They moved slowly, the sound of the propeller no more than a soft hum behind them.

The fissure was not straight, but zigged and zagged, eventually ending in a sudden right turn into the much wider crevasse. Still they crept along at minimum speed, although Wilton could hardly bear the waiting. They were almost in the heart of the enemy formations; surely someone would see them soon?

"Here we go," Gerrand said, the first words since they had left the base, the first breaking of radio silence. That no longer mattered.

Water churned in front of them and propellers spat ice particles as the hovercraft squadron powered up to attack speed.

"Arm your weapons," Anderson said, clicking her tongue. "As soon as we jump, it's weapons free."

"Weapons armed." Wilton confirmed the instruction. His heart was racing; his mouth was dry. From now on, every fraction of a second was life and death.

The Spitfire's nose came up and it lifted off the water, on the tail of the aircraft in front of it. The wind lashed viciously at them as they rose out of the fissure, flying, for a few meters at least, as the craft cleared the cliff and rocketed across the ice, right between two Bzadian battle tanks that were starting to react to this new threat in their midst. One tank flashed by, then another; then they were through the flanks of the formation and racing across the ice toward row after row of SAM batteries. There were soldiers everywhere, mostly on snowmobiles, and they were quick to react. Bullets were already smashing off the armored glass of the windshield. It was small-arms fire and shouldn't worry the Spitfire, but Wilton engaged them with the front gun as they spread out with the other hovercraft, racing toward the SAM units.

In the thick of the battle, in the thick of the storm, it was like driving in a heavy fog, with giant battle tanks appearing out of nowhere.

One of the Spitfires turned sharply to avoid a rotorcraft that materialized in front of it, veering right into the path of another Spitfire. There was a ball of flame as the two craft collided.

The SAM batteries looked like the Bzadian tanks, although slightly smaller. There were at least a hundred of them. He ignored them. The sidewinder missiles would not penetrate their thick, spinning hulls. He concentrated on their defenders, the rotorcraft and snowmobiles that buzzed around them in the storm like mosquitoes on a foggy night.

"Target acquired," the gunnery computer told him, and Wilton pulled the trigger. A sidewinder leaped off the right wing and left a smoky trail in the air as it closed in on a rotorcraft. Another sidewinder from another Spitfire was on the same trail. There was a flash, followed immediately by another as the missiles struck. White lightning occupied the place where the rotorcraft had been. One of the missiles had hit the ammunition store inside the vehicle.

Wilton whooped with excitement. His first hovercraft kill.

"Concentrate!" Anderson said. "There's plenty more where that came from!"

The gunnery computer found another target but lost it almost immediately, then found a third. Wilton squeezed the trigger a second time and saw the missile miss by a meter and go spinning off into the distance. Another target, another missile, and this time success.

"Rotorcraft, three o'clock," Anderson said.

"Got it," Wilton said.

He pinged it with the target acquirer and was rewarded with a steady tone. He fired just as the enemy craft let loose two missiles toward them.

The sidewinder spiraled toward the rotorcraft as their Spitfire leaped into the air, using height to evade the Bzadian missiles that scorched through underneath. The sidewinder streaked into the rotors of the enemy craft and exploded. The craft shimmied in midair, then dropped onto the ice.

"Couple of snowmos on our tail!" Wilton yelled. Two snowmobiles were right behind them, trying to line up shots as Anderson jigged the Spitfire around, in between Bzadian tanks.

"Take a deep breath," Anderson said. "Stay calm. Drop a couple of mines. I'll reverse flick at the same time."

She straightened to give Wilton a good line. He punched out two landmines, and as he did so, Anderson cut the power to the propeller and spun the hovercraft 180 degrees, sliding backward over the ice at seventy kilometers per hour.

The first snowmobile ran straight over one of the landmines, which leaped off the ice, magnetically attracted to the hull of the machine. There was an explosion and the snowmobile erupted in flames. The second machine swerved around the first and kept on coming, until Wilton took off its right tread with the machine gun. It flipped violently and smashed into a mound of ice.

"Nice shootin'," Anderson said, spinning them back around and gunning the engine just in time to avoid a collision with a SAM battery.

"Nice drivin'," Wilton said.

[MISSION DAY 3, FEBRUARY 18, 2033]
[1550 hours local time]
[ACOG Emergency Operations Center, Raven Rock Mountain Complex, Pennsylvania]

THE OPERATIONS TABLE AT RAVEN ROCK WAS SHAPED like an elongated doughnut. In the center, in the hole of the doughnut, a small group of uniformed personnel sat at computer workstations, running the communications for the command center.

Russell was the only person at the table without bandages. He was the only person lucky enough to have been out of the bunker when the bomb exploded.

The rest of them sported a variety of dressings, some starting to stain red with blood. Watson had a broken arm and looked shaken. Hooper's head was wrapped so thoroughly she could have auditioned for a role in *The Mummy*. Hundal's hands were heavily bandaged, and even now one of his arms was being attended to by a medic.

Bilal and Whitehead were missing.

No one, apart from Russell, had escaped unscathed, despite the elaborate and sophisticated defenses of the Pentagon bunker.

"It's not rocket science," Russell said. "We blow the mines; that will force them to bring up the bridgers. We wait until the bridgers are in place, then drop in a tactical nuke."

"The oversight committee will never allow it," Gonzales said.

"The oversight committee has no say in the matter," Russell said. "Since the bombing of the Pentagon, we are in a state of martial law. Government powers have been suspended. With Whitehead incapacitated, I am the senior ACOG commander, and right now what I say goes."

"You'll still have to answer to the committee after the fact," Gonzales said. "When martial law ends."

"That's fine with me," Russell said. "They can complain about it afterward and hold an inquiry and run around in circles with all their usual red tape. But we are losing the fight for our lives and we are not stopping for a rubber stamp from a bunch of old women who are too afraid to do what needs to be done to win this war."

"You'll use artillery?" Hundal asked. "I doubt my planes could get near."

"Yes, they are already in place," Russell said. "We drop the nuke five klicks offshore with a blast radius of four klicks. That takes out ninety percent of their attacking force. They'll think twice before trying to cross the Bering Strait again."

"But they won't think twice about using a tactical nuke on the battlefield," Hooper said.

"Hooper, are you with me, or should I have you removed from this room?" Russell asked.

"I will obey your orders," Hooper said. "But I want it on the record that I disagree."

"Done," Russell said. "What's our wind situation?"

"Westerly, about ten knots," Watson said.

"Excellent," Russell said. "That will blow any fallout toward the Bzadians on Chukchi. But get our ground forces into MOPP suits just in case."

"What about the locals?" Gonzales asked. "The Inupiat."

"What Inupiat?" Russell asked. "We relocated all of them years ago. If some of them want to break the law and go into a military zone without permission, they deserve whatever they get."

"Check your six!" Anderson shouted, and Wilton scanned the rear screen to see a rotorcraft hard on their tail.

Anderson jigged the hovercraft left and right, in a way that the rotorcraft could not match, preventing its guns from locking on.

"Landmine?" Wilton asked.

"You can try," Anderson replied. "You might get lucky."

The Spitfire circled around a battle tank, then straightened out. The moment Wilton was sure the rotorcraft was right behind them, he dropped a mine. In the rear screen, he saw it land, but the rotorcraft lifted up, well over it.

Bullets peppered the propeller behind them.

"It's stuck on our tail!" Wilton yelled.

"Don't worry about it," Anderson said. "They can't turn as fast as we can. Get ready to drop another landmine, on my go."

"Landmine ready," Wilton said.

Anderson spun the hovercraft around in a wide slide, heading right for another battle tank, which tried to engage them with its machine guns. But they were too close and too fast. She veered away at the last moment and whipped the craft in a tight circle around it.

The rotorcraft followed, but Anderson was right: its rotor system, although agile in the air, was clumsy so close to the ground.

Anderson circled the tank twice and said, "On my mark, ready . . ."

They spun around the tank one more time, emerging right on the tail of the rotorcraft, which veered off and tried to build up speed. But the Spitfire was on a collision course with it.

"What are you doing?" Wilton cried out.

"Ready . . . ," Anderson said. She hauled back on the controls and the machine lifted, soaring into the air over the top of the rotorcraft. "Now!"

Wilton punched out the mine and heard the explosion as it fell into the blades of the rotorcraft. He yelled with excitement.

"Okay, we're out of here," Anderson said.

"We were just getting started," Wilton said.

"We've been pulled out," Anderson said. "Everybody is being pulled back, effective immediately."

"Why?" Wilton asked.

"They didn't say," Anderson said. "But it's not hard to work out."

"Guys, we have a problem," the Tsar said. "ACOG has ordered all units back to a perimeter of no closer than five kilometers."

They were a hundred meters behind the Bzadian lines and closing fast, a long row of rounded hulls ahead of them, blurred by the driving ice and snow.

"Pulled them out? Why?" Wall asked.

"Oh my God, they're going to nuke the place," Barnard said.

"So what's wrong with that?" the Tsar asked. "That'll stop them."

"The Pukes have nukes too," Price said.

"So?" Wall asked.

"It's called escalation," Barnard said. "We use a nuke, even just a tactical one, and they respond with a tactical nuke of their own. So we use a bigger one. Next thing you know there's missiles raining down out of the skies and the only winners will be the cockroaches."

"Better that than handing the whole world over to the Pukes," the Tsar said.

"Why do you say that?" Price asked.

"They're going to kill us all anyway," the Tsar said. "Let's go down fighting."

"And leave planet that will be toxic for hundreds of thousands of years," Monster said.

"They're not going to kill us all," Wall said. "They need us. They're trying to take over, not destroy us."

"Did they teach you that at Uluru?" the Tsar asked.

"As it happens, yeah," Wall said.

"I bet they told you a lot of things," Price said.

"They wiped out everyone in Indonesia," the Tsar said.

"I know," Wall said. "To show the rest of the world what would happen if they did not cooperate. Since then they have subjugated but not exterminated the countries they have overrun."

"You sure you're on our side?" the Tsar asked.

"Don't be a moron," Wall said. "I'm just saying that it's better to be alive than dead."

"It's better to be dead than a slave," the Tsar said.

"Why?" Barnard asked. "How is that an improvement?"

"At least if you are alive, you have the chance to fight back," Wall said.

"But once we start down the path of nuclear weapons, there is no turning back," Barnard said.

"So what do we do, LT?" the Tsar said.

"This changes everything," Price said. "We agreed to have a go. To do what we can. But we didn't agree to this. We didn't sign up for nukes."

There was silence.

"I don't think it changes anything," Monster said. "We stop bridgers, or die trying. We die by gun or nuke, no matter, we still dead."

"I'm with the big guy," the Tsar said.

"If we stop the bridgers, they won't need the nukes," Barnard said. "It still comes down to us. I'm in."

They all looked at Wall.

"Are you guys mad?" he asked.

The Tsar shrugged. The rest stared.

"You are mad," he said. "But it's my kind of mad. Balls and all. I'm in."

"We'd better hurry," Monster said. Then he did something that was very un-Monster-like. He moved to Price and put his arms around her, hugging her, not minding the stares of the others.

"We do the right thing," Monster whispered in her ear. "But I don't think we coming home from this one."

31. THE RUN

THE COAST OF ALASKA WAS SLIPPING QUICKLY PAST. Wilton felt cold, and it was not from the temperature, which was comfortable inside the cabin.

"When we get back to base," Anderson said, "stay in the Spitfire. We should be well away from the blast, and the hills should protect us from any shock wave, but the Spitfire will keep us safe from any fallout."

"Captain Anderson, can you please look at the tactical map," Wilton said. "At the rear of the Bzadian lines."

"What the hell is that?" Anderson asked. "One of our troop transporters? What is it doing all the way back there?"

"It's the Angels," Wilton said.

"Your old mates?" Anderson said. "I thought they were shut down."

"Don't believe everything you read on the Internet," Wilton said.

"What they hell are they doing there? They're way behind enemy lines," Anderson said.

"They're a recon team," Wilton said. "They're supposed to be behind enemy lines. They're going after the bridging units."

"They'll never make it," Anderson said.

"Not on their own, they won't," Wilton said.

"Uh-uh, no way," Anderson said. "This place is about to go nuclear popsicle. We've been ordered to get clear."

"I know that, Captain," Wilton said. "I bet the Angels know it too."

There was silence for a moment; then Anderson reached out and flicked the comm onto the open channel, so all the other members of their squadron could hear.

"Wilton, repeat what you just told me," she said.

Price watched as a line of tanks slid past, the rear guard. The bridging units were next. Monster swung the machine into a turn, drifting like a stock car.

"Here we go," Barnard said, pulling on the cables to operate the de-icing. "Is it working?"

"Yes," Wall said. From his position in the rear gun turret he had the best view of the liquid spraying onto the ice behind them.

An explosion hurled huge shards of ice into the air behind them as one of the tanks finally realized that there was a cat among the pigeons. More explosions sounded as other tanks joined in, but the firing was wild, the radar-controlled guns unable to lock on. The Angels' hovercraft was too fast, too stealthy. The guns on the tanks fell silent.

"Watch out for rotorcraft," Price yelled.

Even as she said it, one of the Bzadian slow movers appeared, skimming along the ice between the rows of SAM batteries.

Wall began to fire from the right rear turret and sparks flashed on the armor of the rotorcraft.

Soldiers on snowmobiles appeared behind them, angling in on their trail. Coil-gun rounds clattered off the shield of Wall's turret and he ducked down instinctively before getting back on his gun and letting off a long burst that had the Bzadian soldiers diving for cover.

Price, in the top turret, swung the twin heavy machine guns around to the left and poured fire at a snowmobile that was angling across their path to cut them off. She hit the vehicle's fuel tank and a fiery explosion scattered bits of the machine across the ice.

Wall's guns were chattering constantly as the Bzadian craft poured in from the right-hand side, but Price saw that more were swinging around in front of them.

Ahead, a two-man snowmobile skidded to a halt, the rear soldier bringing a missile launcher to his shoulder. She swung her guns toward them and pulled the trigger but heard only a click, followed by a whir as the automatic reloader began to change out the ammunition case.

"Wall! Missile team! Ten o'clock!" she shouted.

Glancing back, she saw that Wall could not bring his gun to bear; he was blocked by the huge fan. Still her gun whirred and clicked and now the missile launcher was trained directly on them.

There was a flurry of snow around the two men and she thought the missile had fired, but there was no streak of light toward them, no impact. Her guns came back online as the flurry subsided and she could see that the missile team was down, the launcher lying uselessly on the ice.

Behind them, disappearing into the fog of the battle, she caught a glimpse of a tall man in furs, his head masked by the skull of a white wolf. Then he was gone.

More Bzadian rotorcraft gunships flowed in. Price took aim at the closest one and saw the front windshield explode. The machine dipped, hit the ice, bounced up, and went spinning off into the distance.

Two more took its place.

"Watch out!" she yelled, and Monster swung the machine around in a tight curve, sweeping in and around the SAM batteries to their right.

The sudden change of direction confused the Bzadians, and a snowmobile, screeching around to match them, bounced up off a hump in the ice, hurtling through the air at a rotorcraft. There was a flash and a ball of fire and blackened bits of wreckage spun off in all directions.

Monster turned again, bringing the craft back on its original course.

Price glanced back, trying to judge how far they had come. She estimated they were almost halfway there. A burst of shots slammed into her turret and a mule kicked her in the chest. She fell backward and when she picked herself up, she saw that her armor was shattered. One more shot like that and she was dead.

She nestled her shoulders into the stocks of the twin machine guns and exploded a snowmobile that had just appeared in front of her.

32. SACRIFICE

"WE'RE NOT GOING TO MAKE IT!" WALL YELLED AS A wave of snowmobiles swept in from the right. The side windows cracked, then shattered. The Tsar ducked down below the controls, but Monster stayed where he was, steering the hovercraft right at their attackers as Price emptied her magazines at them.

One snowmobile exploded, a second narrowly avoiding the debris, but now the vehicles were scattering in every direction.

"What the hell?" Price yelled.

The Tsar picked himself up and examined the scopes. "It's the cavalry!" he shouted.

Pouring out between the rows of SAM batteries were fast-attack hovercraft, Spitfires.

Sidewinders were flying into the Bzadian ranks, leaving a tangled ball of cotton-like smoke trails in the air. Other units emerged, Vipers, and as Price watched, one got close enough to a command tank to launch its weapon. The sticky bomb flew straight out at the tank, clinging to the rapidly spinning surface. It wound the reel of det cord out in less than a second, the cord wrapping itself around and around the tank.

The crump of the explosion was like a thump in the chest and, at first, she thought it hadn't worked, but half a second later the armored hull of the tank, warped by the explosion, shook itself to pieces in front of them.

The de-icing unit was scraping over the ice behind the hovercraft, and Price was acutely aware that if the hoses were damaged, they would be wasting their time, and probably their lives.

Barnard was at the open side door and at regular intervals hurled C4 packs out onto their trail. Glancing back, Price saw the packs sitting like a row of ants behind them, gradually sinking as the fluid melted the ice underneath.

Around them was a whirling circus of Bzadian and human craft. The air was full of tracers and bullets. Explosions rocked them from the left and the right. The Bzadian command tanks were starting to fire as the bridging units moved forward, giving them a clearer field of fire.

Through the maelstrom raced the Angels on a hovercraft that was starting to disintegrate around them. The bulletproof glass of the side windows was gone and the rubber of the air cushion was peppered with shrapnel holes.

"How's the de-icing going?" Price called back to Wall.

"It's not working," Wall said, looking at the trail they were leaving behind them.

"It has to work," Price said.

Or had she thrown away all their lives for nothing?

"It's not working," Wall said again.

Behind them, the massive tracks of the bridging units were rolling across the slush-filled trench the Angels had cut in the ice. It wasn't deep enough or wide enough, or they were just too fast for it, but as Price watched, more and more of the huge bridgers rolled across the gap.

"We're not finished yet," Barnard said.

A series of explosions rippled along the trench, spraying slush into the air like geysers as the C4 packs exploded.

One of the bridging units was caught by a blast and lifted into the air, shunted sideways, and slammed back down into the ice, apparently undamaged. Otherwise there was little effect. The bridging units continued their march toward the front lines.

"Incoming!" the Tsar yelled.

A rotorcraft was heading right for them. It fired and Monster dodged to the left as an explosion blasted ice and snow over them.

A Spitfire screamed out from behind a SAM unit, veering onto the tail of the rotorcraft. A missile leaped a short distance and the rotorcraft exploded. But already there was another one, this one right behind the Spitfire, which shuddered under the impact of heavy guns.

Price poured fire into the rotorcraft and had the satisfaction of seeing it shudder and dip, the front edge catching the ice and flipping it over. It disintegrated in a tangle of broken metal. The Spitfire, completely out of control, spun in circles before embedding itself in a crushed pile of ice. It did not move again.

Several of the Bzadian bridging units had already crossed the trap that the Angels had so carefully laid and were passing through the lines of the SAM batteries. The others followed and Price could see that they had wasted their time. It was too late. It hadn't worked.

Then a fearsome sound split the air, louder even than the explosions of shells and the boom of the tank guns.

The ice on the far side of the channel shuddered and began to dance, shivering as if cold. All of the fluid in the trench drained away in an instant, leaving a narrow chasm in the ice, an artificial canyon where none had been before.

The edge of the ice sheet started to sink, weighed down by the combined weight of the bridging units and SAM batteries arrayed on it.

Seeing what was happening, the bridgers increased power, a roar coming from all along the line as they tried to drive away from the crack behind them.

More and more the ice dipped, the edge disappearing down into the water. As it did so, the angle of the ice sheet increased and the heavy Bzadian machines started to slip as they tried to climb the icy slope.

The SAM units began to slide backward first, then the heavy bridging units.

As they got close to the edge of the ice sheet, Price heard more of the tremendous cracking sounds, and it was clear that the ice floe was breaking in two, the weight at the back too much for the middle. It gave way in a rush. The ice tilted up sharply and none of the Bzadian vehicles had a chance.

Huge spouts of water erupted as the bridging units and most of the SAM batteries slid down the near vertical slope into the black waters of the sea.

Wilton opened his eyes.

The windshield was shattered and the cold, subarctic wind whistled in through the empty space in the front of the cockpit.

The Spitfire was dead.

And as far as he could tell, so was Anderson. She was slumped sideways in her seat and there seemed to be a lot of blood on the sidewall.

He looked at his fingers and saw that they were covered in ice. He clapped his hands together to dislodge it, but couldn't feel anything in his fingers when he did so. The skin on his hands was a blotchy patchwork of white, yellow, and red.

He found the starter switch on the control panel and pressed with a nerveless thumb. To his surprise, the engine started immediately, and soon warm air was blowing up around him. It was fighting the wind and the wind was winning, but it was still better than without.

The main screen lit up, showing damage to the craft. Apart from the windows, the Spitfire was in good condition. The front gun was gone, but the remaining sidewinder missile seemed to be active.

More heartbeat indicators lit up. According to the sensors, he was still alive. So was Anderson, although her heart rate was slow and erratic.

With frozen fingers, he switched the heaters to full, although it still seemed to make little difference. He flexed his hands and was relieved to find that they still worked, despite the numbness of the skin.

He rubbed them together in front of an air vent, trying to get some feeling back into them.

In the back of the cockpit, Anderson grunted once, a half-choked cough, and the heartbeat monitor on the control panel paused, restarted, then stopped flashing altogether. His own heartbeat continued to flash, a tiny beacon of hope or maybe a warning light.

A large hovercraft rushed past just to his left. It was taking fire and sparks were flying from armored panels. It showered Wilton with snow as it passed. It was the Angels. It had to be.

"Hi, guys," he called, knowing they had no way of hearing him.

He laughed as the craft slewed from side to side in evasive maneuvers, machine guns firing from three turrets.

"Go on, get out of here!" he yelled. "I never liked you anyway."

He began to laugh again, but stopped because it hurt his chest and the icy air burned his lungs.

They were almost there, almost free; only one Bzadian tank remained between the Angels and a wide-open plain of ice.

And then the tank began to fire.

It was barely a hundred meters away from the Angels' hovercraft.

The tank rocked as the main gun lashed out three times in quick succession.

The hovercraft was heading toward the tank, running sideways across its path. The first shell overshot the hovercraft's nose by a good six meters, ricocheting off the hard ice and exploding in the distance.

The second shot did all the damage, passing through the rubberized skirt of the aircraft and out the other side before exploding on the ice.

The nose of the hovercraft disintegrated and the entire machine flipped up, pointing skyward. The propeller at the rear shattered and spat itself out across the ice as the cage that surrounded it was crushed.

The hovercraft continued to slide across the ice, on its tail, like a dog standing on its hind legs, before toppling over backward, landing on its roof, facing the direction it had come from. Even now its momentum kept it sliding until it came to a rest directly in front of the tank.

Wilton waited for the next shot. The one that would finish them off. But it didn't come. Instead, the tank began to move. At first Wilton couldn't understand what it was doing; then he realized the commander of the tank intended to crush the broken hovercraft.

"Guys!" Wilton shouted, grabbing at the controls.

There was a moment of indecision as the air cushion inflated and strained to break the grip of the ice, but then with a cracking sound, the little Spitfire was moving. But something was wrong with the fan and he had to steer hard right to go forward. There were scraping noises from below, but he was still moving.

Ahead of him, the giant Bzadian command tank rolled straight at the downed hovercraft.

It wasn't going to crush it, he realized. Instead, the tank shoved it forward, the spinning hull grinding into the smaller craft, bulldozing it toward the broken edge of the ice floe and the cold waters beyond.

"No!" he shouted, and before he thought about what he was doing, he gunned the Spitfire. He considered firing his last remaining sidewinder, but it would have little effect on the thick spinning hull of a tank.

The nose of his hovercraft dipped as he accelerated, the wind shrieking, a heinous banshee noise, through the smashed windshield.

His face was completely numb and he sensed ice particles growing on his nose and cheeks. Only the visor of his helmet protected his eyes and he had to rub at it with a frozen, rigid hand to keep it clear.

His face would not move. It was frozen in a grimace, and still he gave the machine full power. A burst of machine-gun fire from one of the tanks ripped along the side of the craft, shattering his armored window, and he felt a jolt in his right arm followed by a numbness that quickly spread down that side of his body.

His left hand still worked and he could steer with that. He aimed the nose of his craft at the front of the Angels' hovercraft, which had flipped around and was facing him. The armored windshield of the craft was intact and he was close enough to see inside. Price was there; she was still alive. So was the Tsar, hammering at the side door of the craft, trying to get it open.

Price looked up, her eye catching the sight of Wilton's hovercraft approaching.

There was a crunch as the nose of his craft slammed into that of the Angels', now teetering on the edge of the ice floe.

The impact hurled him forward in his seat, slamming him against the harness. The other craft was bigger, heavier, and jammed against the front lip of the Bzadian tank, but the impact of the crash was enough to jolt it free.

Still he kept the power on, driving forward, wrenching the Angels free from the grasp of the tank, pushing them. Ramming them out of the way.

Price saw him, and knew him—he could see the recognition in her eyes just before the craft spun out from the front of the tank, sliding away from the edge of the ice. Price's eyes were wide as the craft slipped out of his sight.

But now the tank had him. It ground into the Spitfire above the rubber cushion, pressing it down, squeezing the air out of it. He gunned the engine, wrenching the steering to the left and right, but the grip of the tank was remorseless.

He was on the very edge of the ice. The thin wedge gave

way underneath him, and the tail of his craft dropped. He was looking skyward, at a gray arctic sky that quickly turned to black, eclipsed by the crescent that was the front of the tank.

If anybody had seen the expression on Wilton's face at that moment, they would have seen a frozen face, a face in which the skin and muscles no longer had any feeling or any movement. It was a rigid mask beneath a visor that was icing up, as if to hide his eyes from what was to come.

But if anyone had seen that expression, as fixed and forced as it was, they would have thought that Specialist Blake Wilton, of Vancouver, Canada, was smiling as his hand found the firing button on his steering controls.

Nothing happened at first. The sidewinder missile leaped from its cradle on the stubby wing of the Spitfire, clanged against the underside of the tank, rebounded down onto the ice, jammed against one of the big ball wheels as its rocket motor blasted, and seared the underside of the tank, melting the ice around it.

The arming delay counted down and the fuse activated. Sensing that it was in proximity to a target, it did the only thing it knew how to do. The one thing it was made for. It exploded.

The nine-kilogram warhead, loaded with titanium fragmentation rods, pulverized the ice beneath the tank.

The ice cracked, then gave way, and as Wilton's craft disappeared into the depths of the Bering Strait, the front lip of the tank slowly followed it, toppling, overbalancing, and sliding off the broken ice shelf into the water. It stayed there briefly, wedged between the ice on either side of the channel; then with another ear-rending crack, the ice gave way beneath it, and it was gone, joining the gigantic bridging units and SAM batteries. A permanent metal graveyard at the bottom of the sea.

Somewhere below it, in the debris of his craft, Blake Wilton was still smiling.

33. THE END

MILLIONS OF TONS OF ICE, ABRUPTLY FREED OF THE weight of the bridgers and SAM batteries, began to regain its equilibrium. The submerged edge of the ice sheet rose slowly, ponderously, out of the water, sucking up seawater with it, cascading over the edges. It rose higher and higher like a breaching whale before falling back in something like slow motion.

As it landed, an immense wave of water flooded up through the gap in the ice, washing over, around, and through the Angels' downed hovercraft; icy water poured through the shattered side windows and open hatch. Caught up in the flow, the craft washed away like a toy boat on a beach.

. . .

The door to the command center opened and General White-head entered. He was in a wheelchair, pushed by an adjutant. He seemed frail, but his eyes were focused and his hands were steady.

"Situation report," he demanded.

"We have scattered reports coming in from Spitfire teams," Watson said. "The Bzadians just lost all their bridging units."

"How?" Whitehead asked.

"That's unclear, sir," Watson said. "A gap opened up in the ice and they fell through, according to the reports we're getting."

"I believe it may have been Recon Team Angel that did it, sir," Watson said.

"Stand down your nuclear weapons," Whitehead said.

"Sir?" Russell asked.

"Stand them down." Whitehead's voice was firm. "The Pukes can't get to Alaska without those bridgers. We can do this without nukes. How is their SAM cover?"

"Hovercraft teams have taken out a lot of their SAM batteries," Watson said. "And they lost more when they lost the bridgers."

"Get those remaining Tomahawks in the air," Whitehead said.

"Straightaway, sir," Russell said.

Without the bridging units, the Bzadian tanks could not move forward. Without SAM cover, they were vulnerable.

Unable to advance or retreat, the Bzadian tanks would be an easy target for the cruise missiles.

"Those Angels may have just saved our hides," Whitehead said. "Again."

"What Angels?" Gonzales asked in all seriousness. "They were never there."

34. GREATER LOVE

THE STORM HAD BLOWN ITSELF OUT, IN THAT FICKLE WAY of weather in the arctic. The skies were gradually shedding themselves of the dense black clouds. Even the sun was out, hovering low above the horizon as always. The Angels were heading toward it, which made a bright orange glare across the windshield of the pickup truck.

They had taken it, with Bowden's blessing, from the hangar at Little Diomede. It was not really designed for driving across the broken ice floes of the Bering Strait, but they didn't have a lot of other choices.

The cab was large enough for only three of them.

Monster drove. Price, semiconscious, was beside him, her head on his shoulder. Barnard drew the long straw and got the other seat. Wall and the Tsar lay on the back tray, in the space left where the de-icing tank had been removed.

They went as far south as possible before the ice got too rough and ridged. Even so it was slow going, keeping a close watch out for crevasses or fissures. As slow as it was, it was still safer here in the south than north of the islands where the battle still raged.

It was a different kind of battle now. No longer an invasion, it was a fighting retreat and the Bzadians were taking heavy losses.

"Did you know the ice floe would crack the way it did?" Monster asked.

"I kind of hoped," Barnard said. "There was a lot of weight sitting on the edge."

"Shame about your friend Wilton," Wall said.

"On Operation Magnum," Barnard said, "Wilton told me that he would give up his own life for his buddies. For us. If he had to."

"I remember," the Tsar said. "I said that was the mark of a great man."

"I told him he wasn't a man yet," Barnard said.

"Yes, you did," the Tsar said.

Monster strained his eyes, uncertain of what lay ahead. A gray blur on the horizon gradually resolved into snow-covered slopes and rocky falls.

"Greater love hath no man than this," Barnard said. "That a man lay down his life for his friends."

Around them the crushed and cracked floes of the ice field

were gradually healing themselves. What had happened here today was no more than a flicker of an eyelid in the endless grind of the ice and the eternal flow of the sea.

"Is that Shakespeare?" the Tsar asked.

"It's from the Bible," Wall said. "I think Emile would have appreciated that."

35. RUSSELL

[FEBRUARY 19, 2033]
[0930 hours local time]
[Operations Command Center, Pentagon, Virginia]

RUSSELL WAS IN HIS OFFICE, STARING AT A TACTICAL MAP of the Bering Strait when Bilal arrived.

Bilal was in a wheelchair. He was flanked by two MPs.

"Daniel," Russell said. "Glad to see you're up and around."

Bilal smiled. "It's good to be out of that hospital. The food was all right, but the wine selection was terrible."

Russell laughed. "How can I help?"

"I have a question for you," Bilal said.

"Shoot."

"Why did you do it?" Bilal asked.

"Do what?" Russell asked.

"We think we know, but I'd like to hear it from the horse's mouth," Bilal said.

"You're going to have to give me a clue here, Daniel," Russell said.

Bilal had been holding a plastic folder. He opened it and withdrew a large photograph, handing it to Russell, who had to walk around the desk to take it.

He studied it before returning to his chair and placing it on the desk in front of him. He leaned back in his chair and pressed his fingertips together.

"How did you get on to me?" he asked.

"It wasn't me," Bilal said. "It was Wilton. That kid I had working for me. Ex-Angel."

Russell nodded. "So he survived."

"No." Bilal's expression was hard. "You sent him to the strait. Assigned him a frontline combat role, even though he was just out of his Spitfire training. He should have been in the reserves. A convenient way of getting rid of a witness, without any tough questions."

"The battlefield can be a fickle thing," Russell said. "Some live, some die."

"And you thought you'd play the odds," Bilal said. "You got him killed to protect your own hide."

"And yet here you are," Russell said.

"You know, I didn't really trust Wilton," Bilal said. "Occupational hazard. And you don't give someone top security access without keeping an eye on them. Everything Wilton did, every key he pressed, every area he accessed, was copied to my computer."

"Ah," Russell said.

"And you still haven't answered why."

"It was a last resort," Russell said. "I wasn't prepared to see the human race wiped out. Nukes were our only option, and if the high command couldn't see that, then the high command had to be replaced."

"Turns out nukes weren't our only option," Bilal said. "We had the Angels."

"It's easy with hindsight," Russell said. "There's no way I would have done what I did if I had thought we had a chance any other way."

"But you did it," Bilal said. He wheeled himself close up against Russell's desk and leaned forward, putting his elbows on the desk. "You want to know a funny thing? Wilton thought you were working for the Bzadians."

"For the enemy!" Russell was shocked.

"Someone made sure that Able was on Little Diomede," Bilal said.

"Not me," Russell said.

"I know," Bilal said. "We are already closing in on who was responsible."

"Good," Russell said. "That's treason."

"Treason," Bilal said, "still carries the death penalty. One of the few crimes that do. Some kind of historical anomaly, I guess."

Russell went white. "I cannot be accused of treason."

"You bombed your own command center. Killed your own colleagues," Bilal said. "Can you think of a better definition of your crime?"

"I acted in our best interests," Russell said. "Not against them."

"That, clearly, is a matter of opinion," Bilal said. "And opinion can be a fickle thing."

36. CHISNALL

CHISNALL WAS DOING PUSH-UPS, BUT STOPPED AS THE door opened and Doctor Royz entered. He appeared fit, she thought. For someone recovering from a broken spinal cord, he had thrown himself into the exercise program he had been given, and he looked much better than when he had arrived.

"Any news?" he asked.

"Success," she said. "You're going to Canberra."

The Bzadians had long ago taken over the Australian parliament as the seat of their own government on Earth. Azoh himself resided somewhere in the capital, although the location was a closely guarded secret.

"Why are you doing this?" Chisnall asked. "Aren't you betraying your own species?"

She shook her head. "Not all of us believe in this war. Millions of people are dying when we believe there are alternatives. A peaceful alternative between our races."

"When do I leave?" Chisnall asked.

"Tomorrow," she said. "We have found you a position in the kitchen at the government building."

"I don't know much about Bzadian cooking," Chisnall said.

"You'll get on-the-job training," she said. "The important thing is to trust no one except your contact."

"A kitchen hand," Chisnall mused. "And after that?"

"That will be up to you," she said.

He went back to his push-ups as she left.

Kartoz stopped her in the corridor outside Chisnall's room and spoke quietly to avoid being overheard.

"Do you think he believed you?" he asked.

"I think so," Royz said. "Yes."

GLOSSARY

Everything about the Allied Combined Operations Group (ACOG) was a mishmash of different human cultures: tactics, weapons, languages, vehicles, and especially terminology. The success of many missions depended on troops from diverse nations being able to understand all communications instantly and thoroughly. The establishment of a Standardized Military Terminology and Phonetic Alphabet (SMTPA) was a key factor in assisting this communication, combining existing terminology from many of the countries involved in ACOG. For ease of understanding, here is a short glossary of some of the SMTPA terms, phonetic shortcuts, and equipment used in this series.

ACOG: Allied Combined Operations Group
Cal: caliber (of weapon)
Clear copy: "Your transmission is clear."

Coil-gun: weapon using magnetic coils to propel a projectile

Comm: personal radio communicator

DPV: driver propulsion vehicle

EV (Echo Victor): exit vehicle

Eyes on: to have sight of

Fast mover: fixed-wing aircraft such as a jet fighter

FFC: forward fire control

GPS: global positioning system

How copy: "Is my transmission clear?"

ICBM: intercontinental ballistic missiles

Klick: kilometer

LCAC: landing craft air cushion (hovercraft)

LOT: lock-out trunk

LT: lieutenant

Mike: minute

MOPP: mission-oriented protective posture—protective gear used in toxic situations

MPC: marine personnel carrier

NV goggles: night-vision goggles

Oscar Kilo: okay

Oscar Mike: on the move

PFC: private first class

Puke: military slang for a Bzadian

Rotorcraft: helicopter with internal rotor blades at the base of the craft

RPG: rocket-propelled grenade

SERE: survive, evade, resist, extract

Slow mover: rotary-wing aircraft such as a helicopter or rotorcraft

SONRAD: sonar/radar

Spec: specialist

NOTE ON PRONUNCIATION

There is no equivalent in English for the buzzing sound that is a common feature of most Bzadian languages. As per convention, this sound is represented, where required, with the letter z.

NOTE ON BZADIAN ARMY RANKS

The ranking system and unit structure of the Bzadian Army are markedly different from those of most Earth forces. Many ranks have no equivalent in human terms, and the organization of units is different. For simplicity and ease of understanding, the closest human rank has been used when referring to Bzadian Army ranks, and Bzadian unit names have been expressed in human terms.

CONGRATULATIONS

The following people won the grand prize in my school competitions and have had a character named after them in this book:

Emile Attaya

Point View School, Auckland, New Zealand

Retha Barnard

Albany Junior High School, Auckland, New Zealand

Daniel Bilal

Woodcrest State College, Queensland, Australia

Gabrielle Bowden

Hebron Christian College, Auckland, New Zealand

Holly Brogan

St. Cuthbert's College, Auckland, New Zealand

Ryan Chisnall

Belmont Intermediate School, Auckland,
New Zealand

Courtney Fox

St. Peter's School, Cambridge, New Zealand

Emily Gonzales

Santa Gertrudis School, Kingsville, USA

Lynette Hooper

Ipswich West State School, West Ipswich,
Australia

Elisabeth Iniguez

Vista Del Valle Elementary School,
Los Angeles, USA

Janos Panyoczki

Kaiwaka School, Kaiwaka, New Zealand

Trianne Price

Woodcrest State College, Queensland, Australia

Jake Russell

Santa Gertrudis School, Kingsville, USA

Hayden Wall

Padua College, Queensland, Australia

Harry Whitehead

Waimea College, Richmond, New Zealand

Blake Wilton

Orewa College, Orewa, New Zealand

Also to:

Jaylen Gerrand

and

Kamaljeet Hundal

ABOUT THE AUTHOR

BRIAN FALKNER, a native New Zealander, now lives in sunny Queensland, Australia. His keen interest in military history inspired the futuristic "history" of the Recon Team Angel books. Find him online at brianfalkner.com.